THE SHARK CALLER

ZILLAH BETHELL

USBORNE

COPPER MINE

TO TOWN

LAWATBULUT TREE

MAPLE HAMELIN'S HUT

SIRINGEN'S HUT

THE SEA

BLUE WING'S VILLAGE IS IN PAPUA NEW GUINEA.
PAPUA NEW GUINEA IS AN ISLAND COUNTRY
BETWEEN THE PACIFIC OCEAN AND THE
CORAL SEA, AND LIES, AT ITS CLOSEST POINT,
150 KILOMETRES FROM AUSTRALIA.

THE SEA

CHIMERA'S CAVE

BURIAL GROUND

PAPAYA GROVE

MR JEFFREY'S SHOP

BIGMAN'S COMPOUND

MAP OF BLUE WING'S VILLAGE

GLOSSARY OF PAPUAN PIDGIN ENGLISH TERMS

bikpela = big

hambak = annoying

hat = hot

kapiak = breadfruit

kapul = small marsupial

kasaman = rope and wood device used in shark calling

kaukau = sweet potato

kol = cold

larung = coconut rattle used in shark calling

liklik = little

longlong = silly, foolish, crazy

lukim = look

mobeta = better

Moroa = Papuan god

namba wan / tu = first / second

nogut = bad

oltaim = always / all the time

orait = all right

raskol = criminal

saksak = milk and honey pudding

snek = snake

soldia = soldier

taim = time

tambu = traditions

tarangau = eagle

taur = conch shell

telefon = telephone

tru = true / very

NAMBAS (NUMBERS):

wanpela = one

tupela = two

tripela = three

fopela = four

faipela = five

sikispela = six

sevenpela = seven

etpela = eight

nainpela = nine

tenpela = ten

wanpela ten wan = eleven

wanpela ten tu = twelve

tupela ten = twenty

tripela ten = thirty

wan-handet = one hundred

BLUE WING

I stand on the edge of the moonflower coral and take a cormorant dive into the blue. My ears fill, my nose bubbles and my eyes sting; but I can see *tru* clear in this underwater kingdom and I can hold my breath for a very long *taim*.

I somersault over an angelfish, then float for a while – sway, sway, sway – like a ribbon of seaweed in the beautiful cool. How many secrets live down here? How many tight-shut oyster shells? Nobody knows. Not even me.

I climb back onto the reef, careful not to cut my feet on the coral that looks like chewing gum. The sun hits me with a slap. It is going to be a rude and uncivil person today, the sun.

Soon the motorboat will come, bringing the tourists. "Blue Wing," Siringen will say if I am close, or if I am far he will blow the *taur* shell to announce *"It is time."* And I will dive off the coral, swim hard to the shore, take my place in the canoe.

I look across the *bikpela* blue, beyond the leaping place, beyond the shark roads. There is a *liklik* black dot growing bigger and bigger, like a pupil in the darkness. *Sea Ballerina* is coming! I smile at the name, because this boat is no dancer on the waves.

I turn to the shore. Siringen is waving at me. I wave back. Standing at the edge of the sunflower coral, I dive into the sea and start swimming fast...

It is time to call the sharks.

PAT NAMBA WAN

THE SAND

WANPELA

The Man-From-England sits in the outrigger canoe with Siringen and me. Sometimes the man smiles and sometimes he frowns, his hands covering his eyes as he looks out over the dazzling water.

Siringen doesn't smile.

He doesn't smile much anyway, but today he doesn't smile at all. The Man-From-England does not make him happy. I know Siringen feels it is all wrong. The man is dressed too well. His face too clean. His hands too soft. He has more money than anyone in the village could ever dream about. More money than the god Moroa could ever imagine. And because he can pay, he can do what he wants. That's what the Bigman tells Siringen, and that is why Siringen has to take him out onto the shark roads.

Because the Man-From-England wants to kill a shark.

The man sweats. Even in his rich clothes made for the heat, he still sweats. His forehead shines with it and he has made his shirt wet. Sometimes he reaches over his round shoulders and pulls the shirt away from his skin, shaking it all off. It doesn't work because he keeps doing it. And he makes *hambak* blowing noises – I think he thinks it keeps him cool.

"Is it always this hot?" the Man-From-England asks Siringen.

"*Hat*, yes." Siringen nods. "*Hat oltaim.*" He pushes the paddle into the sea and turns us to face the land.

I can sense the smile in the man's eyes. He hides it as well as he can, but I can sense it around him like a cloud. He finds Siringen funny. He is laughing at him, within himself.

I suddenly feel angry and hate the Man-From-England, who has swooped in like a *tarangau* spotting *kapul* in the forest. He has come to take what he likes and wants, before leaving behind what he doesn't like and doesn't want. I feel my fingernails digging into the palms of my hands.

Siringen stops paddling.

"What're you doing now?" the man says, watching Siringen taking up the coconut rattle.

"Larung."

Siringen puts the rattle into the water and shakes it hard. The seawater gurgles and froths, and the coconut shells knock against each other. He stops for a short *taim* before doing it again. And again. Then again.

"Makes sharks come," Siringen explains to the man. "They think fish are in trouble, so sharks come."

"Cool," the man says, before drinking the ends of his cola can and throwing it into the sea. Siringen shakes his head at the man's action but the man doesn't see. Or pretends not to see. "I hope we get a big one."

Siringen shivers the rattle one more *taim* before starting his chant. The chant is part of his magic to make the sharks come. His uncle taught him the magic chants many years ago, when Siringen became a man. Siringen's eyes half close, and the magic words start coming out of his mouth, up and down like a song played on the *taur* shell.

The man laughs out loud. He doesn't even try to hide it. He laughs out hard at the noises Siringen is making.

But none of it stops Siringen. With his half-closed eyes, the magic streams from his mouth and down into the depths of the sea below. I have seen him do this a *handet taim*. And every *taim* the words bring sharks to the surface.

After a while, the man stops laughing, and all that can be heard are Siringen and the soft slaps of the waves against the side of the canoe. I crouch in the corner, my legs tucked into my arms, my mouth against my knees.

I keep myself silent.

There is no wind. Out here, sometimes, when shark magic is happening, the wind blows itself away, so that the sharks can hear the words the old shark caller speaks. It is like Moroa understands, and allows the natural things to flow around the ancient tradition like a river around a rock.

"Ah." The man breathes in like a knife and points. "There! Over there."

Far off, the sea is cut with the tip of a fin.

"Here it comes!" says the man. His hand reaches down into the bottom of the outrigger and pulls up the spear.

Siringen, opening his eyes a little, waves at him to put it down and, without asking any questions, the man does so.

Slowly the shark nears us. It is not a *bikpela* shark, as the man had hoped, and his face tells me he is disappointed. The shark dives under the outrigger and comes out the other side before turning back on itself, drawn towards us by Siringen's magic. Softly, Siringen takes up the spear and puts the day-old bait fish onto the end of it.

"What happens now?" asks the Man-From-England. "Are we going to kill it with the spear? Or should I bash it to death?" He grabs the wooden club and sweeps it about in the air like it is a paper windmill. Suddenly I feel sorry for the people who know this man well.

"No!" Siringen almost spits by speaking so quickly. "Not yet. First, we must tempt the shark into the *kasaman*."

I can see that Siringen is hating all of this.

"What's the...*kasaman*?"

"This." Siringen shows the man. It is a loop of cane rope passing through a small hole, in what looks like the wooden propeller of a plane. I think of the propeller on the plane which brought this man to the islands – and which I hope will take him away again *tru* soon.

"What's that do?" The man taps the wood with his finger.

"Watch," says Siringen.

He lowers the loop into the water and pushes the bait fish at the end of the spear in behind it. The shark circles, the fish tempting it near.

The man says nothing. He doesn't even move. His eyes watch the shark as it swims beneath the canoe, twisting back and around. Slowly getting nearer the bait. Waiting to take it.

Suddenly the shark strikes, but Siringen is too quick for it. All his years out on the seas calling sharks have made him quick, even if he is an old man staring into the window of death. As the shark bites at the bait, Siringen lets it swim through the loop before pulling hard on top. The loop tightens and the wooden propeller is tied to the shark's back.

The shark panics and swims away, fighting with the float, kicking up the surface of the water and making it foam.

"What do we do?" shouts the Man-From-England. "Do we kill it now? Why are you letting it get away?"

Siringen puts his fingers to his lips and sits as calm as the breeze, watching as the shark struggles with the *kasaman*.

"Shouldn't we kill it now?" the man asks again, pointing and frowning.

Siringen shakes his head. "The shark is powerful," he says. "*Much* more powerful than any man. If you want to kill a shark, you must make it weaker. You must make the battle…" He searches the sky for the right words. "You must make the battle more fair."

The man watches as the shark shakes and fights with

the piece of *kapiak* wood.

"But…isn't that cruel?" the man asks. "Isn't it better to kill it straight away? Not to let it suffer?"

Siringen smiles to himself, and I know why he is smiling. The man wants the kill to be easy. But the problem is he does not understand what it takes to make the kill easy. He wants the honour without doing anything honourable. He wants to be a warrior without knowing what is needed to be a warrior. He wants to take away the life of something, but he does not want the blood on his hands.

It is like he is not real.

"The shark does not eat man," Siringen says, his fingers cleaning off the end of the spear. "It is not…in their nature. They eat fish. But…" He puts the spear in the bottom of the boat and picks up the paddle. "They will defend themselves against man. Too many men and women and children I have known have been bitten or killed because a shark has felt…" His eyes look at me. "Has felt…risked."

"Threatened." The man puts the word right. "I think you mean 'threatened'."

Siringen nods. "*Kasaman* stops the shark from diving. It makes the shark tired. But only a willing shark would ever come. A shark not ready to be caught…it would not come. There is respect between the shark callers and the sharks. A shark caller knows the shark, and the shark knows the caller. Respect."

We all sit there quietly as the splashing starts to stop. The shark is tiring.

At that moment, Siringen puts his eyes upon me again and speaks to me without saying anything.

I know what it is I have to do.

Softly I lower myself over the side of the boat and into the water. The man doesn't notice me go. I dive beneath the surface, the blueness and silence of the world below the waves like another home to me. I kick hard and keep as far down as I can.

Soon I am directly under the shark that is giving up its life. With the light of the day above it, it looks like a bird in the sky. A bird caught in a snare. The outrigger canoe, like an aeroplane.

I swim up towards the shark. It is not fighting any more. It has accepted that today it will die.

But it will not.

It is my job to make sure it will not.

As I get nearer, it sees me and thrashes its tail. But it cannot get away because of the *kasaman*, and it knows that. Its eyes are glossy like milk and its teeth – shown to me as a useless warning – sharp and flat and uneven.

She is a young shark. I can tell. No one knows how long the sharks live, but this is a young shark. I can feel it. The size. The shape. The way she moves. She is young.

I come up alongside and stroke her. She struggles no longer and lets me. Her skin is rough. Like every shark's skin.

I want to talk to her, tell her that it will all be good soon. But this is a place of silence and no words are ever spoken. So I stroke her some more, and then I begin.

I reach down to my ankle and rip the knife out of its sheath. With my other hand I hold the top of the *kasaman*. The cane rope is tough, but I know that if I keep cutting away at it, it will eventually split. The shark pulls a little but, accepting it is about to die, quickly stops and lets me continue. I drag my little knife over the rope, up and down, and as I do it, the canoe comes always nearer.

I need to be fast.

Up and down. Up and down…

And then—

It splits. The threads of the cane come away in my hand and I pull the rope back through the hole in the *kasaman*, letting go the hold on the shark.

Feeling the loop about her loosen, the shark comes

back to life and shakes herself free before swimming away scared into the dark distance of water. I wave towards her and slide my knife back into its sheath.

I wish I could shout to her and tell her to take care and not to come back until this man has left. But I cannot. Because this is a place of silence and no words are ever spoken.

I dive deeper and swim to the place beneath Siringen's canoe. The sun flickers above and, as I surface just behind the boat, its warmth bursts onto my face.

"Sometimes it happens," I hear Siringen saying. "The shark can be very strong. So sometimes it happens."

I pull myself gently into the back of the boat and tuck myself in once again. The Man-From-England never saw me leave and now he doesn't see me return.

Siringen is picking the broken *kasaman* out of the water, inspecting the cane rope like he is surprised even though he isn't surprised.

"What about another?" the man asks. "Do your coconut shake and try to get another one. A bigger one this time."

"No. It is too late." Siringen pulls the *kasaman* into the canoe. "The magic has gone."

Back in the village, the Bigman is standing on the beach with his arms crossed. As the canoe comes in closer to the shore, I can see he is frowning.

"No shark again, eh, Siringen?" he says as Siringen climbs out and drags the outrigger onto the sand. "How many trips is it now? Seven? Or eight?"

"I cannot remember."

"No."

The Man-From-England helps pull the boat out of the shallow water.

"We had one," he says. "But it got away. Broke the float."

"Did it? Well, well." The Bigman still stands frowning with his arms crossed like they are knotted together and holding back his anger. "Your *kasaman* are not so strong these days. It is strange how many of them break. You must be losing your magic, Siringen."

"Yes." I notice that Siringen doesn't look the Bigman in the eyes.

The Bigman doesn't look at me at all.

"It's a pity," says the Man-From-England. "I've shot elephants and giraffes in Africa. I've shot bears and wolves in Canada. I would have loved to have caught a shark. Had it stuffed and flown back home. Shown my friends and told them all about this place." He gives the Bigman a jokeless stare. "They'd all be coming over and paying good money to catch one themselves. Such a shame."

A *nogut* word comes to my lips, so I press them together before it escapes.

TUPELA

My name is Blue Wing and I live in my *waspapi*'s house. A *waspapi* is someone who looks after you if your parents are dead. My *waspapi* is Siringen – the shark caller. Close to seventy-five ages old. From the clan of Tarangun. Son of the maker of paddles and the calmer of seas.

I cried when I first came to my *waspapi*'s house, saw the sharp coral fence, the tree fork for a door and the shark carvings, dirty with smoke and hanging from the ceiling.

Now I smile when I lie on my sago mat while Siringen chews betel nut and tells tales of *tumbuna* time, when the god Moroa hung the sun in the sky and – when the sun was asleep – hung the moon in its place. I smile because I am glad. I smile because it is my home.

"Why not?"

It is a question I have asked a hundred thousand *taim*.

"You know why," Siringen replies for the hundred thousandth *taim*.

"Because I am a girl?"

Siringen uncrosses his legs, goes outside and takes another ember from the dying fire to relight his pipe.

"That is one reason, yes." The smoke from the pipe fills the hut as he returns and almost hides him from me.

I sigh and pick splinters out of the floor. "But you have no nephews to pass the magic on to. Not even any sons. When you die, all the magic will die. There will be nobody left in the village who can call the sharks."

"Huh!" Siringen blows an angry smoke ring which floats up towards the blackened rafters before disappearing. "Nobody in the village would care. Things are different."

"But *I* want to be able to call the sharks. You know this. I have told you for so long now that my jaw aches whenever I say it. *I* want to call the sharks. Teach me the magic and show me the ways.

"I may be a girl but I can do as well as – no, I can do even *mobeta* than – a boy." I stick my chin out to show him I am tough and fierce.

But he knows all this anyway and just shakes his head for the hundred thousandth *taim*.

"No, Blue Wing. You know what the traditions say. I am already breaking many of the *tambu* by taking you out on the outrigger with me. Isn't that enough?"

"No. It isn't. I want—"

Siringen holds up his hand to tell me to stop. He has heard too much.

Outside, the daylight is almost dead and the moon's reflection shivers over the sea. I can see a dark shadow walking along the beach.

"Of course," says Siringen, rubbing the smoke from his eyes, "being a girl is not the only reason, is it? There is even more of a reason – a greater reason – why I do not teach you the magic, yes?"

And, of course, it is *tru*. My *waspapi* knows me far too well.

"But—"

His hand stops my voice again.

"It would not be right for me to teach you, when you have such anger in your heart. You cannot use the magic for such purposes, Blue Wing. It would not be right."

"Aha!"

We both jump. Suddenly the shadow on the beach has filled itself into the doorway and is staring into the hut.

"So this is where you sit in the evening, eh, Siringen?

After your busy day shark calling." The Bigman taps the wall with his knuckle. "It's not very...spacious, is it? Not for an important person like the village's shark caller."

Siringen chews on the end of his pipe for a moment. "What do you want, Lungadak?" he says eventually.

"Aren't you going to ask me in to smoke with you, Siringen? Isn't that the right thing to do with the Bigman of your village?"

Siringen takes another puff of his pipe before sweeping his arm across the floor, inviting the Bigman to sit with him.

Of course, the Bigman doesn't look at me at all.

"You know," he begins, pulling some cigarette papers and a shiny packet of American tobacco from his T-shirt pocket. "If we had more money, we could always knock this place down and build you something more suited to your position. Something with more than," he looks over his shoulder, "two rooms."

"I do not need more than two rooms."

The Bigman stuffs the tobacco into the paper and lights it with a pink plastic lighter. "Everyone needs more than two rooms, surely?"

"I don't."

The Bigman sucks on his cigarette long *taim*. Even from behind, I can feel his eyes blazing into my *waspapi*.

"Siringen," he says. "I do not understand you. You hold on to your old ways like one of the sharks you used to catch. But why? It has been many years since the people of the village have needed to eat the sweet meat of shark. Even I, who have always lived here, cannot remember the last *taim* I found shark in my bowl. I don't know if you've noticed through those old eyes of yours, but these days many of us keep pigs and chickens. And most other things we can buy from the trade store or from town."

Siringen says nothing.

"As Bigman of the village, it is my responsibility to keep the village alive. It falls on my heavy shoulders to make sure that all the men and women and children have futures and lives to make their ancestors proud. You must understand this?"

Siringen gives a small nod.

"So why must you fight the new world like it is an enemy? You need to embrace it like a friend. That man today – and all the others who have come here before – they are people who have heard about us. They have heard about you. They know that you are the best shark caller in the whole of New Ireland."

"Please. Do not flatter me, Lungadak."

The Bigman sighs. "Siringen." His voice sounds darker

and deeper. "Shark calling is dead. Nobody needs it any more. It is not the old *taim* when people's stomachs depended on it to live. That *taim* has gone. Accept it."

He seems to shuffle in closer to Siringen.

"If you are willing to see the world through different eyes, shark calling can become something else. Something new. The westerners who come here, they are rich. All they want to do is kill a shark and pin it on their wall like a trophy. What is so wrong with that?"

I curl my fingers into my fists and feel the muscles in my arms go hard. As if he is sensing my anger, the Bigman looks around for a moment before turning back to Siringen.

"It is cold in here. Why is it so cold in here?"

Siringen shrugs and stares at his feet.

"Anyway..." the Bigman continues, his cigarette hanging from his lips. "It is good for the village and it is good for you, and you are a fool if you do not see it."

"I am an old man," Siringen whispers. "I see very little."

"Pah!"

Suddenly the Bigman stands up and flicks the cigarette out through the doorway and onto the sand below.

"And these things," he says, reaching up and pulling on the old shark carvings Siringen has hung from the ceiling. "You would do better to sell them to the tourists in town. They might fetch you a lot of money."

"No. I do not think so."

"Why does that not surprise me?" The Bigman stands in the doorway and jabs his finger towards Siringen. "I was right. You *are* a fool."

I open my mouth to say something but Siringen's eyes flick quickly across to me, so I obey and back down.

"I am going to teach you a lesson," continues the Bigman. "If you cannot see the worth in bringing outsiders here, I will *make* you see the worth. Soon we are to be joined by an American professor. A professor of coral. He will be spending some *taim* here, studying the reefs. As you are so keen on the ocean, Siringen, I am making you entirely responsible for him while he is here. Take him out onto the sea when he wants. Cook for him. Clean for him. Do anything he asks. As chief of your village, these things I order you to do. Perhaps then you might get to see that these people are our future."

Siringen still says nothing.

"Do you understand?" The Bigman steps out through the door and turns, hoping for an answer.

Siringen simply nods. And even though I feel, deep inside, that I want to shout something *tru* rude at the Bigman, I keep my tongue still.

"Good. Oh, and this professor... He'll be bringing his daughter with him. Take care of her too." The Bigman walks away, but as he goes he calls back, "You know, Siringen, I think it is warmer outside than it is in your tiny cold hut."

The dream is so frightening that it stops itself by waking me up. I sit straight on my mat and I can feel that my hands are wet and my neck is wet like I have just been swimming even though I have not been.

It is dark both inside and outside the hut – the only light comes from the stars and the fluttering reflection of the moon on the sea. The sea on the sand is the only noise. I sense that Siringen is asleep in his room.

There are some dreams that, when I wake up, have slipped from my mind like they were never even there. Like flowers with thin stems, blown away in the breeze. There are other dreams which seem to be like these but which flicker back to life at some *taim* during the day – the flames made to grow by some small thing said or done.

But this dream...this dream, I can remember it all straight away. It doesn't disappear or hide away like a shy child. It stands in my mind like a proud warrior, refusing to move out of my path.

Everything about it is still there.

My mama and papa, both standing in the waves on the beach in front of our hut. It is not a hot sunny day. Instead it is cold and there are clouds that cover the whole of the sky. The trees behind the hut are not green any more. They are black and grey like ash has covered them. No birds are calling. It is like everything has died.

I am out in the deep sea, watching it all. Trying not to be seen. I feel *nogut* and guilty trying not to be seen. I am full of shame.

Suddenly, a wind blows hard and I am being dragged through the water towards the shore. I try to fight against it. I kick and I swim and I push and I shout, but nothing stops me moving.

And then the worst thing happens.

My mama and papa, both standing in the shallow water, begin to melt. The sea around their legs bubbles and froths, and slowly they sink into the water, their faces no different to how they ever were. It is like they have not even noticed they are melting.

I shout harder, my chest like it is about to catch fire. But nothing happens. They just keep going down, down, down into the sea until I cannot see their faces any more. They have gone.

Then the wind stops and I am all alone in the waves.

I do not know which direction to swim. I am lost. I am lonely.

That is when the sea begins to turn red.

And that is the point at which the dream wakes me up with one word echoing around inside my skull.

Xok.

TRIPELA

At first I think it is a coffin. It is shaped like a coffin – long and thin and like a box. And its colour is the sort of colour you imagine a coffin to be – dark brown and shiny smooth.

"Why have they brought that?" I ask Siringen, after poking his arm.

He turns to me. "What? A clock?"

I look again. The men lower it carefully over the side of the boat. The men in the water strain to keep it out of the way of the waves.

Yes. It is a clock. One of the tall ones you can picture sitting in the hallway of an English palace, with the swing that *knick-knock*s back and forth and that bongs to tell you what the hour is.

The men in the water slowly walk up through the surf,

the clock weighing down their shoulders.

Siringen looks at me again and shakes his head.

"I do not know. It is a strange thing to bring to a hot island like this. It will be ruined within the week."

The villagers are all out to help. Everyone, at the insistence of the Bigman. Men and women and children are lined up, a twisting *snek* of people passing strange-looking packages and boxes from the boat, all the way along the beach and past the fishermen's huts. It is the middle of the day and everyone is hot. The Bigman yaps his orders and points a lot.

Siringen is not part of the twisting *snek*. He is the oldest person in the village. Even though the Bigman would like nothing more than to force Siringen to carry the clock on his bent back, tradition says he is not allowed. I am Siringen's helper, so I stand beside him and watch.

"When are they coming?" I ask, as we both turn and follow the long line of strange-looking packages and boxes into the village. The heat is like a roomful of fire, and many of the men and women passing the things along are almost raining with sweat.

"They are coming on the next boat. That is what Lungadak says. They sent all their possessions ahead and are following behind in the next boat. They will be here soon enough." The sand burns under our feet.

The line of people runs past the school building – no children learning anything there today – past the freshly painted church hall with the big white board outside, the word of the missionaries' Lord bleached and faded, with only one or two letters remaining. It weaves through the trees and the papaya plantation. It follows the stream backwards, towards the hills and alongside the road.

It is only as we cross the road over to the place where the land dips that I start to wonder.

"Siringen," I ask. "Where are they staying?"

Siringen tries not to look at me, but he fails. His eyes flutter towards me before staring at the ground once again.

"Siringen?"

He stops moving and gives an awkward cough. "I think…" He pauses. "I think you already know where they are staying."

"No." I shake my head. "No, they can't be. That is not right."

Siringen says nothing with his lips, but his eyes tell me everything.

"No!"

I run off from Siringen, my feet digging hard into the dry earth. I follow the twisting *snek* of people down into the small valley on the beach. Down I rush.

To the hut where I once lived with my mama and papa.

I push past the woman standing in the doorway and look around. It seems so different. I know I haven't lived here in a long *taim*, but it seems so... The whole hut seems smaller. The walls cleaner. The floors scrubbed and bright.

I step through into my room. Boxes and packages are stacked against a wall, and a camp bed with a mattress lies directly under the window looking out over the bay. A man with a mouthful of nails is knocking one into the wall with a rusty hammer. He doesn't notice me looking. Once he's happy the nail is fixed, he bends over and lifts up a framed picture, hooking it into place.

It is a picture of a city. Black and white. A photograph taken from the air. It might be London. It might be New York. It might be Tokyo or even Paris. I don't know.

A city.

Salome – one of the women who normally works in the papaya grove – comes into the room holding some thin, silky-looking material. Kneeling on the camp bed, she starts to pass it over a small wooden bar that has also been nailed into the wall above the open window. The material is white, with colourful shapes over it. I step nearer to see. The shapes are horses. The sort of horses you would see at the fairground. On a ride that goes round and round. I have read about them in books and seen pictures before. Carousel horses, they are called.

Salome tugs the material tight before standing back and admiring the new curtains.

"There!" she says. "Isn't that *mobeta*?"

My room is no longer my room. It has become a room for someone else. Someone who likes to see pictures of cities and carousel horses from their bed. Someone who doesn't understand this place at all.

Someone who doesn't belong here.

I haven't even met the professor and his daughter.

But I hate them already.

Two of the fishermen from the village position the tall clock in the corner of the main room of the hut. I snort to myself as I pass. It looks ridiculous. So wrong. Like a *telefon* in a graveyard.

Outside, Siringen is talking to Miss Betty – another one of the workers from the papaya grove.

I straighten myself up and walk past them with my head high in the air.

"This is not a good thing, *waspapi*," I shout without looking at him. "*Nogut*. Only bad things can come from this."

I sense him looking at me as I pass, but he says nothing.

I cross the sand over to the place where the hibiscus flowers begin to grow – their red and purple heads all heavy and papery at the same *taim*, the sea breeze shaking them gently where they root. Being careful not to trample on them, I pick my way across the glade until I come to the old lawatbulut tree. The same knotty old lawatbulut tree that my mama would let me play on when I was really *liklik* – two or three, something like that. She would balance me on one of the thick, low branches and I would climb up – my tiny bare feet scraping against the dry bark, my tiny, smudgy fingers clutching at the waxy leaves above.

I come around to the front of the tree and rest my head against it.

Why is the Bigman allowing these outsiders into my old home? Why *this* hut? It doesn't seem fair. There are a dozen other old huts in which they could stay. Why should *my* old home be torn and made pretty for these Americans? Why not someone else's?

In anger, I punch the tree and the branches tremble. A couple of the looser leaves twist over and over, falling to the ground. Slowly, the tree stops its shaking, but the pain in my fist takes a little longer.

The Bigman looks almost as strange as the clock in the hut.

Most days he is dressed in one of his far too big T-shirts with the stripes going left and right or up and down. One of his T-shirts and a pair of shorts. Plastic sandals on his feet. A film-director cap on his head.

But today...

Today he is playing his traditional role as chief of the village. A high and wide headdress made from cassowary feathers sways as he shakes his head from side to side. Around his neck hang hundreds of coral-shell necklaces that rattle as he moves. A grass skirt covers his lower half, and in his right hand he holds a long green walking stick of unripe bamboo.

The rest of the village council are in traditional costume too. Even Mr Boas, who dresses in a smart suit and tie most days before walking up to the place on the road where his large Mitsubishi sits parked under a specially made shelter, and driving into the town where he sits behind a desk at the Australian bank. Mr Boas looks especially awkward in his freshly applied ceremonial paint.

Siringen is nowhere to be seen. He has pulled his outrigger off the logs outside his hut and pushed it through the thin, soft sand, down into the water. It is where he feels happiest – out on the sea with the silence and the dolphins and his thoughts. Miles away from all these *longlong* men. It has been a sensible move.

I reposition my feet in the cloth loop before climbing a little further up the betel-nut tree. From this height I can see just about everything. The children practising their singing. The women lining up plentiful bowls of caraway rice on the trestle tables. The smoke coming from the two hogs roasting on a spit. I can also see the boat *Sea Ballerina* bringing the Americans. Nobody else can see it yet, I know, because everybody moves at the same speed as they always do. Once someone sees it, everything will change. The women will hurry, the men in costume will puff out their shoulders and nod to each other, the children will squeal and stand where they are ordered to by their teacher. But at the moment, it is only me who can see it, slightly below the horizon.

I pull myself a bit further up the tree and it tips over slightly. Taking my knife from its sheath on my ankle, I cut some of the betel nuts from a nearby stem, letting them drop to the ground. Like most of the men in the village, Siringen likes to chew betel nut. It doesn't do you any good. Turns the teeth red and stops you from sleeping. I've known men with holes in their cheeks because of betel-nut chewing. And everywhere is covered in red spit.

Looking down into the village, I can see some of the women knocking the sand with brushes, covering up the horrible red strings of their husbands' betel-nut spit. I laugh to myself. How decent of us to hide our true ways for the sake of these American intruders! How…nice.

"Hello, Blue Wing!"

I almost lose my footing, and the tree shudders under me. I turn to see a face. I must be fifteen metres above the ground, but a face is grinning straight at me.

"Thought I'd join you and watch the show from here."

It is Chimera. Chimera is old – almost as old as Siringen, I think. She doesn't live in the village any more, instead choosing to sleep in a cave somewhere in the hills beyond the papaya grove. Everyone thinks she is mad – her father was the village witch doctor a long *taim* ago and, after he died, she carried on with his magic. Only, not so many people believe in it now, and the Bigman has told everyone that they shouldn't have anything to do with her – even though I know for a fact that he went to see her for some problem with his back. So she lives out in her cave and only occasionally comes into the village.

The tree Chimera has climbed wobbles back and forth under her weight (which isn't very much). I stare at her arms, which are oddly strong for such an old woman.

"An American professor, I hear," she says, her yellow

eyes flaring in the sun. "Coming to stay with us for a while." Suddenly she squints and gives a dry laugh. "I don't know... The Bigman owns a jukebox and a mobile phone. The westerners come here to live the way we do. It is almost like two different worlds trying to meet in the middle. Like a tunnel."

She coughs, and the leaves above her shiver.

"Where..." she almost whispers, "is your *waspapi*? Not down there practising his tribal dance with the elders, is he? I can't see him."

I point out to sea. "He is in his canoe."

"Ah. Talking to his beloved sharks, is he? You know, I think he trusts those sharks more than he does any human being."

I'm not sure what she means by this, but she sounds sad, so I nod.

"Siringen is a good man. I have always known it. While most other people in this village have lost their heads to money and jukeboxes, Siringen keeps his out on the sea where his magic is still strong." Her yellow eyes seem to flare once again.

"Chimera?" I ask.

"Yes, Blue Wing?"

"May I ask you a question?"

"If it is a good question and not something stupid like

'What's it like being a witch?' or 'Can you make a pig belch?'"

I shake my head and the leaves above me shake along.

"No. I just want to ask...well... Suppose you went back to your cave one day and found someone else there. Living there, I mean."

"Hmm?" Her eyes are fixed on me.

"Wouldn't you be angry? Wouldn't you hate the person for being there?"

Chimera grins. "Well...for a start, nobody would want to live in my cave. Unless they were completely *longlong*. It is wet and cold and horrible."

"So why do you live there?"

She points to the village below. The boat has obviously been seen, because everyone seems to be rushing about and making much noise.

"Because I would much rather live in my wet, cold, horrible cave than in a village run by a chief with a jukebox, who has forgotten how to wear his traditional clothes."

I laugh as I spot the Bigman picking up his elaborate headdress from the ground and trying to repin it onto his head.

"But," I continue, "if there *was* somebody – a stranger – in your cave...wouldn't you be angry?"

She thinks about this for a minute. "Depends."

"On what?"

"On how much *they* needed a home."

"What?"

"Well, if they didn't have any other place they could live...if they were lonely and sad...well, I wouldn't feel angry. I would feel that they needed my help." She adjusts her tiny weight on the tree. "And if they needed my help, I would invite them in."

It isn't the sort of answer I was hoping for.

"After all," Chimera whispers, "that is exactly what happened with you and Siringen. You know, after," she takes a breath, "after what happened, Siringen invited you into his home, to watch over you. He saw you lost and alone, so he invited you in."

"That's right. He *invited* me in." I say the words so she can hear the difference. "Siringen *invited* me into his house. I didn't just march in like some sort of *soldia*, taking over the place."

Chimera smiles. "Is this all about the westerners staying in your family hut?"

I nod and suddenly I find that I am biting my lip.

"Oh, Blue Wing...Blue Wing, my child." Her eyes are now trying to reassure me. "A home is not a building. It is not a collection of bricks or planks of wood with a roof on the top. It is not the glue or nails that hold it all together. A home is a place where you are wanted. A place where you feel safe. And loved. That is what a home is – not the materials it is made up of or even its location. A home is the place where you are accepted for who or what you are. Please, never forget it."

I turn my head away from her. It isn't right. Chimera doesn't understand. She has spent too much time hidden away from people, up in her cave, and has gone mad.

I say goodbye and let myself slide down the betel-nut tree, just as the boat pulls onto the shore.

FOPELA

It is early the next morning and there is a hard tapping on Siringen's tree-fork door. Without warning the door opens and the Bigman puts his large head round it.

"Siringen!" He glares hard at my *waspapi*, who is busy polishing one of his carvings. "You were not at the welcome party last night. Where were you?"

Siringen says nothing but points past the Bigman to the sea behind. The Bigman twists his head before he realizes what my *waspapi* is telling him.

"I should have known."

He steps into the room and I can see that he is carrying something. A tray. And something on the tray smells good. Sweet and hot. Delicious.

"Don't get excited. This isn't for you. My wife has baked these for our visitors. For their breakfast. I want you to take them over and introduce yourself."

He puts the tray on the floor in the middle of the room and straightens up again. I can see that Mrs Bigman has baked bagels for the intruders. An American breakfast for the American people. Nice of Mrs Bigman to try and make them feel at home, I think to myself. The Bigman gives an uncertain look in my direction, then turns back to Siringen.

"Take them. As you decided not to show yourself yesterday, I think it is the very least you can do for me."

Without saying anything else, the Bigman walks out of the hut.

"Please," I beg. "Just one. They won't miss just one."

"No." Siringen swings the tray away from me so I cannot reach. "They are not for you, Blue Wing. Anyway, they probably taste *nogut*. Most American food tastes *nogut*, like all the goodness and life has been sucked out of it."

"You've never even tasted American food. You are a miserable old man sometimes," I moan.

Siringen looks at me with eyes that say *Remember to respect the old*, so I stop myself from saying anything more.

We pass the lawatbulut tree, cross over the patch of hibiscus flowers and step down onto the small bay in which my old hut sits.

Suddenly I stop.

"What is it?" asks Siringen.

I shake my head. "I don't think I want to see them."

"Why not?"

I think for a few flickers of *taim*. "I don't know."

"Well...just wait here then. I won't be long."

I hold back, trying to hide behind a palm tree while I watch Siringen carrying the tray towards the hut.

"Hello," he shouts, as he gets near to it. To one side of the hut I can see a generator has been started. Another luxury for the spoiled Americans, I think to myself. Bagels and electricity. "Hello!"

The *thup-thup-thup* of the generator seems to reply, but nobody comes out from the hut.

"Hello!"

Suddenly the door swings quickly open, so I tuck myself in closer to the palm tree.

"Hello?"

"Good morning," Siringen says, his English difficult and slow. "I have some...breakfast for you."

"Oh, thank you." I can hear the tray being taken. "That is most kind." It is a man's voice. The professor.

"You must be Mr Siringen? Your village chief said you would be happy to take me out on the water."

"Siringen. Please. Just Siringen. Not mister."

"Okay. Siringen. I'm Atlas. Atlas Hamelin."

There is a *liklik* silence, so I look around the tree to see the two men shaking hands. The professor is tall and thin, but strong. His hair is blond and reaches the top of his shoulders. From where I am standing, I think he has a beard.

"I am…the village…shark caller. I know all the sea here. There is nobody else who can show you the sea like I can," says Siringen.

"Fantastic. I'm going to need someone who knows their way around these waters. I'm having a decent-sized boat brought over from the mainland later this morning. Perhaps tomorrow we can take a trip out?"

It takes a second or two for Siringen to take all this in. Eventually, he nods.

"Excellent!"

"But I have a canoe. Maybe we can use that."

"An outrigger?"

Siringen nods his head again, but the professor shakes his.

"The thing is, I will need my diving gear." He points to some large bottles of gas standing against the side of the hut. "And I don't think an outrigger will take the weight of all my equipment. Don't you agree?"

Siringen looks at the gas bottles before turning back to the professor. "No. Maybe not."

"I'm sure that, between us, we can easily manage this new boat. It's just a basic motorboat. Nothing too special."

"Yes."

Suddenly the professor's voice jumps up into loudness.

"Maple! Come here, sweetheart."

I look round the trunk of the palm tree to see the daughter standing in the doorway. I can see that she is about twelve years of age – similar to me. Her hair is a mosquito shade darker than the professor's. And longer too. It is shiny and straight and falls all the way down her back. I run my hand through my short, thick hair and find a piece of bark caught in it. I pull it out and throw it onto the sand. The girl wears a dress that I think looks pretty – even though I don't know one thing about pretty clothes. It is covered in colourful shapes. Birds perhaps.

I look down at my torn shorts and my dirty T-shirt.

"This is my daughter – Maple." The professor's voice has dropped back to evenness. "Say hello to Mr Siringen... I mean, Siringen. He's going to be coming with me on my expeditions."

"Hi." The girl does not look pleased. Her face is like one of the terrible days that we get in the rainy season.

"Hello." Siringen smiles.

The girl doesn't smile back.

"Look. Siringen has brought us breakfast." The professor shows the girl the tray. "Bagels. Your favourite."

She shrugs. "Who's the girl?" She points towards me.

"What, sweetheart? Oh, yes. I see. Is that your... granddaughter?" the professor asks Siringen.

They can see me!

"Um." Siringen is confused for a second. He turns. "No. That is Blue Wing." He waves for me to come out from behind the tree. "She, um, she is someone who helps me."

Slowly I step out and walk towards them, my head down.

"Hello, Blue Wing." The professor comes down from the steps and holds his hand out to me. "My name is Atlas Hamelin."

"Yes, I know." I take his hand – it feels hotter than mine – and shake it.

"And this is my daughter, Maple."

I nod at the girl who doesn't do anything back.

"Your...er..." Professor Hamelin pauses. "Erm... Siringen has promised to take me out on the ocean tomorrow. So, while we're doing that, perhaps, Blue Wing – what a beautiful name – you might want to show Maple around your village. Keep her out of trouble. Oh, that's if you're not at school, of course."

"Dad!" the girl growls.

"School?" Siringen asks. "No. Blue Wing does not go to school now. Not any more."

"Oh." There is some silence while Mr Hamelin thinks of something to say. "Okay."

"Blue Wing will show your daughter the island," Siringen answers for me. "We will go…to the ocean, and she will show your daughter—"

"Maple," Professor Hamelin reminds Siringen of the girl's name.

"…Maple. Blue Wing will show Maple all there is to see."

I feel my shoulders rising up. I do not know if I want to show this girl my island.

"Excellent!" Professor Hamelin smiles – too wide and with too many teeth. "Well, thank you so much for these delicious-smelling bagels." He lifts up the tray again and sniffs the food. "Wonderful!"

"*Orait*." Siringen points. "I…I didn't make them. Bigman's wife – she make them."

"O-kay…" Mr Hamelin looks confused. "Well, thank

54

you for bringing them and we look forward to seeing you both again tomorrow. Don't we, Maple?"

Maple says nothing, just turns and disappears inside the hut. *My hut. My family's hut.* I chew my lip again.

"Yes. Thank you. Goodbye." Siringen gives a small wave and takes one or two steps backwards. Mr Hamelin goes inside and closes the door.

We walk slowly across the hot, soft sand, back past the palm I had hidden behind.

"They saw me," I say as I shade my eyes from the sun flashing over the rolling of the sea.

"Yes," says Siringen. "I know."

FAIPELA

I watch as Siringen and Mr Hamelin load up the boat with all Mr Hamelin's equipment. Diving gear, including bottles of air, flippers and a face mask. A large black box with a large black screen – some sort of computer, I think. Smaller, scientific-looking grey tubs with writing on them. Two or three square zip cases.

It seems like a *lot* of equipment just to study the coral.

Siringen throws his own small snorkel onto the pile and climbs in.

He looks a little uncertain. He is too used to his own outrigger. I don't know if he has ever used a boat with a motor to power it, but the look across his face tells me it is a strange thing to him. His eyes move from the front of the boat to the back as he wonders where he needs to be sitting.

Mr Hamelin has a wetsuit on. It comes to a stop just below the knees and just after the elbows. He smiles as he passes me and goes into the hut. A few moments later he comes out again.

"She won't be long, Blue Wing." He looks nervous, like he might be lying and she *will* be a long *taim*. "I don't think she got a great deal of sleep last night – new place, new bed and all that. Takes a bit of time to adjust. Especially to this heat." He wipes the back of his hand across his head before staring at the sweat on it. "*So* hot."

I shake my head. "It is not so hot. This is normal for the *taim* in the calendar. At other calendar *taim*, it is much, *much* hotter."

"Is it?" He looks worried. "I don't know how you can stand it."

I shake my shoulders up and down like it is all nothing to me. "When you have spent your complete life here, you are used to it."

Mr Hamelin says nothing else and climbs into the boat, after lifting the rope away from the stick in the sand. Siringen makes room for him and watches as Mr Hamelin tugs a couple of *taim* on the engine cable. The engine starts and the sea behind the boat starts to kick up and foam.

Mr Hamelin waves at me, Siringen nods at me and the

boat begins to slip away from the shore, cutting the small waves like a knife. I stare as they steer their way round the end of the bay, towards the places where the reefs are brightest and biggest.

In the hut, nothing seems to be happening. I walk up the beach towards it, hoping that as I get near I might hear the sounds of the girl getting out of her bed. There is nothing. I wait for a while, sitting on the sand and sorting shells into piles. But still there is nothing.

After a few more minutes, I get up and tap on the door of the hut. It is a door I know well. *Tru* well. The thought that this is really *my* home, and not this lazy girl's, angers me once again and I knock much harder on the door.

"Get up!" I shout. "It is late in the morning. Get up!"

Suddenly the door swings open and the girl is standing on the step before me.

"Look…" She is blinded by the brightness of the sun so covers her eyes with her hand. "Look, whatever your name is—"

"Blue Wing." I spit out my own name like a watermelon seed. "My name is Blue Wing."

"Look, Blue Wing. I know my dad said you were supposed to show me around the village, but…"

"What?"

"Well, I don't want to look around your stupid village. And, if you're being perfectly honest, you don't really want to take me. Am I right?"

"What are—"

"So," she carries on without letting me finish. "Why don't we strike up a deal? If you pretend you showed me around, I'll pretend I've seen it. Then I'll tell my dad and you can tell your grandfather, and everyone is happy. Yes?"

I shake my head. "Siringen is not my grandfather."

"Well, whatever he is." The girl's eyes point directly at mine like two beams of moonlight. "Do we have a deal?"

I frown at her and shake my head for the *namba tu* time.

"Okay. I'll take that as a yes."

Without saying anything else, she closes the door.

I do not know what to do. I am confused and stunned, like a shark with a *kasaman*.

I start to turn, but stop myself.

"No!" I shout, then I hit the door hard with my fist. "I am not going away! I am not going to lie for you."

"Do what you want. I'm not going anywhere with you," comes the girl's voice from inside.

"*Orait!* I shall sit out here until you *do* come out.

59

And when your papa comes back, I shall explain what you said."

"Fine! He doesn't care about me anyway."

I sit myself back on the sand next to my piles of shells. "I can stay here all day," I say in a calmer voice.

There is no reply.

I realize I hadn't been totally truthful to Mr Hamelin earlier. It *is* hot today. Hotter than it usually is for this calendar *taim*. I move along a couple of canoe lengths, until I am sitting in the shade of the hut. Only a tiny breeze tries to cool the day – it is a day of heat and thirst.

I let the sand stream through my fingers and keep one of my eyes half pointed towards one of the windows in the hut. One or two *taim* I see the girl looking out, wondering what it is I am doing. I pretend to ignore her.

Nearly an entire hour goes by and she still hasn't come outside. Although it is nice to relax and listen to the sound of the sea as it tries to reach up the beach, it is beginning to feel as if this waiting could go on long *taim*.

So I begin to sing.

I think of the most *hambak* song I know. It is one that the *liklik* children in the school sing all the *taim*. Siringen says it is a song that the missionaries liked to sing with the villagers.

"Mama says no play,
This is a work day.
Up with the bright sun.
Get all the work done.
If you will help me,
Climb up the tall tree.
Shake the papaya down."

There is no movement in the house, so I carry on, making my voice go *liklik* louder and *hambak*.

"Sweet, sweet papaya,
Fruit of the island.
When all the work's done,
Dance on the white sands.
If you will help me,
Climb up the tall tree.
Shake the papaya down."

I sing my way through all the parts of the song. All through the *Shake them down, shake them down*, all through the *I love papaya, yes I do* – all the way through to the end. And when I reach the end, I begin again. Over and over, I sing until even I am sick of the song. Eight or nine *taim* I sing it, until—

Suddenly the door bangs open and the girl marches out to where I am sitting. She doesn't look happy.

"Okay," she says. "You win. Stop singing that stupid song and show me your stupid village."

It feels a little like dragging a dead cassowary bird around with me. Plenty *taim* she hangs back, not paying attention to me or what I am showing her, and plenty *taim* I have to pull her on.

Many of the villagers smile at Maple and greet her, but she doesn't really smile back or say anything. One of the women who tends the goats says nice things about her dress (a different one to yesterday – light blue with snowflakes all over it) and her wide hat to keep the sun out of her eyes, but all the girl does is give a look like her head is aching and then carry on.

"Why are you being so rude?" I ask as we come to the school building. Inside I can hear the children repeating their times tables.

"What do you care?" The girl stares hard at me like she wants me to fight her.

"Don't you want to get along with people? Do you like people looking at you like you're *longlong*?"

Her eyes close a little.

"*Longlong*? What does that mean?"

I have to think. "It means…" I tap the side of my head with my finger.

"Oh. You mean crazy."

"Yes. That is it. Crazy."

"Ha! *Longlong*. That's weird. Your language is weird."

The anger in me comes up again. "No, it isn't."

She doesn't reply. Instead she stands on the tips of her sandals and looks in at the open window of the school. "Is this the school?"

"School? Yes."

She watches for *liklik taim*. The children inside finish off their *fopela* times table and move on to their *sikispela* times table.

The sound makes me shiver. I do not like Maths.

"You will go to the school when you are here?" I ask. "While your papa is fishing?" I try to sound polite, but really I am asking because I don't want to have to take care of the girl every day. If she went to the school then I wouldn't have to spend more *taim* with her. "Yes?"

"No. I won't be going to this school," she says. "I never go to school. My par—" She stops before carrying on. "My dad, he homeschools me. I learn everything I need from…him."

I feel my belly fall like a rotten papaya.

"Anyway, my dad isn't a fisherman. And, anyway, you don't go to school either."

I say nothing.

"Why don't you go to school?" she asks. "You're still young enough. Does your grandpa homeschool *you*?"

I go in a circle around the question and frown at her. "I told you," I say. "Siringen is not my grandfather. He is my *waspapi*."

"Another weird word from your weird language!"

There is a small bit deep inside me – buried right in the middle – that tells me to punch the girl. It says that punching the girl is the best thing for her and the best thing for me, and that I should do it now.

But there is a bigger part deeper inside me that tells me to be patient and to wait. Like Siringen out on the waves calling the sharks. Let *taim* show the way. Let *taim* put things right.

So I bite my lip again.

"This way, this way." I move her on.

We pass some of the older huts along the beach. Outside one I can see Eliap the fisherman rubbing down his outrigger with some soft white coral. In the hut next to his, Miss Betty is playing with her newest child – a *liklik* girl not even two years old. The child watches as we cross in front of the hut, stops playing with the halves of her coconut shell and smiles at me. I wave to her and she waves back.

The professor's daughter barely notices.

We pass another of the fishermen, who smiles at her with his wide eyes before spitting onto the earth.

She comes alongside me and whispers, "That man is not well."

"What?"

"That man. He spat blood on the ground. That means he's got something wrong with him."

I look over my shoulder.

"No. He has been chewing betel nut."

"Betel nut?"

"It turns your mouth red."

"Ugh! Disgusting! People shouldn't spit. It's disgusting. You can get arrested for spitting in the place I come from. Someone should tell him it's unhygienic."

I try hard like a crocodile skull to ignore her.

Soon, we get near to the Bigman's compound and I let my voice go down and my footprints in the sand get lighter.

"This is where the chief of the village lives."

She looks around at it. "It's big."

I nod. It is *bikpela*. Over many years the Bigman has added extra rooms and buildings to the hut that his papa

– the chief before him – had lived in. Now there are rooms for sleeping, rooms for cooking, rooms for eating, rooms for drinking, rooms for smoking, rooms for dancing and rooms for washing. I can even see bamboo poles and wooden flooring laid out in the sand, ready to add another room to the corner of one of the buildings.

A *bikpela* house for a *bikpela* man.

Two or three generators *thup-thup-thup* away as they feed the compound with electricity.

"Your chief must be an important man to live in a hut that's so much bigger than the others."

I shake my shoulders up and down. "He likes to think so."

She ignores me. "It's a *much* nicer hut than the one we've been put in."

The small bit deep inside me – buried right in the middle – grows *liklik* bigger.

"Oh. What is wrong with the hut in which you have been put in?" I ask, my hands on the belt on my shorts.

"Ha! What *isn't* wrong with it? It's small. It's smelly. It's far too near the sea – all night long all I can hear is *whoosh, whoosh, whoosh*. The waves…they never stop."

I almost feel like I should laugh.

But I don't.

"The sea is always there," I say. "It always has been.

It always will be. People are born and people die. All the *taim* they are being born and dying, and all the *taim* in between, the sea is moving up and down, up and down. All the *taim*. It never ever stops. Never in all *taim*." I put on a smile that makes me feel taller than the girl. "Do you think you have special magic that can stop it? Make it *kwait* for you?"

"Quiet?"

"That is what I said. *Kwait*. Is that what you think?"

"Don't be stupid," she says, her face like a pebble. "I'm just saying, it's noisy. That's all."

"No, it isn't," I say, trying to keep back the anger in my voice like a dammed river. "No, it isn't all you were saying. You were saying that the hut you...you are staying in is small and...stinks. That is what you were saying."

"Well, it does."

"No, it doesn't." I step back from the girl, afraid I might still punch her. "It doesn't! It is the best hut in the village. *Mobeta* than the Bigman's...pretend castle! Why not put your *bikpela* clock in there!" I point my finger to the window above. "Put your clock in there. Let it tell you when it is a new hour. It will be at home in there!"

Suddenly I am turning around and walking away from the girl, my head feeling like it has been spinning all morning.

I am on top of the mountain that looks over the forest and the village and the sea and the sky. My arms ache and my legs ache and they are scratched all across. It has taken me nearly two hours to get here. Some of the way up is steep and I have to climb over rocks that stick out from the earth like blades and drag myself through bushes that feel like they are made with rough wire. Sometimes the only way to keep moving up is to hold the trees by their trunks and pull. In some places the earth slips away under my feet and I fall until my fingers dig into the ground and stop me. In others, I have to use my knife to help me climb.

But, standing on the top of the mountain, I know it has been worth all the hard work.

Because, here, I am higher than everything.

I am higher than the whole world.

Below me I can see the village. The people are dust, but I can just see the tops of the huts. A few dots on the sea in front of the village show that the fishermen are out and it is a good day to fish. The waves might be giants, but from up here it looks as though they don't even exist.

The village is so small – like a toy. Like it is not real. Like I could simply clap my hands and it would slip into the sea without even making any noise. I wonder if the girl is still standing outside the Bigman's compound and, for a second, I worry that I should have taken her back to the hut. My old hut. Wouldn't that have been the right thing to do?

But it is only for a second that I worry.

Looking straight down, I see the way I have just come: pandanus trees, ipil trees, oriana palms, ferns, twisting and curling orchids. A steep, green rug of life and of air.

The sea and the sky are the same colour today and it is difficult to piece them apart from each other. It is only the position of the other islands that shows me where the sea is, and the thin smoke of cloud that shows me where the sky has begun.

The breeze is warm. The sun is hot.

I turn around and walk over to look down on the other side of the island. The mountain is just as steep, the forest just as green and the sky and sea just as blue as each other. I can see the thin *snek* of road that leads from our village to the town, and in the other direction I can see the dry and broken-up skeleton of the long-dead copper mine.

Everywhere I look, the sea goes on for ever.

It is nice.

I close my eyes and listen to the breeze and the soft

sounds of the sea. The birds of paradise *whoop-whoop*ing in the trees below. I stretch my arms way out and feel the wind through my fingers.

No city could ever feel like this.

I do not know how long I am there, taking this in through my skin and my ears, but after a *taim* my mind hooks onto Siringen like a fish and refuses to let him go. I open my eyes. The position of the sun in the sky tells me it is later than I wanted it to be, so I say goodbye to this peaceful place and begin my slow slip back to the bottom of the mountain.

"Where have you been?"

Siringen sees me as I come along the beach to his hut. He is sat cross-legged, smoking his pipe in front of the *mumu* oven in the ground. He is cooking something. Without looking at me, he pokes a stick into the hot stones before throwing water over the banana leaves wrapped around the food.

"To the mountain," I say. "To the top."

I see his eyebrows go up and then down. Still he doesn't look at me.

"And what about Maple?"

"Who?"

"The girl. Maple. Mr Hamelin's daughter. Did she go with you?"

I laugh.

"What is so funny?" says Siringen, wiping the smoke from his eyes. "Did I make a joke?"

I sit down on the opposite side of the *mumu*. "No, *waspapi*. You did not make a joke."

"Then why did you laugh?"

"I don't think the girl—"

"Maple." Siringen looks at me for the *namba wan taim*.

"I don't think Maple would even dream about climbing to the top of the mountain. She would be too worried about getting her nice, pretty dress dirty or getting earth under her fingernails."

"Oh. I see." He doesn't smile at me like I thought he would. "Did you ask her?"

"What?"

"Did you ask her if she would like to go with you to the top of the mountain?"

I find my eyes staring at the parcel of food cooking in the *mumu*. I suddenly feel very hungry.

"Um, no. I didn't ask her."

Siringen taps his pipe out on a nearby rock. "So how do you know that she would be too worried about getting her dress dirty or getting earth under her fingernails?"

I stop myself laughing.

"*Waspapi*, you should have heard the way she was talking as I took her into the village. She was—"

"How do you know?" he asks again.

I look at him. He is still not smiling.

"I…" I trip over my own words. "I…don't."

"No. You do not know. Because you didn't ask her." He sighs and pokes the *mumu* again. "Blue Wing, because you find someone to be uncivil doesn't mean you have to be uncivil back."

"But, Siringen—"

He puts his hand up to stop me from talking.

"And I understand that you are upset about your family hut being used. I understand. But that is just a fact that you have to accept. Mr Hamelin and his daughter had no fingers in that decision. Blame the Bigman, if you like, but not the girl. Do not go around thinking that is her fault. It isn't."

I sit there and say zero.

"And anyway," he adds, refilling his pipe from the small bag he carries around with him. "If the girl – her name is Maple, remember – is uncivil, maybe there is a reason for that, yes? Something that has made her so."

He lights the pipe with a smoky ember.

"You see, Blue Wing, sometimes you have to dive a

72

little deeper to find the treasure you need to find. Don't just think it should always be in your hands."

The food is not for me. It is for them. As a punishment, Siringen makes me take it to them.

I tap on the door and Mr Hamelin answers it.

"That really is so very kind, Blue Wing. Thank you." He takes the package from me. It smells delicious. It is chicken and taro with herbs from Siringen's garden.

"However, you must tell Siringen that he shouldn't feel the need to cook for us all the time."

"Okay."

"We have a small stove and I've just discovered your local trade store. Between that and the fish and meat I can buy from the villagers, I think we can manage ourselves. In fact..." He turns around. Behind him I can see the girl – Maple. She looks like she might be frowning at me but I'm not sure. "In fact, one night, I would like to invite both you and Siringen to eat *here*. With us."

"Um..."

Maple suddenly disappears from behind her papa.

"Thank you," I say with my voice but not with my heart. "That is very good."

SIKISPELA

The trade store has been in the village for long *taim*.
More than fifty year, according to Siringen.

"It was not even a hut to begin with," he says to me
as we walk through the village together. Even though it
is a story he has told me a thousand *taim*, I try not to
sigh. "It was a boat. The trade boat would come up to the
village from the mainland. It would go to all the villages
along this coast.

"It would bring things in tins. Lots of different things.
Many of them I'd never even heard of. At first, the people
were not certain. 'Fruit in tins?' they would say. 'Why
would we need to buy fruit in tins? We have fruit that
grows on trees, and anything else we need to eat we can
find or grow for ourselves.' But then people got curious,
and the missionaries who lived among us encouraged them.

So they tried the fruit in tins and found that the fruit in tins was much sweeter and *mobeta* than the fruit in the trees, which would rot if you didn't eat it in *taim* and which you had to cut down yourself. Then the children tried the condensed milk, which came in tins too, and they liked it so much. They would open the tins and spoon it around. '*Mobeta* than betel nut!' their parents would say.

"So the men in the boat opened up the trade store. They built their own small hut. And then, when they learned they could earn lots of money, they had this... thing...brought here." Siringen nods towards the trade store. "Such an ugly thing."

The trade store is a long, red metal container. I have seen pictures of such things on the tops of *bikpela* ships. Freight containers, I think they are called. Used to carry things all across the world.

But this one doesn't travel any more.

Instead it is stuck in the ground at the edge of the village. A window has been cut out of one of the longer sides and, in the morning, when the shop opens, Mr Jeffrey who runs it pushes the window open and serves people through it. Mr Jeffrey sells many things through the window. He still sells the tins of fruit, but there are plenty other things too. Packets of potato chips,

PK chewing gum, bottles of South Pacific beer, Kellogg's corn flakes, boxes of tea leaves in little bags, jars of coffee, tubs of dried milk, cans of Coca-Cola and Pepsi. Plenty different things that we couldn't get otherwise.

As we get near to the trade store, I can see Mr Jeffrey pushing a metal stick into the window to stop it from falling shut.

"Aha, shark caller Siringen! This is a rare honour." Mr Jeffrey grins wide and I can see his row of uneven, yellowing teeth. "I can't remember the last *taim* I sold you something. Let me think...let me think..."

He clicks his fingers and looks as though he is struggling to pull something out of his mind.

"Ah, yes. *Oktoba*. Nine year ago. No! Wait... *Novemba*, nine year ago. Yes. That is it. I sold you two tins of fragrant Double Phoenix lychees. Am I right?"

Siringen shakes his head. "I do not know. I cannot remember, Jeffrey."

"Aha! But I can." He taps the side of his head like he is *longlong*. "Memory the size of an elephant in there!"

Mr Jeffrey does not live in the village. He has a large stone house on the edge of the town, so people say. Every sunrise, he packs up his van and drives along the thin coast road to open up his *liklik* shop. He sits behind his counter reading the newspaper, listening to the radio and

76

serving customers until an hour before sunset, when he shuts up the shop, puts a heavy padlock on the door and drives home again. I do not know if he has a wife or children. To work such long hours, I imagine he doesn't.

"What can I serve you with today, my dear sir?"

I hold back as Siringen stands in front of the window of the shop. Siringen reaches in and pulls something small onto the counter.

"Aha! An excellency choice, sir. Not one that I would have thought you would make, but an excellency choice all the same. That will be three kina."

Siringen puts the coins onto the counter and takes his purchase.

"A very goodly day to you, sir. Perhaps, next *taim*, I might see you in sooner than the nine year?"

"Unlikely," Siringen mutters as he comes back to where I am standing.

"What did you buy, *waspapi*?" I ask.

"Here." He throws something to me and I catch it out of the air.

It is a chocolate bar. An American one.

"Three Musketeers," I say, reading the wrapper. "What does that mean?"

Siringen's shoulders go up and down.

"Is this for me?" I ask.

"Who else would it be for? Yes, it is for you."

I rip the silver wrapper and bite into the chocolate. It is delicious.

"Thank you, *waspapi*."

Siringen looks at me and smiles. "Don't eat it too quickly. You will make yourself sick."

I watch as the boat with Mr Hamelin and Siringen turns in the opposite direction from yesterday.

"I suppose you're here to keep an eye on me again."

I look behind me and see that the girl – no, *Maple* – is standing in the hut doorway with her arms crossed like they are angry.

"Um…"

"Well you made such a good job of it yesterday, didn't you?"

She marches onto the sand. Today she is wearing white shorts and a white vest. They are cleaner than anything I have ever seen in my life. On her wrist hangs a silver bracelet with *liklik* figures on. I try to see what they are, but she moves too quick for me.

"Leaving me stranded like that."

"Were you *orait*?" Today I am going to try as hard as a whale shark to be good. I am going to think about

Siringen's words and not do anything *nogut*. Suddenly I realize why Siringen bought me the chocolate bar – to remind me that he knows *mobeta*. That I am thankful for him. He is a very clever man, my *waspapi*.

"Of course I was all right," Maple says. "I can take care of myself. Anyway, just after you went, your chief's wife took me in, gave me food and showed me around her house. I have to say, even though it is big, it's not exactly the sort of place I'd like to live in. Still," her eyes are on me like moonbeams again, "it's much nicer than *this* shack."

I think she is trying to see how I react, but because I do not know the word "shack" and I am busy thinking of the word "shack", I just look confused.

"This is far too small and noisy."

I chew my lip.

"And smelly."

"Would you like to climb to the top of the mountain with me?" I spit the words out quickly, before I say something *nogut* instead. "To the top, up there?"

She looks up at the mountain that stands up into the sky behind her.

"What? All the way up there?"

"Yes."

"You've got to be kidding me. That must be, like,

four kilometres up or something."

"No. It is not that tall. It is not that far really. Would you like to climb it?"

Her face doesn't smile. "No. I would not."

I am trying hard, Siringen. I am trying hard.

I think of something else I could show her.

"There is the old copper mine. We could...explore that."

"A copper mine?"

"Yes."

"An old copper mine? Like, shut down?"

I shake my head. "I do not understand."

"You know, shut down. Closed. Finished. You know, not working any more."

"Yes. Finished. We could explore the copper mine."

"Isn't that a bit dangerous? I mean, at home, anything like that would be off limits to members of the public. Especially kids. There'd be a wire fence all around it and big signs saying *Keep Out*. That kinda thing. People who break in would be arrested."

She talks so quickly that it is difficult to keep up with what she is saying. "We could go there. If you would like."

She stands silent for a short *taim*.

"Well," she says in the end. "I don't suppose there's

80

anything else to do around here. All it is is sand and sea and some green jungle stuff. So…yeah. Okay. Why not?"

It feels like I have just struggled to pull an oyster from out of its shell.

The copper mine is almost on the opposite side of the island. To get there you have to take the main road out of the village, towards the town, and then, nearly two kilometres out, take a wide track through some of the forest that was ripped away for the mining trucks. The track is hard to walk along – the tyre marks in the mud are dried and deep and it is difficult not to fall into them.

Maple falls all the time.

"You didn't say it was going to be so far away!" she says as she gets back up again. "When you said we could go there, I assumed it was nearby."

"It *is* nearby," I say as I help her. "Only about one kilometre now."

"Ha! One kilometre might as well be a million along this stupid path."

It doesn't take a long *taim* because of the track. It takes a long *taim* because Maple always seems to stop to take her water bottle from the bag she carries on her back. She drinks more water than a boar trapped in a pen.

"I can't believe how hot it is." She looks at me through her *bikpela* sunglasses. "I don't know how you can do anything in this heat. Can't you feel it? And the bugs!" She slaps the side of her neck and checks her fingers to see if there is something dead between them. "Always bugs and mosquitoes buzzing about."

I ignore her and carry on walking.

After some more water-drinking and falling into the tyre tracks, we come around the corner to where the copper mine used to be. The ground has been dug out and the wide space – which starts all the way over where the trees end and runs all the way across to where the other trees begin – is below the ground level where we both stand. To get down into it you have to be careful and watch where your feet are placed on the light, clay earth.

"Here," I say, sticking out my hand to her. She is bound to fall and hurt herself. "Hold my hand."

Maple looks at my hand like I have offered her the most *nogut* food in the world.

"Don't you trust me? Do you think I'll fall?"

"Yes."

"Ha!"

She doesn't take my hand and begins to slowly make her way down to the bottom, a *liklik* behind me.

This place is silent, apart from the noises of the birds up in the trees on the edge of the site. All the machinery left here to die makes it feel like a graveyard. Some of the *bikpela* trucks and diggers are standing around like they are waiting for the workers to return. But they never will. They are *longtaim* gone. Gone back to their own lives in Australia and America, not thinking about the machines they left here to die.

I am surprised, but Maple doesn't fall.

"There. See. Told you so," she says, just before taking another drink from her bottle. "Woah! This place is weird. What did you say it was again?"

"A copper mine. The mining company used to dig under the ground and bring up the copper. I do not know what for. I suppose they make things out of it."

Maple walks away from me a little. "Nobody here now though, is there?"

"No. They left. Ten year ago. It's been like this since then. They must have taken all the copper that was here. Some of the other islands had a war because of the copper mines." I say this last thing with the thought that she might be interested. But she isn't.

"And you're allowed to come here?" She takes her sunglasses off and I can see the brown of her eyes. "Nobody stops you?"

I shake my head. "Why should people stop us? There is nothing anyone needs here any more."

"Cool."

Maple punches one of the *bikpela* tyres of a yellow machine that looks like it was used for moving rocks.

"This is colossal," she says, before climbing up the ladder into the driver's seat. "Come on up."

I follow her and sit next to her on the broken seats.

"It's a pity we can't get this thing going," she says, reaching around under the steering wheel for a key or a button to get the truck moving. "If we could, we would probably get around this tiny island in twenty minutes or something."

"No. It won't move," I say. "When the men went, they made sure it couldn't move any more. It has also been a long *taim* and the salt in the air would have stopped it moving anyway."

Maple holds the steering wheel – which makes her look like a doll – and pretends to turn it. "That's a shame. I kinda like the thought of trampling over all the trees and things in this monster."

I look at her and shake my head. "Are you not well?" I ask.

"What do you mean?"

"I mean what I am saying. Are you not well? Is there

84

something wrong inside you? Why would you want to break over all the trees? The trees give us air. The trees hold life. Why would you want to break them over?"

Maple takes her hands off the wheel. "I wouldn't expect you to understand."

I feel she is just trying to flick my question off, like one of the mosquitoes she hates so much. So I buzz back at her some more. "Why wouldn't I?"

"What?"

"Why wouldn't I understand? What is it you know so well that I could never – in all the tides' history – understand?"

She stares at me through the sunglasses that remind me of insect eyes. "Don't worry about it."

"I *am* worrying about it."

"Oh, be quiet." She pulls herself out of the door and begins climbing down the ladder.

I find myself saying something cross under my breath. I know Siringen wanted me to try *mobeta* today, but this girl is just too *too* difficult. I think back to the chocolate bar and try to wrap my anger back inside its cage.

"Would you like to look inside one of the mines?" I ask her, down on the rocky ground, my voice quiet and trying not to make more waves. "We can go down into one if you would like."

She looks at me and even from behind her bug sunglasses I can tell that her eyes have been crying. Suddenly I feel like it is my duty to stop her tears in some way.

"There are some torches that still work, I think. We can use them to look into the tunnel together." I smile, thinking that by smiling I can make her smile also.

She doesn't smile. But she doesn't continue crying either.

"But surely that *is* dangerous," she says, putting her hat straight on her head. "Gas leaks and all that kinda stuff."

"No, we won't go that far," I say, my smile still stuck like dried ceremonial paint onto my face. "No one ever goes that far. We will go in and around a corner. Just to where the air becomes really dark. Then we can come back again. Yes?" Siringen is going to be *tru* proud of me today!

"Okay." She nods. "Let's do it."

I find two torches with the dying ends of battery still left inside and hand one to Maple. She takes it from me like she's never held anything so heavy before.

"Ready?"

She nods.

The entrance to the mineshaft is wide, with a track for wagons running *stret* along the middle of it. It is almost level, only going downwards a *liklik* bit at a *taim*.

"I used to come here a lot when I was young," I tell her. "All the children did. They still do. Their parents do not like them coming here, but they still come."

We step into the tunnel, and the heat immediately disappears into a coldness.

"Woah! That is nicer." Maple pulls her sunglasses off and puts them into the bag on her back. "So much cooler."

We walk on a few steps. On each step, the air around us becomes a tiny bit darker and the light from our torches grows a *liklik* bit stronger. The ground in front of us gets more difficult to see and I worry that Maple will start her falling over once again.

We work our way around some abandoned oil drums filled with rubble and rubbish. It gets colder the longer we go. Colder and darker, until the entrance to the tunnel has shrunk down to a *liklik* square behind us. The only noises are our feet on the grit and our breath in our mouths.

"Is there much more?" she asks. "Do we have to go further? I'm not sure I like it very much." I cannot see her face, but her voice tells me it has a scared look all over it.

"There is more," I answer. "Much, much more, so they say. These mines go down into the ground beneath us as far as the mountain grows above us." I shine the torch up into her face. Her eyes still look as red as the hibiscus. "But we are getting near where the corner turns. At that place there is no light from the entrance. If we turn off our torches at that place you will see what *tru* darkness looks like. Do you want to see?"

I start to walk again, but Maple doesn't move.

"I...er..."

I can see she is still trying to be the strutting cassowary she likes to be in front of me, but the redness around her eyes says that this *taim* she cannot pretend. A part of my spirit says I should be happy that this rude girl who wants to trample all the trees on the island has slipped like a mudslide right in front of me.

But another part of my spirit...

"It's okay," I say. "We do not need to go on. It is not very interesting. And you cannot see *tru* much anyway. Maybe we should go back."

"You didn't answer my question yesterday."

"What question?" I ask, as we come back out onto the main road between the village and the town.

"About school," she says, before stopping and finishing the end of the water out of her bottle. "About why you don't go there any more."

My shoulders go up and down. "I have nothing more to learn from school."

"So you know everything, do you?"

I stop and look at her. "I have nothing more to learn."

"So what do you do all day, if you're not at school? Do you go fishing with your grandfather?"

"I have already told you about *wan-handet taim*, Siringen is not my grandfather. He is my *waspapi*. He looks after me."

"But you go fishing with him, right?"

I continue along the road.

"No. I do not go fishing with him. Siringen is not a fisherman. He is the village shark caller."

"A what?" She seems interested by this and runs up alongside me. "A shark caller? What's a shark caller? Sounds cool. Does he give them all names?"

I don't bother to look at her.

"Don't be *longlong*."

"I'm not being *longlong*." She grins at me. "Just interested. So what does a shark caller do?"

"Siringen goes out onto the ocean and calls to the sharks. Then they go to him."

"Then he kills them, yeah?"

I find my face frowning at her. "No. Not these days. In the past, yes. Back when the people of the village would eat shark, Siringen and the shark callers before him would kill the shark and bring it back to the village for the women to cook."

"But not now?"

"No. Now he calls to them out of respect, to keep the traditions alive. And sometimes to show the tourists. Siringen calls the sharks, they come, then they go."

I see a questioning look on her face.

"Doesn't sound like it's the best-paying job in the world. So your...*waspapi*...he doesn't kill *any*? Not even the man-eating sharks? You know, the huge ones like in *Jaws*?"

Suddenly a large truck roars up behind us, the driver pushing hard on the horn. We jump out of its way and it rumbles over the dusty road beside us, towards the village.

"I do not know what you mean by this *Jaws*," I say as we continue.

"You know. *Jaws*. The film. About the shark." She starts to sing. "*Da-duh. Da-duh. Da-da-da-da—*"

"What are you doing? I think you really are *longlong*!"

"Hey, Blue Wing." Her brain jumps like a rat onto a different raft. "Have *you* ever eaten shark?"

I think. "A*ting*."

"A*ting*?" she asks.

I think again for the English word. "Probably. A long *taim* ago. Probably."

"What was it like?"

I shake my head. "I do not know. I cannot remember. I don't know if I really have eaten it."

She goes quiet for a while and I am pleased that she is not *whoop-whoop*ing in my ear like a bird of paradise. I think, maybe, I like her more when she is not happy to be with me and does not talk.

"Hey, Blue Wing," she begins again and my muscles inside seem to moan. "Are *you* a shark caller? Do you call sharks?"

"No. I am not. Girls are not permitted to become shark callers."

"What?! That's ridiculous!" She stops and changes the position of the rucksack on her back.

"Yes. It is," I agree.

"Now *that* is *longlong*. A girl can do anything any stupid boy can do. In fact, they can usually do it a whole load better."

"That is *tru*! That is what always I tell Siringen! I tell him that he has no sons and nephews to pass his magic on to. I tell him that I am the only one who is wanting to become a shark caller – nobody else in the village wants to do it. So why not change the *tambu* and let me learn."

"*Tambu?*"

"Um…traditions. I am wanting to do it. And I can do it better than anyone else."

"If you *did* become a shark caller, would you kill any sharks? You know, the big *Jaws* sort of ones? The ones that eat people?"

"No," I lie. "No I would not. No, no, no. Definitely not."

I think it is better not to name Xok.

As we come into the village, I can see the truck that passed us sitting alongside Mr Boas's Mitsubishi.

"I've got something you might like to see," says Maple. "In the hut. Come on." Suddenly she starts to run ahead of me, down the path towards the beach. I follow her.

I see her in the doorway of the hut, her sunglasses and hat gone, waving me on. When I get there, she goes inside.

The hut is dark compared to the outside light. Thin curtains are pulled together, trying to block out the day. It takes a *liklik taim* for my eyes to start to see.

It looks so strange. There is the clock, yes. I hear its

slow, low ticks and tocks as the thing inside it swings left and right. But there are other things too. A table with chairs. A small cooking area with knives and forks and plates and bowls and spoons. A soft chair to sit on. Pictures and posters pinned to the walls. An electric light, wired through the bamboo beams. A plant with shiny leaves sat in a pot.

Everything is so different. Not like when I lived here.

Maple pulls the curtains apart and light explodes into the hut.

"Wait here," she says and goes through the doorway into her room. The room with the picture of the city and the carousel horses over the window.

My room.

"Here he is." She comes back a few seconds later holding a small cage. "Meet Trinket."

I look inside the cage and see a *kapul*. It is white with brown spots along its furry back, and its wide, black eyes look all over the room as if it is lost. It hangs on to the side of the cage with one of its paws and eats a leaf that it holds in another of its paws.

"He's a spotted cuscus. A possum. We bought him on the mainland. Isn't he cute?"

I stare at the poor lost animal. "Why is he in a cage?" I ask, trying to keep my voice low.

"Well, we've only just got him, so Dad thought it would be best to keep him in the cage until he's been tamed a little. Otherwise he might just run away. Not that he runs at all. Just does everything really slowly. Isn't he sweet? I think he's the nicest pet I've ever had."

She puts the end of a finger in through the wire and moves it about in front of the *kapul*. "Yes you are." She puts on a strange voice like she has pebbles in her cheeks. "You are the sweetest little thing *ever*."

I shake my head. "It is not right."

"What?"

"It is a free animal. A free creature. It should not be kept in a cage for you to…" I think of the right word. "To…wriggle your finger in front of."

"Oh! Why not?" She puts the cage on the floor.

"Because it is not right! It is a wild animal. It should live in the trees with other *kapul*!" I feel the anger rushing out. "It shouldn't be kept as a pet."

"Is that right?"

"Yes! It is."

"But you just told me your grandfather – and let's face it, he's more or less your grandfather, whatever you choose to call him – goes out on the sea and calls the sharks to him. He calls the sharks to him *like they are his pets*!" Her face turns almost as angry as mine.

"That is different!" I shout.

"How is it different?" she shouts back. "I can't see how it is different. In fact, your grandfather" – she says the word "grandfather" just to make me angrier – "used to call the sharks in, *and then eat them*! He would tease them into shore, pretending to be their friend, *and kill them*! That's a lot worse than having a possum to feed and love and take care of, wouldn't you agree?"

"No. I would not!"

"Then you are *stooopid*!" She taps the side of her head. "Really really *stooopid*! You are the most *longlong* of everyone! If you honestly believe that killing sharks is better than loving something, then..." She trips over her words. "Then you don't know anything."

I turn my back and step towards the door. "It is *you* who do not know anything! *You* are an American." I walk outside and away from the hut.

Behind me I can hear Maple shouting.

"That shows how wrong you are! I am not just American! I am Japanese-American!"

"What now?"

Siringen knows there is something wrong as soon as he comes into the hut.

"There is nothing wrong," I say, rolling over on my sago mat so he cannot see my face.

He throws his diving mask into a woven basket.

"Blue Wing. Lying is not a good thing, and you are not a good liar. I suppose it is the girl?"

"Maple," I remind him, the way he reminds me.

"Yes. Maple. You have disagreed again?"

I say nothing.

"Did you find out?" he asks, using a cloth to wipe down his face.

"Find out? What do you mean?"

"Do you not remember our conversation yesterday? If Maple Hamelin is as uncivil as you are saying, there must be a reason for it. Well? Did you find out what it is that makes her so uncivil? Did you ask?"

I spin back around on my mat to look at him. "I talked to her, *waspapi*. I was good to her all day. Even when she was saying how she wanted to trample down all the trees, I kept my tongue behind my teeth and kept my words inside. I did try, *waspapi*."

"That is good, Blue Wing. But maybe you should now start digging for the treasure. Find out more. Be interested. You never know, you might be more the same than you are different…"

Suddenly a voice calls from outside. "Hello!"

"Who is that?" I ask, sitting up.

"Oh, no," says Siringen. "It is Chimera. Sit still. Be quiet and maybe she will go away!"

I have never seen him look so shaken as a coconut rattle before.

"Hello! Siringen!" A face comes around the tree-fork door and grins. "There you are, Siringen! You are a sticky man to find sometimes."

"Oh, hello, Chimera." He licks his lips with nerves.

Chimera comes around the door and into the room. "And Blue Wing too! This is good!"

I smile at her.

"I am very pleased to find you both home. Three *taim* I have visited today and found your hut empty. I know you have been out on the sea with the American professor, Siringen. And Blue Wing…"

"She has been with the professor's daughter," Siringen says quickly.

Chimera looks at me then back at my *waspapi*, who nods.

"I see… That is good too."

"Is it?" I ask, getting up from my mat. But Chimera ignores me.

"But now, at last, I have you both here."

Siringen sighs. "What do you want, Chimera?"

"I have made you supper." It is only then that I notice the pot she is holding in her hands. "It is just broth. Nothing much. But I thought that if you have been busy diving with the professor all day then you would not have the strength to cook food." I also notice the paint she has put on her face is thicker than normal.

"That is kind, Chimera," says Siringen, reaching out to take the pot from her. "You have thought kindly." His hands go around the sides of the pot but she doesn't let it go. For a *liklik taim* they are both standing there holding the pot like stone statues, saying no words.

Suddenly my mind tells me what is going on.

"Would you like to stay and share it with us, Chimera?" I ask. Siringen's eyes stare hard at me. "You have been very generous and have probably given us too much broth. Maybe you will stay and eat with us. Yes?"

"Oh, you are a very kind girl, Blue Wing," she says. "I would very much like to eat with you."

Siringen lets his hands slip off the pot and Chimera gives him a *bikpela* smile.

SEVENPELA

In the morning, the sun is lazy for the village. It hides behind the mountain, leaving us in its shadow. Slowly the shadow gets smaller and smaller, moving from out over the sea, over the beach, over the huts and the trees and the papaya grove until the heat of the day is upon us and the light is hard to escape.

Siringen is always up before the heat and the light. He spends long *taim* getting his outrigger canoe prepared for shark calling. He paints it with coral – inside and outside. The coral makes it turn white and stops it drinking in the seawater so quickly. He polishes his *kasaman* and his paddle. He tests the strength of the *larung*.

Then he performs all the magic needed to make the shark calling successful. He takes a piece of heavy, thorny vine found only on the bushes clinging to the mountain and rubs it over the *fopela* stone shark-gods he keeps in an enclosure outside the hut. By doing this he puts the teeth of the real sharks on edge, making them hungry for the day-old bait fish that sits in the canoe. Then he takes his many-pronged spear and makes holes in the sandy beach, from the stone sharks' enclosure all the way to his canoe. This fastens all the devil sharks to the floor of the ocean. They will not now be able to approach his canoe as they have been pinned to the bottom of the seabed. Finally, Siringen takes a piece of wild ginger and throws it into the sea. The wild ginger makes the sharks hungry too.

Once all these things have been done – and only once they have all been done – Siringen pushes the canoe through the soft sand into the gentle waves, before climbing in and paddling out onto the shark roads.

This morning I watch him as he does all these things.

"You are not going out with Mr Hamelin today?" I ask as he wipes the dried coral from his fingers.

"Not today. He has other things to do."

I try to be interested, like he says. "How is the diving with Mr Hamelin? Has he seen the things he has come to see?"

Siringen picks up his spear and starts stabbing the sand between the hut and the sea.

"I do not know completely," he says, his eyes pointing down to the ground. "I don't understand what it is he is looking for. As a professor of the sea he seems to know *tru liklik* about it."

I start to think about Mr Hamelin and I start to think about Maple. And questions slither into my mind like *sneks*. Why has Mr Hamelin brought his daughter with him to the island? Why has he made her follow him across the world so that he can do his work? It doesn't seem right. Why doesn't Maple stay in America with her mama? Why is she here?

I shake the questions out of my mind and watch as Siringen wipes the sand from the tips of the spear.

"No one knows as much about the sea as you, *waspapi*," I say to him.

He looks up at me. "You sound like Lungadak, Blue Wing. Try not to. It is not a good sound. Too full of hollowness," he says, throwing the spear into the canoe and starting to push it towards the sea.

I join him, holding on to the outrigger part and pushing it into the water. Siringen climbs in and takes the paddle, turning the canoe around to face me.

"Can I come with you today?" I ask. "If Mr Hamelin has given you the day off, can I come out and call the sharks with you?"

"No," answers Siringen, keeping the canoe still. "Professor Hamelin has had a truck brought to the village. He needs to go into the town and get supplies. He wants you to go with Maple and him. To help."

"To help, *waspapi*?"

"Yes. I know. Just do what you can."

He begins to spin the canoe around.

"Siringen," I shout towards him. "If you see Xok today…"

"No, Blue Wing. I won't kill him for you."

"Then let me do it. Please! Teach me the magic words. Show me the ways. I can do it. I *need* to do it."

Siringen looks away from me, shakes his head and then paddles away, leaving me alone on the beach just as the shadow of the mountain passes over my head.

The truck is one of the ones with a large, flat, open back for carrying things. A Nissan. Bright white, with fat wheels. Seats in the front and seats behind.

"You girls can sit in the back together, if you'd like," says Mr Hamelin, opening the door for us. "You've probably got things you'd like to talk about."

Maple looks at me and I look at Maple. We say nothing as we climb onto the seats.

"Better strap yourselves in," says Mr Hamelin over the part where the driver's head is meant to go.

I watch as Maple plugs the seat belt into its socket, and I do the same.

Mr Hamelin starts up the engine and the truck roars off. Inside the truck it feels warm and the shiny leather seats smell. Mr Hamelin presses a button and makes the windows go down into the doors. Then he twists another button and cool air starts blowing all over us.

"How's that? Better? It's so hot. I really don't know how you can take it, Blue Wing." He smiles at me in the mirror and I smile back. "I always feel like I am going to faint."

Maple just stares out of her window at the trees we are passing.

Mr Hamelin pokes his finger at some more buttons and the radio comes on. On the screen the words *Nau FM* flash up and a song I've never heard before starts playing. Pop music. Western music. It is loud and sounds like someone is hitting the side of a lawatbulut tree with a broken pan. The singing seems no better. Like the person has stepped on a *mumu* fire and is in pain.

"Oh, I like this one," I hear Maple say against the glass, and she begins to sing along with it.

A few kilometres outside the village, Mr Hamelin

makes the car stop suddenly. Maple is thrown forward hard and I have to put my hands out to stop myself from hitting the seat in front of me.

"Dad! What are you doing?"

"Sorry, sorry. Didn't mean to scare you both. Only," he points out of the window, "I spotted *that*."

Just off the road, trying to hide among the trees, is a *bikpela* metal tube, pointing to the sky. It is old and rust-coloured, and green vines have tried to grow themselves along it.

"What is it?" asks Maple.

Mr Hamelin opens the car door and gets out. I unplug my belt and climb out too. So does Maple.

"Wow," says the Professor. "That is fantastic! Really, really fantastic."

"Yes. But what is it?" Maple asks again.

"It is a gun for shooting down planes," I answer. "A Japanese gun. During World War Two the Japanese took over these islands. There were many battles. Many people dead. That is what Siringen tells me."

Mr Hamelin walks off the road into the bushes. He reaches up and touches the gun.

"You're right, Blue Wing. It is a World War Two Japanese anti-aircraft gun. In fact, it is a Type 96 twenty-five millimetre anti-aircraft gun. Not the greatest gun the Japanese navy had at their disposal, but…wow. I've never seen an actual one outside of a museum before. This is fantastic!"

"There are many of them all over the island," I say. "When the Japanese army went from here, they left many things behind – guns, tanks, trucks. Many things. I can show you others, if you would like."

"Oh, Blue Wing. That'd be great," he says, patting the gun like it is a dog one more *taim* and going back to the car. "I'd love to see more of them."

Maple looks at me like I've just poured goat's milk all over her rainbow dress.

I do not like the town. I have never liked the town. Ever since I was *liklik* I have seen that the town is not a good place to be. Too many buildings, too many people, too much noise, too much to see. The town is a place where there is too much of everything and it fills your head until it hurts and stops working. There is no space and no silence.

Cars and trucks zoom up and down the roads, trying not to hit the people on bicycles. Music comes out through the windows and doors of the bars where *raskols* sit about drinking South Pacific beer and Jack Daniel's whiskey and smoking cigarettes. Old men and women zigzag across the streets.

Nothing is still. Everything moves.

Mr Hamelin takes us into a shop selling equipment for diving. As he talks to the man behind the counter, Maple pulls on the sleeve of my T-shirt.

"What?" I ask.

"I see you're trying your best to make my dad like you better than me."

"I don't understand what you are saying."

"You know perfectly well what I'm saying. You're trying to get back at me by getting on with my dad. Well, it won't work, you know?"

What she says makes no sense to me, so I ignore it and make the talking go in a different direction.

"How is your *kapul*?"

"You mean Trinket? *My pet*?"

"Is he still sad? Is he still in his cage? Or have you let him free?"

"Actually, if you must know, last night we let him fully out of his cage for the first time."

"And did he go back into the trees with the other *kapul*?"

"No. He slept on my bed."

"Did you sleep with a lamp on? As you are so very afraid of the dark." As I say this, I feel straight away bad.

"I am not afraid of the dark!"

Mr Hamelin turns around and looks at us.

"Is everything okay, girls?"

"Fine. Everything's fine," says Maple, although she does not sound as if everything is fine. This makes me feel less good.

"That's my daughter," Professor Hamelin says to the man behind the counter, "and her friend. They've come to help me load it all onto the back of the four-by-four."

The man serving looks down at us. His face folds up, confused.

"No need. No need, sir. My boy can do that for you, sir. He put it all in truck for you. Easy as a pie. No need for…your daughter to do this."

"Really? Thank you. That's very helpful."

Outside, the shopkeeper's boy lifts the air tanks into the back of the truck.

"I need to go to the supermarket," says Mr Hamelin. "Then there's a man I've arranged to speak to. You two can go off and do your own thing, if you'd like. Shall we say meet back here in an hour? Great."

He doesn't say anything else. Instead he starts helping the boy with the equipment.

Maple walks away, trying to make the gap between us as wide as possible, but I run and catch up.

"Where are you going?" I ask. "You do not know where to go."

"Away from you. *Far* away from you. That's all you need to know."

"Maple." I try to catch her arm but she pulls it away from me. "Maple, I am sorry. I am sorry that I said you were afraid of the dark."

She stops. "Are you actually *apologizing* to me?"

I have to think what "apologizing" means, for a short *taim*, but then I nod my head. All the *taim*, in my mind, I am thinking of what Siringen has said to me. *Find out more. Be interested.*

"I am sorry. It was *nogut* of me."

She looks at me, confused, like the man in the diving shop.

"You are. You're apologizing to me." She folds up her arms like she doesn't know what to do.

Also, I do not know what to do.

We both stand in the street – cars and bicycles passing us like we are both invisible – for minutes.

Then I smile and say: "Shall we walk? Together?"

"Is it *orait* if I ask you a question?" I say, as we leave the main street and cross through a park with short grasses and *bikpela* squares of frangipani flowers.

"Well, I suppose that depends on the question." Maple doesn't look straight at me. But she doesn't look away either. "What question are you going to ask me?"

"Mr Hamelin is your papa, yes? But…" I think of how to ask the question. "But where is your mama?"

"My mother?"

"Yes. Your mother. Is she back in America?"

She stares down hard at the path.

"In a sense."

"What? I do not—"

"Her body is back in the States. In Vermont."

"Oh."

"She's dead."

"I am sorry."

We say no more until we come out the other end of the park, near the place where the American golf course meets the sea. Everything here looks neat and clean. For the tourists, of course.

"How long ago…?"

"A year." Maple says the words quickly, like she knows them very well. "A year ago next month."

"That is not long," I say, thinking of my own mama

and papa. *Two year and five month.*

"No. You're right. It isn't long." She looks at me for the *namba wan taim.* "Not long at all. Far too soon to be selling the house, putting everything into storage and then travelling two-thirds of the way around the world to a place you've never even visited before, don't you think?"

I sort the words out in my head and nod.

We walk over the road and down into the place where the people who own the golf course have put two long concrete arms out into the sea to stop the waves from getting too fat on the beach.

"How did she die? Was she old? Was she sick?"

Maple doesn't answer straight away. "A tumour. In her brain. She was thirty-six."

I do not know what a "tumour" is, but I know the word "brain" so I paint a picture in my head.

"There was nothing they could do." She talks like she needs to talk. Like all these words and thoughts have been stuck inside for a long *taim.* "When the doctors found out, it was too late and there was nothing they could do to get rid of it." Her voice sounds like she has some *kaukau* stuck in her throat. "They were going to bring her back home to die, but they were too slow. Paperwork. Forms to be signed – that kinda thing. So she died in the hospital."

She coughs.

We walk down onto the sand, which looks whiter than any sand I have seen before. Tourists are sunbathing under giant umbrellas, rubbing creams and liquids onto their skins. It is not like the beach on which I was born.

"Maple," I say, taking off my sandals and feeling the sand between my toes. It also *feels* different to the sand of the village, and I wonder if the Americans who own the golf course had it brought from America in containers and put here. "Maple, I have not been good to you, I'm afraid. Before you came, I already hated you. You see, the hut in which you are staying...it was my family hut."

"You used to live there?"

"Yes. I was born there. Your room was my room."

"And now your parents are both dead."

I am surprised. "How did you know this?"

"I guessed, I guess. I mean, what other reason would there be for you to live with your *grandfather*."

My mouth starts to tell her again that Siringen is not my grandfather, but stops when I see that on her lips is a tiny smile.

"Ah. You are playing a trick on me."

"Yes. Siringen is your – let me see if I can say it correctly...*waspapi*?"

I nod. "*Stretpela!*"

"Straight what?"

"Correct. It means correct."

"I don't think I'm ever going to get your language, you know."

Maple takes off her own sandals and puts her feet into the still water.

"One thing my mom did like to do was swim. She was a great swimmer. What about a race?" She suddenly looks different to me. She has changed. Not angry. Not sad.

"Where? What sort of race?" I ask.

"In there." She points to the sea. "A swimming race." She throws the sun hat and sunglasses down and pulls her rainbow dress off. Underneath she is wearing a swimming costume. "Come on!" She runs into the sea.

"Wait!" I say. I take off my T-shirt and shorts down to the costume I always wear and follow her in. The water is as warm as it always is.

She swims slowly to the middle of one of the concrete-arms-that-stop-the-waves, where she holds on to the bottom of a metal ladder. I am soon right next to her.

"What are you doing?" I ask her. We both feel the soft swell of the *liklik* waves under us.

"Swimming. What does it look like?"

"You can swim then?"

"Of course! Let's race right the way across this bay to the other jetty over there. See the place like this one? The point where the ladder is?"

"Yes. But…"

"But what?"

"I have been swimming in these seas since the *namba wan* day I was ever born. When I was a baby my mama threw me into the sea and I have been swimming ever since."

"What's your point?" Maple says, with a question between her eyes.

"I am saying that I am a *tru* strong swimmer. I can dive very deep and hold my breath for three minutes. I swim with the dolphins and the sharks. I do not think I have blood in my body. I think I have seawater instead."

"You think I don't stand a chance in a race against you. That's what you're trying to tell me, isn't it?"

"Well…um…yes."

Maple grins and I can see her rows of clean white teeth.

"You're probably right. I don't stand a chance. Still… let's race anyway. Ready? On the count of three. One. Two. Three!"

Maple pushes off from the wall the width of a butterfly's wings before me. I kick hard against the water, pull even harder with my arms and I move in front of her. I move easily and strong, reaching out into the sea. I try not to be too quick – I know she is sad inside and wants to show herself to be brave – so I let myself hold back.

Behind me I can hear her strokes. They sound fast. And smooth.

Halfway across the bay, I look back over my shoulder and see that she is still with me. So I speed up.

Halfway of what is left, I see that she is coming up next to me, her fingers cutting into the water with hardly a *liklik* splash.

I stop holding myself back at all and use all my strength and speed to try and win the end of this race.

That is when she really begins to swim.

Suddenly I realize that I was not the person holding back.

She was.

With every stroke, she moves forward ahead of me, like a dolphin. She swims so easily and without any tiredness that I think I must look like a whale next to her. I see her face as she passes. She looks like nothing could distract her. Her body and mind are thinking only of this race. Everything else has gone from her: the thoughts of her mama, of me, of where she is. She is completely inside herself.

I try to kick stronger, my legs hurting with each flick. But it is *nogut*. Maple Hamelin is just too good at swimming. *Mobeta* than even I am.

She reaches the ladder about two seconds before me.

I wipe the water out of my eyes and see her smiling. It is not a horrible smile that says, *That will teach you a lesson for thinking things about me that you couldn't know.* It is a nice smile. Like the smile of a friend.

Also, she is not fighting for her breath as much as I am.

"*Orait.* You win," I say, once I have enough air to say it. "You are *mobeta* swimmer than I am."

"Vermont State squad," she says. "Silver medallist for my age group two years running."

"Silver medal? That is good."

"It's not bad. That was before my mom died, of course."

"Yes," I say with *tru* feeling in my heart. "I understand."

"Before you came, I was angry. More angry than anyone in the world."

We walk back through the park with the short grasses, getting wet with the hosepipes spitting water.

"I was thinking it was wrong for anyone to come and live in my hut. That was *my* hut and my mama's and papa's. No one else should live there. But then you arrive

115

and I am surprised because you were more angry than I was. It made me confused. You had no reason to be more angry than I was. It didn't seem right."

We step back into the busy street and the noise makes my voice go loud.

"It was strange. I was the most angry person in the world, and then you took that name from me."

"I'm sorry I've been so angry with you."

Maple stops to let a bus pass before crossing the road.

"It's not your fault, I know, and I shouldn't take it out on you. After my mom died, I felt like I needed time to adjust. I wanted everything else in my life to stay the same. I needed my home and my friends. I needed the swim squad. All those little things that would remind me of her, keep her with me so I wouldn't forget. You see, one major part of my life had just disappeared, and I *really* didn't need anything else to change."

"So why have you come here?" I ask.

"Honestly? I don't know." She holds the sun hat on her head as the wind from the cars tries to blow it off. "I think it's my dad's way of coping. He got kinda stressed – as you can imagine. Took time off work to look after me – all that stuff. Then he started reading around and got kinda obsessed with this part of the world. I don't really know why. He's pretty secretive about things sometimes. Just kept saying that the best way to move on was to move on. Not get too buried in the past. That we should just clear out and go someplace else. That way we could refresh our memories of her."

"Sounds strange."

"I know. Ever since we left Vermont, I've been mad with Dad. I've tried to understand, trust me. I realize he's hurting as much as, or even more, than I am. But I still feel it's not the right thing to come here. We needed more time back home."

We get back to the *bikpela* white Nissan. All the diving equipment and boxes of food are now strapped in the back, but Mr Hamelin is not there.

"Where is he?" says Maple, looking up and down the road.

"He said that he was going to talk to a man. After the supermarket."

"Oh. There he is."

At the furthest end of the road, Mr Hamelin is standing talking to a short and round man. The man nods a lot and Mr Hamelin nods a lot back. After a short *taim*, the professor puts his hand into the pocket on his jacket-without-arms and pulls something out. It looks like a roll of kina notes. He hands it to the man who takes it and nods a few *taim* more before handing something back.

"What is that?" says Maple.

"It looks like paper."

"It's an envelope."

The man smiles and bows at Mr Hamelin, then turns and disappears behind the next road. Mr Hamelin folds the envelope up and slides it into his pocket before walking along the street towards us.

"What did that guy give you?" Maple asks, as soon as her papa is close enough.

"What guy?"

She points behind him. "That guy. The one who just gave you something."

"It was nothing, sweetheart." He pats the place where the envelope is. "Just an old map of the coral around these parts. That guy is an expert, that's all."

"Jeez, Dad," says Maple, pulling open the car door. "How is it you're *sooo* interested in coral nowadays?"

We all climb in and we all drive off and we all say nothing else about the map.

But I think we are all thinking about it.

ETPELA

"What do you think?"

I am trying not to laugh. Siringen owns two T-shirts. He never wears them. He likes to be traditional and have the sun burn down on his bare chest.

But tonight he is trying out his two T-shirts and trying to pick which of them he will wear. The first T-shirt has words on it.

PNG INDEPENDENCE 1975, it says.

"When did you get that T-shirt, *waspapi*?" I ask.

He points to the 1975 on his belly.

"That is old! How many times have you worn it?"

His shoulders go up and down. He does not know.

"Oh. It has a hole in it." Siringen puts a finger in the hole and moves it about.

"Maybe you should try the other one."

"Yes."

The other T-shirt looks *mobeta*. It has a collar around the neck and a pocket on the chest and buttons up the front. Also it is clean and doesn't have holes in.

"I do not know if it is the right sort of thing," he says, pulling on it to make it straighten. "I have never been to another man's hut for dinner before. Village celebrations, yes. I have been to many of those. But never to another man's home to be fed."

"I'm sure it will be *orait*," I say. "Mr Hamelin and Maple will not care what you are wearing. They are being nice to us. They are rewarding us for being nice to them."

Siringen's eyes go wider in his face. "Nice? You? I thought you hated Hamelin's daughter?"

"Yes. I did."

"*Did* means in the past. *Did* doesn't mean now." He smiles and I see his betel-nut stained teeth. "What has made this change?"

"I did what you told me to do. I asked."

"I see. And what did you find out?"

"That Maple is sad."

Siringen nods – not like he is agreeing with me, but like he is drinking this information.

"So you found something that you both have in common."

I look at him. "I am not sad!" I say, my voice squeaking up like a fruit bat. I feel like he is saying something I have never thought before and I do not like it. "I am always smiling. Look!" I open my mouth wide and show him my own teeth back.

"A smile does not mean you are happy," he says. "A smile can mean many different things. Happiness might not be one of them."

I stop smiling. It hurts my jaw.

After a few minutes where I manage to stop Siringen from taking Mr Hamelin some betel nuts as a gift, we leave our hut and walk the *liklik* distance across the beach and the ground where the hibiscus flowers grow. As we get closer and closer to the place where I used to live with my mama and papa, I can hear Maple's voice. It doesn't sound its usual sad or angry. It sounds like it has a laugh within it.

Suddenly she comes from behind the hut with something strange on the top of her head. I think it is a strange hat – something that people in America wear when the snows come down and cover everything.

But then I see the hat move.

"Blue Wing!" She waves at me. "Mr Siringen! Dad, they're here!"

"Hello, Miss Maple," says Siringen.

Maple lowers the *kapul* from her head and holds it like it is a baby. It looks like it is happy to be there.

"This," she says this to Siringen, "is Trinket. He's a cuscus."

"Yes." He reaches out and strokes his finger across the top of the *kapul*'s head. "Hello, Trinket." I look at Siringen like he has gone *longlong*. Siringen is not a soft man. He is tough and treats people and things with no gentleness. I don't think I have ever seen one tear in his eye. But now he is patting and *talking to* a *kapul*!

Siringen sees me looking and nods his head at me as if he is saying *Now you*.

"Hi," I say and let the animal wrap its claws around my finger. It feels very tight.

"Come on in. I think Dad's about to set the table."

We start to walk towards the hut, my finger still trapped in the *kapul*'s nails.

Inside the hut, Mr Hamelin has been cooking over the small gas stove. The food smells warm and delicious and I think my belly is thundering.

"Siringen. Blue Wing." Mr Hamelin takes off a pair of cooking gloves and shakes Siringen by the hand. "So glad you could come."

"It is very kind of you to ask us to come," says Siringen.

"Not at all. You've been a great help to me over the

past few days. And I know that Blue Wing, you've been extremely useful in keeping Maple out of trouble!"

I look at Maple and she looks at me and we both say nothing, but I think we are thinking the same things.

"This is just a small way of saying thanks."

The room is busy with all the furniture. In the middle of the room is a table with four chairs around it and on the table are bowls and forks and knives and spoons. Siringen looks at it all nervously.

"What would you like to drink?" Mr Hamelin asks Siringen. "I've got a bottle of white wine cooling in the fridge, or there are some beers." I see there is a small fridge tucked into a corner, plugged into a wire that goes out through a window to the *phut-phut-phut*ing generator.

Siringen shakes his head. "Thank you. No. I do not drink alcohol. Water would be nice."

"Sure." Mr Hamelin opens the fridge and takes a *bikpela* green bottle of water out. He pours some out into a plastic cup and hands it to Siringen, who takes a sip.

"Oh," he says. "Fizzy."

"What about you, Blue Wing? Would you like water? Or would you prefer some Coca-Cola?"

"Coca-Cola," I say quick before Siringen answers for me. "Please."

Mr Hamelin picks two cups off the table and fills

them with Coca-Cola. He gives one to me and the other to Maple.

I have only had Coca-Cola two times before in my life. Both times when I had to go to the birthday party of the Bigman's son. All the children in the village had to go – even though nobody was really his friend – and we all had to take presents. But the food was nice and the Coca-Cola was tasty. So we all ate and drank as much as we could – I had two *bikpela* glasses of the drink. Afterwards I felt sick.

"Thank you," I say and take a *bikpela tru* mouthful and swallow.

"I've not made anything too special," says Mr Hamelin, stirring something hot and bubbling on the stove. "Just a split pea and ham soup. It's a Vermont specialty. And I've bought some breads to eat with it."

"Smells good." Siringen's tongue is on his lips. I am thinking that he might find it easy to eat in another man's house after all.

Mr Hamelin smiles.

"Perhaps, while you're waiting, Maple, you could show Blue Wing your room."

"Sure."

I find my fingers nervously straightening the grass band in my hair.

There are different things to look at in my old room but, thank Moroa, it still feels the same.

"Is that the city you are from?" I ask, pointing to the black-and-white photograph pinned to the wall. "It looks very busy."

"Yes. Burlington. It's not that busy really. Not like some of the other cities I've been to. Chicago's busier. And New York is even worse. We did once take a trip to Tokyo, and that was ridiculously busy. I quite like cities though. All the people. All the things going on. All the noise. Feels alive."

"I have never been to a city," I say. "I have been into the town a few times. That is the nearest I have been."

"You should come to Burlington one day. You'd love it."

I shake my head. "I don't think I would. The town is too much noise for me. I don't really like all the buildings. I prefer the trees and the mountains and the sea. They are the things that feel alive to me."

"It is beautiful here," says Maple. "But I don't think I could stay here for ever. I think I would go nuts."

"Nuts?"

"*Longlong*," she explains.

"See? You are learning to understand our language!"

Maple grins and puts Trinket down on her camp bed with the mosquito net.

"So this used to be *your* room. Where did you sleep?"

I point to the corner. "There. By your pretty curtains. I had my mat on the floor there."

"I think it was empty before we arrived. What happened to all your stuff? Did you take it over to Siringen's hut?"

"Oh, no. When…when it all happened…after it all happened, the Bigman came and gave all our things away to the other villagers."

"After what happened? The death of your parents?" I nod. She looks mad. "Why would he do that? Why would he take all your stuff and just give it away like that? That doesn't make any sense."

"Well, I suppose nobody was going to need it any more."

"No. *You* needed it. It all belonged to you." She shakes her head. "Did he really give *everything* away?"

"Yes. Everything. My papa's canoe. My canoe too. The people in the village all have them now."

"That's mean."

"No. It is fine. I do not need them now. It does not make me sad."

It goes quiet between us for *liklik taim*. Then I see her looking at me.

"Blue Wing. Your parents." She looks like she isn't going to smile or laugh. "How did they die?"

I suck air deep into my chest. "Well—"

"Okay, girls!" Mr Hamelin's head comes around the corner. "Dinner's ready. Come on through."

"The cage?"

As I come around the side of the table to my seat, I notice that the cage for the *kapul* has gone.

Maple points to the small window at the back that faces the trees. Outside, underneath it, the cage lies on its side, the *liklik* door hanging open.

"What happened?" I ask.

"I agreed with you," says Maple. "It wasn't right having Trinket all caged up. He needs to be free. But I don't think he can ever go back into the trees with the other cuscuses. He was already tame when we picked him up on the mainland. He wouldn't be able to cope out in the wild. It wouldn't be fair on him."

"No. It is *tru*," I agree. "You need to take care of him. I see that now."

We all sit at the table and make polite *aaah* noises about the smell of the soup.

Then we begin to eat.

127

It is *mobeta* than I would have imagined. It is hot and creamy and the meat is soft and easy to chew. The bread is also soft and almost disappears in my mouth when I put it in. I look at Siringen, who seems to be focused *wan-handet* per cent on the food.

Mr Hamelin gives us all more soup and we spoon like hogs until it has gone and the bread is nothing but crumbs.

After the soup, Mr Hamelin takes a large chocolate cake out of the fridge.

"It looked so good I just had to get it."

He cuts it up into *bikpela* chunks and drops them onto plates. It is probably the tastiest food I have ever eaten. When I have finished, I want to ask for more but I know that my *waspapi* would think it was rude, so I stop myself and drink down the rest of my Coca-Cola.

"More cake, Blue Wing?" Mr Hamelin has another piece ready to push onto my plate. My eyes go to Siringen, who doesn't look at me.

"Yes. She would like some more, Dad." Maple speaks. "So would I."

"Siringen? What about you?"

Siringen shakes his head. "That was enough. Thank you, Hamelin."

The *namba tu* slice of the cake is even more delicious than the *namba wan*, and I suddenly feel like there is nothing else that can fit inside my belly. We all sit back on our seats and stay there like whales that have come ashore.

After some *taim*, Mr Hamelin pours himself another glass of the wine. He takes a sip, then leans forward over the table.

"So, how long have you lived with Siringen, Blue Wing?"

"*Tu yia.*"

"I'm sorry?"

"Two years, Dad," Maple answers. "Blue Wing's lived in Siringen's hut for two years. Before that she used to live here. With her parents."

"Did you really? What? This used to be your home?"

"Yes. Since the moment I was born."

Suddenly Mr Hamelin gets up from the table and goes over to the large clock that *knick-knock*s in the corner. He reaches up and pulls a round glass door away from the face.

"This clock seems to be getting slower and slower." He moves one of the hands around, checking the *taim* with his watch.

I can see that on the shiny brass face of the clock there are the shapes of the sun and the moon, with stars in between. When he is happy, he pushes the glass door back into its place and then sits down on his chair. It is only then that I notice the other clocks in the room. Four or five of them. Some *liklik*. Some *bikpela*. Some old. Some new. All of them with hands twisting around their faces.

"So," Mr Hamelin speaks like he hasn't just got up and fixed the clock, "if it's not a personal question, Blue Wing, where are your parents?"

"Dad!" Maple uses the same eyes on her papa that she has used on me over the last few days.

"No. It is *orait*," I say. "I want to tell you both. They are dead. You know this already, Maple."

"I am sorry, Blue Wing." Mr Hamelin looks like he has done something rude and quickly hides behind another sip from his glass of wine. "I think I assumed, but I didn't want to ask Siringen or Maple, because I wasn't sure... that it was their place to tell me."

"No. Please. It is okay. Do not say sorry. My parents died two year ago."

"They died together?"

"Yes. Together."

Everyone sits there in the quiet for a short moment, listening to the *phut-phut-phut*s, the *knick-knock*s and the *whoosh* of the waves. In the end, it is Maple who asks the question.

"How?"

I look at Siringen, who looks straight back at me. His eyes tell me that it is my choice if I want to say. I try to drink the last bubbles of Coca-Cola from the bottom of my glass, and then I begin.

"I never liked school. All the mathematics and the reading. It was too much thinking, thinking, thinking. Sometimes my head would hurt from all the thinking and I would not be able to find the right answer. So the teacher never smiled at me and never gave me ten out of ten.

"Because, you see, I always found being outside *mobeta*. Outside, I could run and jump and climb up trees. I could take my canoe out onto the sea and pretend I was a great fisherman, like my papa. Being outside makes more…"

"Sense?" says Maple.

"Yes. Being outside makes more sense. Everything that happens in this village happens outside. All the fishing. All the fruit that grows. All the cooking. All the working. All the playing. It all happens outside.

"So sometimes I did not go to school. Sometimes I would pretend to go and then do something *mobeta* instead.

"That is what I did on the day it happened."

Mr Hamelin leans over and pours some more Coca-Cola into my glass.

"I think there was to be a mathematics test, and I was never good at mathematics. I knew I would fail. So I thought I would swim instead. I knew I wouldn't fail at swimming. I walked out of the village along the road to the bay beyond the small hill. It is quiet there and nobody would see me.

"I got to the bay and went into the sea. It was a hot day – *tru* hot – and it was nice to get cool in the water. The waves were still and the breeze was zero. I dived under the waves and explored the bottom of the ocean. The rocks. The fish. It was blue and beautiful and *mobeta* than any mathematics test. It felt like life, and it felt like Moroa was on my side and agreeing with me. For long *taim* I swam and dived. A family of dolphins came with me out to where the cliff pushes away from the land. They thought I was one of them, I think. They went in and out and around me before they realized I was not one of them, then they left.

"It was a good day. A *tru* good day."

I take a sip from the Coca-Cola. Then I say more.

"I was floating on my back, just feeling the sun on my face when I heard the voices. A man and a woman. Calling my name. I looked to the beach and saw my mama and my papa. Zephyr was my mama's name. Jeremiah was my papa's name. My mama was named after the pretty pink petal flowers. My papa was named after his papa before him.

"They were calling me. Trying to find me.

"You see, the teacher at the school had told the Bigman I was missing the mathematics test and the Bigman had gone and told my mama. She went and got my papa and they were both looking for me. Angry that I was not at school. Again."

Siringen is looking at me with a tiny distant star of worry in his eyes. I know he thinks that I should not be saying this. He thinks it will hurt me to say.

I ignore his eyes. Telling the story is making me feel good, I realize. *Mobeta* in a way. It is like I *want* to say it, so I carry on.

"I tried to stay still in the water, hoping they wouldn't see me. They might think I was a strip of wood just washing up on the shore. But they *do* see me. They see me and wave their arms at me to try and get me back to the beach. But I am far off in the water and it will take me some *taim* to swim back.

"Then they both start waving harder and their voices sound like the screeches of boobook owls. I see my mama rush into the water. Then my papa follows her. They have not taken their shirts off. It is like they have turned *longlong*, and I feel like I should laugh.

"But I don't. Something is *nogut*.

"As my mama slaps the water with her arms and legs, I can hear one word that she screams.

"'Shark!'

"I turn. Behind me, further out to sea, a *bikpela* shark's fin is coming fast through the water. *Tru bikpela*. I have seen sharks many, many *taim*, but not a shark as big as this.

"Suddenly I feel scared. More scared than anything. I cannot move. The only moving I do is keeping myself floating.

"I see Mama swimming hard, making a lot of splash. My papa is a fisherman and swims much better than Mama. I see his arms and his feet. My parents are trying to come and get me."

Maple sits with her hand over her mouth like she cannot bear what is going to happen. Mr Hamelin's eyes are vast.

"The fin gets closer and closer and closer to me. And then, when I am about to feel it next to me…it just goes past. It leaves me alone. I breathe out. It has missed me. Inside there is a piece of me that feels happy. But it isn't happy for long.

"Because my brain tells me the thing that everyone in New Ireland knows about sharks. That they will always go to the splashing. It is how shark callers make the sharks come. They shake the *larung* rattle in the water and the sharks will go to it. And that is what it was like with my mama. Making too much noise. Making too much splash.

"In that second, I wished that the village shark caller was there to lead the shark away."

Siringen is looking down to the floor.

"But it is not to be. We are alone in the bay. There is no one else to help us.

"I shout to them to go back to shore. But they keep coming. Even when they know that the shark has passed me and is going to them instead, they keep swimming out to me. They keep trying to save me."

I do not cry any more. It has gone beyond me to cry. Crying is a hoping. And when things have moved beyond hope, there is no need to cry. Everything is already scratched into the rock. It cannot be unscratched.

"I have known sharks," I say. "All my life I have known sharks, and it is *tru* what Siringen says, that sharks do not attack man. Sometimes they make mistakes and think that a kicking man is a cloud of fish. Sharks are not meant to attack people. It is not within their spirits.

"But I saw this attack. I saw the way this shark…I saw

the way it attacked Mama and Papa. It was not the way of a normal shark. It attacked because it *could* attack. It *wanted* to attack. It was not natural."

My throat is hurting. I have another *liklik* sip of the Coca-Cola, and think of the *taim* my mama had to take me to the Bigman's son's birthday party. I put the glass back down on the table.

I look at Maple and her papa. They are as still as Siringen's stone shark-statues.

"The shark that killed my parents had killed many *taim* before. And I know in my brain and my heart that it will kill many *taim* again. It is filled with evil spirits and will not stop killing until someone stops it. Always it hides away. But I know it will attack again."

I stop. I can hear blood in my ears.

"The shark has a name. It is called Xok."

"For many generations, the shark callers have believed that some sharks have evil spirits within them."

Siringen's voice is slow and deep, like what he has to say is important and needs to be listened to.

"Rogue sharks, they are called. Sharks that do not follow the normal ways of the shark. They attack other sharks as well as humans. There is no reason for what they do. They do it just because they have a badness within them.

"Xok is *not* one of these rogue sharks."

"*Waspapi,*" I start to argue. "You know what Xok has done. You know what—"

Siringen holds his finger out to me to stop me from saying more. Mr Hamelin and Maple look surprised at this movement.

"Blue Wing. This world is a difficult and complicated place. There is the sand. And there is the sea. But there is also the place where the sand meets the sea, and that place is changing all the *taim*. It is never always in the same position.

"Xok is not a rogue shark. I have had enough years of shark calling to understand this."

"Then what is he?" I ask, even though Siringen has told me not to speak. "What sort of shark is he? What sort of shark attacks people if it is not a rogue shark?"

"A damaged shark."

I make a noise through the top of my mouth to show that I do not agree with him. "You have told me this before, *waspapi. Oltaim* I find it difficult to believe you."

"What do you mean, a damaged shark?" asks Mr Hamelin, his forehead covered in lines of confusion.

Siringen pulls his chair back and crosses his legs.

"Blue Wing has told you the story of her parents, so I shall tell you the story of Xok," he says. "Then you can decide yourselves if he is a rogue shark."

Maple sits with her lips over the edge of the cola glass, but still she doesn't move. Mr Hamelin lets his hand run through his hair like he does not realize what his fingers are doing.

"Thirty or forty year ago," Siringen starts, "I cannot remember exactly when *bikpela* American companies came to the island to take the copper from out of the ground. They had their *bikpela* machines to dig under the earth and to pull the copper out. Copper is worth a lot of kina, so they wanted to get it all if they could.

"The companies bought up pieces of land to mine. They brought many workers with them. So many workers that they had to build a place for them to live. On the other side of the island, near the mines, they put a small town. There were huts made from iron, and stores and rooms for the men to drink in. They also built a place out in the sea for the ships to rest. A harbour.

"Now the men who worked for the copper companies would work all day then drink in the nights. They did this for years until they got bored. Then they felt like they needed something else. A different type of fun.

"One day, a young shark swam into the harbour. The

men saw it and, instead of trying to help it swim free, they trapped it. They put nets across part of the harbour and stopped it from getting back to its family. They fed it with the meat they didn't eat and stuck it with sticks to make it mad. They kept it and treated it badly. It got more *bikpela* and more *bikpela*, and more angry and more angry."

I have heard this tale a *handet taim* before, so I shake my head and I bite my lip.

"Then," Siringen continues, "some of the men would go out in boats and catch small sharks – they could only catch *small* sharks; they were not shark callers so they did not have the skill to catch anything else. Then they would throw the small shark into the part of the harbour with Xok – that is what they named him – to see them fight. They would drink beer and place bets, but Xok would always win. Xok was angry and would kill anything they gave to him.

"This the men did for long *taim*. And when the companies had dug all the copper they could from under our feet, they left the island and took all the workers back home with them. But before they went away on their ships, they set Xok free."

Siringen stops and reaches for his fizzy water. He sips it before putting it back down on the table.

"Since then, Xok has been swimming in these seas. Still angry and still confused. That is why I say he is damaged."

The sky is moving towards the dark and the stars are starting to open themselves up again. The breeze is falling and the air is cooling. Nobody says anything.

We are standing in a line with our bare feet on the wet sand, the dying waves washing between our toes. Maple has Trinket hanging on to her head. Mr Hamelin holds on to his glass of wine.

We watch the sea as it breathes in and out, the last of the sun and the first of the stars sparking its surface.

"Maple's mother died recently too," Mr Hamelin says, finishing up the wine in his glass.

"Yes," I say. "I know. Maple has said."

"She was the most wonderful person I have ever known." Mr Hamelin is hypnotized by the sky. "So clever. So good. So funny. So caring. We miss her very much, don't we, sweetheart?"

Maple strokes the *kapul*, who climbs down into her arms.

"What about you, Siringen?" Mr Hamelin asks. "Have you ever lost anyone close to you?"

Siringen says nothing for a minute. He stares out at the sea before looking over at Mr Hamelin and nodding.

"Yes," he says. "A long, long *taim* ago."

"Your wife?" Maple says.

He nods again. "But it has been so long...I cannot remember her now. *Taim* slips like a river, and I am an old man. If you turn your head to look back, the land has all changed."

A bat flaps its shadow across the sky, from one tree to another.

"It is a strange thing, time." Mr Hamelin talks like he is letting his thoughts come out through his mouth. "Time, life and death. Impossible for the human mind to fully understand. Unattainable things to grasp. No matter how much science tries to chase them, they always seem to escape. And I wish they wouldn't. I really do."

"I do not know," answers Siringen. "*Taim* is just a basket which carries life and death. And no one can live their life without being touched by death – that is... impossible. So death is just a part of life." He makes his shoulders go up and down. "It is only when we can accept this that life can become real. Life. Death. *Taim*. They are simple things really."

We stand there saying nothing else until the sky is at its darkest and the stars are at their brightest.

PAT NAMBA TU

THE SEA

NAINPELA

Today Maple is wearing clothes that are less pretty but more useful. A T-shirt with a horse on the front. Light trousers with plenty of pockets. A cap with *Vermont Bucks* written across the forehead. Stiff boots for walking. And a brown rucksack across her back.

Oh, and her big bug sunglasses. I think she loves her big bug sunglasses.

"The only things for sandwiches I could get from the trade store were crab paste and a sort of meat paste," she says, her hand reaching into the rucksack. She pulls out a shiny foil package and shakes it about in front of me so that I see it. "Might be disgusting, but I've made eight each. Do you think that's enough?"

"Maybe," I say.

She puts the shiny package back into the rucksack,

then pulls out a large, yellow pack of corn chips. *Fritos. The Original,* it says in bright white letters.

"God, I love these sooooo much. I eat them all the time back in Vermont. When I saw them behind the counter I could have cried. Ever had them before?"

I shake my head.

"And when I saw that they sold US candy bars..." She pushes the corn chips back and reaches around for something else. "You ever tried one of the candy bars the guy sells?"

This *taim* I nod. "Yes. I have tried a *Three Musketeers* bar. It was *tru* good." I wet my lips.

"I'm not so keen on those. Have you ever tried one of these?" She takes a long red packet out and holds it up to me. "I got four of these. Two each."

I look. *Pearson's Salted Nut Roll.*

"They are just...divine, I tell you. You'll love them."

"What about water?" I ask, remembering how much she drank on the road to the copper mine. "Have you got water?"

"Yeah. Loads. Don't worry. I'm not *stooopid.*"

We set off early, while Mr Hamelin and Siringen are preparing the boat. It is cool – the shadow of the mountain still stretching out over the sea.

"Have a good day!" Mr Hamelin kisses his daughter on the head. "Be careful on the mountain."

"Dad!" She pulls away from him and pretends to hit him with her mobile phone.

"Try to get shots all around the coastline if you can, sweetheart," he says. "And definitely take pictures of any large dark shapes under the water. I'd be keen to see those."

We had been given a job to do. Mr Hamelin had instructed us to carry Maple's phone to the top of the mountain and to use it to take pictures of the sea. I do not know why, but I assume it is something to do with the coral that he is here to study, though it seems strange to look for something so low down from a place so high up.

"Sure, Dad. And if we come across another Japanese gun, I'll make sure I get a selfie with it." Maple grins big and holds her thumb up in front of her face, pretending she is already in the picture. She turns back to me. "Dad loves all the old war stuff." Her eyes go up into her head like she thinks her papa is *longlong*. "But then he would do. He *was* a professor in Modern History at Vermont Univ—"

"Maple!" Mr Hamelin's eyes look scared. "No. What have I told you?"

"Oh. Yeah. Sorry." She looks confused, like the sun

has just blinded her. Then she starts to shake her head slowly, like she is sad.

Her papa nods. "That's okay." Then he kisses Maple on the head again and she pulls away again. "Enjoy yourself, sweetheart."

I do not know what it is I have just seen. I do not understand. But I pretend that I did not notice and I smile at Mr Hamelin as he walks back to the boat.

"Come on," Maple tells me, like she is suddenly the Bigman. "Let's go climb this mountain."

Three hours after we start, we reach the top.

"Wow! This is *sooooo* high!" says Maple, wiping sweat from under her cap. "You can see everything."

I point places out to her and take her across to the other side of the mountain.

"Isn't that the copper mine?" she asks.

"Yes."

"And what's that place there? On the coast?"

"That is one of the towns where the miners lived. I think it is the place where Xok was kept prisoner."

"It all looks so small from here."

"And if you look out to sea you can see some of the other islands."

The breeze is cool and I feel it around my face.

Maple soon remembers to pull her phone from out of her bag and she starts holding it up and pointing it out towards the sea, the shiny black screen making *liklik* clicking noises as she pushes the button.

"Are you hungry?" Maple asks, when she has finished. "I am *staaaarving*. Shall we eat before I collapse?"

"You know what?" Maple says with some crab-paste sandwich in her mouth. "Now I come to think of it, I don't think I've ever seen you talking to any of the kids in your village. Don't you like them?"

I wipe the crumbs of a sandwich from my hands and take another one from the shiny foil package. "I do not know if I do not like them. Some of them I used to be friends with, but not any more. It is a different *taim* now. They have all moved on."

Then I point out ahead to a small dot on the sea near the village. "But I do not think I was ever a friend of *that* one."

Maple stretches her neck to see. "What one? What are you saying?"

"On the canoe. You see?"

She covers her eyes with her hand. "Oh yes," she says. "I *think* I see. Who is it?"

149

"It is the Bigman's only son. Moses." I look at Maple. "You see the canoe he is *trying* to control?"

She nods.

"That is my canoe. The one my papa made for me. Moses owns it now, but I can see that he does not use it *tru* often."

"That's mean," says Maple. "They shouldn't have taken it from you. It belongs to you."

I shrug like it is not important – even though I know it is – before taking a *bikpela* bite from the sandwich and looking away from Moses's *hambak* paddling. "What about you?" I ask, my mouth full of bread. "Did you have many friends in America?"

"Some. A few really close ones from the swimming squad, who I miss. I'd send them emails but the Wi-Fi here doesn't exist. And as for the phone signal..." She rolls her foil up and puts it into the rucksack. "The other kids in your village seem to be staying away from me at the moment. Think they're trying to suss me out from a distance before getting too close."

"'Suss me out'?" I ask.

Maple thinks. "Understand me."

"Oh."

Maple rips open the corn chips and takes a handful. I notice the pretty chain on her wrist.

"What is that?" I point.

"This?" She rattles it. "My charm bracelet. Mom gave it to me a few months before she died." She pushes the chips into her mouth then wipes her hands on her trousers. "Here," she starts to unclip the bracelet, "have a look."

She moves across the rock on which we are sitting so that she is next to me and then hands me the chain. It has *liklik* figures and shapes all along it. All shiny, like the foil.

"What are they?" I say, feeling some of them between my fingers.

"They're the charms. My mom chose them. You see, each one of these signifies something special about Mom's life or my life. Or about us both. Look." She takes the chain from me and shows me one. "This is the Eiffel Tower. In Paris. When I was nine, Mom took me to Paris. Without Dad. He was off at some tedious conference or other and couldn't come. So we went on our own. We went shopping and drank hot chocolate in cafes and ate a lot of cheese and ham. We went on boats up and down the Seine. And one day we went to the very top of the Eiffel Tower."

Her eyes are looking at the *liklik* tower, but I don't think they are seeing it.

"You've probably never been but the Eiffel Tower is tall – it's not as high as *this* – but for the middle of a city it is really tall. And I was scared. I didn't want to go to the top. Mom said it was fine, that we didn't have to go all the way to the top if I didn't want to. 'Be a shame not to go to the first floor, though,' she said, and persuaded me that the first floor wasn't that far up at all. So, up we went in the lift, Mom holding my hand all the way. The first floor *was* a bit scary – I didn't even go on the glass floor that they have there – but after a short time I got used to it.

"'What about going up to the second floor?' she asked, and I shook my head. No way! No thank you! The first floor's enough for me! But then she said, 'Why not just pretend you're on the ground right now and you're just going up to the first floor again?' It took a load more convincing than I'm letting on here but, in the end, I agreed to go up to the *next* 'first' floor."

Maple is smiling.

A smile does not mean you are happy. A smile can mean many different things. Happiness might not be one of them.

"Anyway, the next 'first' floor was *really* scary. It was so far up that you could almost see all the way around the world to the back of my head! But still, after a while, it wasn't so bad.

152

"'Wanna go to the *next* first floor?' Mom asked me when I was okay with it. So, sure enough, we went all the way to the top and got some great shots to show Dad."

"And you were not scared?" I asked.

"No. In the end it was all fine." She is smiling still. "That was the thing with Mom. She knew how to win me round. Dad isn't like that. He tells me what he thinks we should do, and goes ahead and does it anyway. Then he's surprised when he finds out I'm annoyed with him."

"It was the same with my mama and papa," I say. "Mama was always the *wan* who would be as still as a lake. Whatever I said, she would be calm and gentle and try to understand. But Papa... He was a fisherman and loved the stormy seas. He was like a typhoon sometimes. A red-hot head and quick to say what he thought he should say."

"Dads, huh?"

I nod.

"What is this one?" I point to a *liklik* figure of a book hanging from the chain.

"It's a book."

"Yes, I know it is a book. What does it mean?"

"My parents homeschool me. That means I don't go to school. I stay at home and my mom or my dad teaches me stuff. Don't ask me why. I think it was because the schools near our house were all terrible and they thought they could do a better job of it.

"So it was my mom who taught me to read. That's what that stands for. It's a reminder that we learned a lot of things together. That little book reminds me that all through my life anything new I learn will be learned on top of the stuff *she* taught me. And," she turns the chain around in her hand, "you see that clock?"

There is a figure of a clock. With hands.

"That symbolizes the idea that, wherever I am and whatever I am doing, Mom is always with me. For ever."

"The long now," I say.

"What?"

"It is what my mama would say when she meant *for ever*. The long now. I think her mama before her used to say it. And *her* mama before *her*."

"The long now? That's cool. A bit weird, like all your language. But...yeah. I like that. The long now."

We sit for a *taim*, looking at the other figures on the chain. A diving woman. A dog. A bicycle. A star. All of them with a special meaning between Maple and her mama.

"You know," she says after a few minutes of quiet. "Even though Mom gave me this bracelet to remember her by, there are some moments on some days when I can't even remember the details of her face. And, even though the little clock is meant to mean that she is always going to be with me...well..." She shakes her head. "I've never felt her presence. Never felt her nearby. Not once." She ties the chain back around her wrist. She is not smiling again. "What about you, Blue Wing? Have you ever felt your parents around you since they died?"

I look down at my sandals. I can see my toes are dirty.

"No," I say with truth in my heart. "I have not."

We rest a *taim* on top of the rock, our eyes closed, the sun on our faces. Then we make our way back down the mountain.

Slowly.

When we are most of the way down, I hear someone singing. Maple hears it too and we stop to listen. It is one of the songs from long ago. A tribal song. A sad song about how the women have to work all day while the men go off to fight in wars.

"Who is it?" asks Maple.

It is then that I come to know where we are.

"Follow me," I say and take a step off the path.

We walk through the forest, over the soft ground dressed with leaves and moss. As we step around the trees, the voice gets louder. We turn around a rock covered in tough, scratchy shrubs and see an old woman hanging some wet cloths on a piece of string stuck between two trees.

She sees us as soon as we see her.

"Well… Hello, Blue Wing! *Tru* nice to see you! What are you doing here? And your friend too! Hello, my dear. This is a surprise."

"Chimera," I say. "This is Maple."

Maple comes near and stares at the old woman with the *longlong* hair, strings of beads around her neck and the thin piece of bone that goes through her nose.

Chimera takes Maple's hands and squeezes them together.

"Hello. It is so very good to know you." She closes her eyes and breathes in air like she is sucking Maple into her body. Maple's mouth is open like Chimera's cave. "So very good." Chimera's eyes jump open again and her hands let Maple's fall. "What is it you are both doing here?"

"We have been to the top of the mountain, taking photographs for Mr Hamelin," I say. "I have shown Maple what it is like to be so above everything."

"Is this *tru*? Well, well." Chimera starts to turn. *"Plis.* Wait here." She goes into the start of her cave and Maple comes next to me.

"Who is she?" she whispers.

"It is Chimera," I whisper back to her. "She lives here, in the cave. She is a witch doctor."

"Woah! Hold on. She lives in a cave?"

"Yes."

"And she's a witch doctor?"

"Yes."

"You mean she's a *witch*, don't you? Like she puts spells on people and stuff. Turns you into a toad if she doesn't like the look of you."

I do not understand. "Chimera helps people who are sick," I say. "She uses medicines from the plants and trees, and talks to the spirits to heal."

"She talks to the spirits?" Maple asks like her eyes have interest. "Really?"

Suddenly, Chimera comes back out, waving us towards the cave. "*Plis*. Come and cool off inside. You both look *tru* hot. Come."

I have never been inside before, but I can see that Chimera's cave is not as wet or as cold or as horrible as she said. Instead it is quite nice. A curtain made of beads covers the entrance and there is a long sago mat that covers the floor. Hanging from the roof of the cave are pots and pans, and all along the walls are baskets filled with foods and herbs and dried insects used in her medicines. A long block of wood is pretending to be a table and stumps of logs are pretending to be seats. A small oil lamp is hooked over a nail in the wall and further back in the cave I can only just see the blankets where Chimera must sleep.

As we go into the cave, Chimera ties the curtain made of beads to one side to let the light in.

"Please," she says, pointing to the logs. "Please, sit down. It is good to have visitors."

We both sit down on the seats. On the block of wood in front of us, Chimera has put two bamboo cups filled with coconut milk. I realize I am thirsty, so I thank her and I start to drink. So does Maple.

"Now," says Chimera. "How is that *waspapi* of yours, Blue Wing?" Her eyes have sparks in them.

I put the cup down. "He is well."

"Helping your friend's papa, I suppose? Such a good, helpful man, Siringen."

"Yes." Maple talks like she should be saying something. "They are out on the sea right now, looking at the coral. I'm not sure what my dad expects to find there exactly…"

Chimera looks at Maple and smiles. "And what about you, my dear? How are you?"

"Er…" Maple looks like she has just seen something strange. "I'm…okay, I suppose."

"Only," Chimera leans in and takes Maple's hands again, "I can see the pain in your eyes."

Maple smiles. "Er…can you?"

Chimera shakes her head. "There is no need to smile or joke or pretend. You do not have to do those things here. Your pain is clear to me."

The smile on Maple's mouth goes away.

"Poor girl. You have felt loss so very hard, I can see."

Maple looks down at the mat. She says nothing. I say nothing. Suddenly the air inside the cool cave feels even cooler.

"Blue Wing…" Maple says after some *taim*. "Blue Wing…she said that you can speak to spirits. Is it true?"

Chimera rubs Maple's hands together. "There are many who can see or speak to the spirits," she says. "Many people. But I have found – from my life, learning – that they all fall into one of three baskets. Those baskets are the very young, the gifted and the guilty. The very young – small children no more than one or two year old. The gifted – people like me who have such magic through their family. And those who feel guilt deep, *deep* in their hearts. These are the people who can see or speak to the dead."

"Can you speak to my mother?" Maple's voice is small and dry. "Is it possible?"

Chimera smiles. "The spirit world does not work the way we hope it would. It is never as simple as that. It does not follow the same rules as *this* world. Those people who see or speak to the dead...they do not always see or speak to the dead that they wish for. You can desire it to happen, but that does not mean it *will* happen."

"But can you speak to my mom? That's all I need to know. Please. If you can...tell her that I love her...that I miss her... Tell her I want her to come back home and to...and to..."

Tears are dropping onto the sago mat.

"Ssh."

"Tell her that I'm sorry for—"

"Hush, child." Chimera's long thin fingers brush the side of Maple's cheek. "Do not talk."

"But...but..." Maple is saying things like she is swimming and coming up to breathe. "But...can...you speak...to her? Please?"

Maple is so sad that my heart starts to hurt for her and I want *tru* much for Chimera to say that she can call out to her mama. To call out and to talk to her. Maybe then, I think, she could even call out to *my* mama.

But...

Chimera shakes her head gently. "No. I am sorry. She is not here with me."

"Why not? Why doesn't…my mom come…to you? Why doesn't she come to *me*?"

"I do not know. Nobody who lives and takes air into their lungs and feels with their fingers can understand the way that the spirit world works. It is an impossible thing for us to know."

I watch all this like it is a show on a television. I do not feel like I am a part of it, so I just watch.

"But…what about ghosts? Can people come back as ghosts? Why hasn't my mom come back and why can't I see her?"

Chimera wipes Maple's cheek on the other side. "You cannot look for ghosts, my dear. If they wish to be seen, they will come to you. But do not go looking for them."

"If my mom loved me so much, surely she would want to tell me that she is okay. Or that there is nothing for me to worry about. Surely she would see the sadness that I can't push away and would want to come back and make me better. Why doesn't she do that?"

"Maple." Chimera uses Maple's name for the *namba wan taim*. "Ghosts are just the dead that haven't accepted they are dead. Or they are the dead who have something they still need to do to feel worthy of their death. Your mama is not a ghost, which tells me that she has both accepted her death and that she has nothing to prove.

If you cannot see your mama, my dear, it means that she is happy."

This makes Maple cry more. But, even though my eyes are on Maple, my mind seems to be on my own mama and papa.

And when my mind is on my mama and papa, it is also always on Xok.

TENPELA

It is the day after we meet Chimera, and Mr Hamelin is going out to sea in his motorboat. Alone. Siringen says he doesn't need him any more, which is *hambak* because nobody knows the seas better than my *waspapi*.

Maple and I stand on the beach, watching her papa disappear.

"There's something I need to show you," Maple says to me and turns.

"What is it?" I ask and follow her back towards the hut.

She opens the door and goes through into her papa's bedroom.

"That." She points to a *bikpela* wooden chest that sits on the floor next to Mr Hamelin's camp bed. It looks old. And heavy. There are old things marked into the wood.

I think they are pictures but they might be words. I do not know.

"What is it for?" I ask Maple.

"That's the thing," she says. "I'm not sure. The only thing I do know is that Dad spends a lot of time looking through it and shuts it up whenever he hears me coming."

"Have you asked your papa what it is for?"

"Sure I have. But he just mutters some rubbish about personal possessions and Mom's memory. But if there were things to do with Mom in there, why doesn't he let me see? I've got as much right to see this stuff as he has, haven't I?"

I nod, even though I do not fully understand some of what she has said.

"What are you going to do?"

"I'd've thought that was obvious," she says. "I'm going to look in it."

"Is that the right thing to do?"

"I don't really care. I don't think it's right for Dad to keep things from me. Or from other people."

I nod again. I understand what she is saying this *taim*; and I want to ask why Mr Hamelin pretends he is a professor of coral when Maple says he is *tru* a professor of history. It seems strange to me that a man like Mr Hamelin should be telling a lie.

"The problem is, I've already tried it but it's locked," Maple says. "And I couldn't exactly go searching for the key while my dad was around."

"No."

"So? You gonna help me look for it?"

"Well…"

"It must be in this room somewhere, don't you think? It can't be far away."

She gets on her knees and starts to look under the camp bed. She stretches her arm under the bag-for-sleeping, then searches inside.

"Come on. Are you going to help me?"

"I do not know," I say. "It does not feel right to me."

"But you would be helping me. Isn't that what a friend would do?"

"But…"

"Dad doesn't have to know anything about this. There's no need for you to feel guilty. *Please.*" There is something about the way she says the word "please" that makes my heart go faster. "Please, Blue Wing. Help me look for it."

I sigh. "Okay. I will help."

"Great. You check out his bags in the corner there and I'll see if there's anything hidden in his clothes."

I open up one of Mr Hamelin's zip bags. Inside are two

or three books that look hard and full of words that I could never understand. There are empty pads of writing paper, some of them getting bent in the corner from being kept and squashed into this bag. Sun hats. Sunglasses. A pen. Nothing else.

"Anything?" Maple asks.

"No. There is nothing."

"Try another one. It would be a long, thick key. Heavy too. I think Dad once said that chest is eighteenth-century or something."

I open up another of the bags. This *taim* it is full of T-shirts and shorts.

"There is still nothing. There is no key here."

Maple is now looking inside some small boxes that are stacked one on top of another next to Mr Hamelin's bed.

"You are not trying hard enough. Look harder. It must be here."

I pull out a *namba tri* bag and start unzipping it.

"What are you doing?!"

We both turn around. Mr Hamelin is standing in the doorway looking at us like his mouth cannot shut and his forehead is old.

"Er…" Maple says.

I say nothing.

"What's going on, Maple?"

"Dad. What are you doing back? I thought you were going off to look at some coral or whatever."

"I'm sure you did." His face looks angry and I slowly pull my hand out of bag *namba tri*. "But I came back because I forgot something. Now are you going to explain what it is you're doing ransacking my room?"

Maple says nothing.

"Maple?"

She still says nothing.

Then Mr Hamelin looks at me.

"Blue Wing," he says. "I'm sure whatever it is that's going on here wasn't your idea. I'm pretty certain that Maple has roped you into this. However, I think it might be best if you went home right now so that I can discuss this with my daughter. Okay?"

"Yes," I agree and get up from the floor and leave the hut without looking back at Maple.

I hear voices.

One voice doing plenty of talking and another voice not saying *tru* much at all.

So I stay outside and wait behind Siringen's hut, listening.

"People have seen her come down into the village."

The voice doing plenty of talking belongs to the Bigman. "They have seen her and they have told me."

"One *taim* only that I know." The voice not saying *tru* much belongs to Siringen.

"That is one *taim* too many, Siringen. You know what I feel about this. About her. She is a witch and we do not want witches in this village."

"Her father was the witch doctor in your father's *taim*," says Siringen back. "Your father had great respect for the witch doctors."

"But my father's *taim* is long past," says the Bigman. "We have moved on from those undeveloped days when waving feathers over your head could cure you from warts. Now we go into town and get medicine – *real* medicine that scientists have proved works. From doctors. *Real* doctors who have studied at a university. Not *longlong* women who think that crushing up herbs into *kaukau* can make you better. There is no place for someone like Chimera in a village like this. This village is not stuck in the past. It is looking to the future."

"I would have thought that the tourists you encourage to come here would *tru* much like to see a traditional witch doctor, waving feathers over people's heads. Isn't that what they like? To see the old ways, to visit the old ways, before going back to their lives."

I cannot see the Bigman's face, but I can imagine it. "Do not mock me and my ideas, Siringen. I am your chief."

"No, Lungadak."

I hear the Bigman moving about inside the hut. "I do not want that witch coming here again. She can stay where she belongs – out on the mountain, in her cave. You can tell her I said that."

The Bigman leaves the hut and I see him walking across the sand back to his *bikpela* compound. When I am certain he is far away, I go around to the front and into the hut.

"Was that the Bigman?" I ask, pretending I don't already know.

"Yes." Siringen doesn't even look up from where he sits, legs crossed on the floor. "He does not want Chimera to come here again."

"What right has he got to tell people what to do?"

"He has every right," says Siringen. "He is the chief of the village."

"Everyone knows that the only reason he does not like Chimera is because she could not cure his bad back. A bad back from carrying too much money and power around."

"That might be. But he is the chief and we are told

by our ancestors that we should respect him."

I look at Siringen as he sucks on his pipe. "But you are older than him, *waspapi*. By plenty year. He should be the one respecting you."

"Pah!" Siringen shakes his head. "You should take your own advice, Blue Wing."

"What? I don't understand."

"Many *taim* your ears do not hear my older words. Many *taim* you decide it is better to ignore them."

"That is not *tru*."

"It is! You know it is so!"

"I think the Bigman has buzzed around your head like a mosquito and you are waving your hands out at me instead!"

Siringen looks like I should not be speaking to him like this.

"See! You talk too openly. You talk too openly and say too many words, over and over and over."

"What words?"

His eyes are on me, saying, *You know what words.*

"Well, maybe it is only because I want someone – anyone – to realize that I could be the greatest shark caller there ever was. Maybe that is why I say these things. Because nobody ever gives me that chance."

Siringen taps his pipe out onto an upside-down shell.

"Why must we *always* have these words? Every *taim* we try to discuss things, these words come out of you."

"And they will always come out of me, *waspapi*. Always!"

Siringen stands up and straightens his back.

"Shark calling is not about the killing, Blue Wing. The killing is the most small part of shark calling. Everything else – the ritual, the respect – is much more important. I don't know why you cannot understand that."

I stand, facing him. I am angry again. "I understand that, but I do not accept it. Not for Xok."

"These words have no purpose."

"I do not accept it fully because if *I* could have called the sharks…if *I* could have called Xok," I reach inside and say the deepest thing inside my heart, "then I could have distracted him away from my mama and my papa. If I could have killed him, then he wouldn't have killed them. They would both be alive now."

Siringen looks at me but says nothing.

"I know that killing him now would not bring them back to me. But at least I would feel that I had avenged them."

"Vengeance is for those whose souls have become as crushed and worthless as frangipani petals."

"Oh please, *waspapi*. Sometimes I think you talk words that should have died a long, long *taim* ago."

Siringen looks offended.

"And anyway…where were *you* on the morning that Xok killed my mama and my papa? You tell me that you were out on the ocean calling sharks. If you had been nearby, *you* could have saved them."

Siringen shakes his head again and looks to the floor. But there is something about his eyes…

"*Waspapi?*" I ask. "What is it?"

"What do you mean?" He still looks down.

"What is wrong?"

"There is nothing. I do not know what you mean."

He is lying. I do not think I have ever seen Siringen lie before, but I know that this *taim* he is lying.

I say nothing to him. I stand there in front of him and wait.

He looks like someone has put sand on his sleeping mat. He stays silent for a *taim*.

"It is nothing." He turns and walks out of the hut.

I follow him closely.

"*Waspapi?* There is something you are not saying to me."

He stops.

"It is not nothing, *waspapi*," I say, my voice more small

and softer. "I can see that it is not nothing. What is it you are not telling me?"

Siringen turns and for the first *taim* I can see his age. He looks like an old man. He looks different to me.

His eyes dance like he is trying to see the right words in the air and to catch them like mosquitoes.

"*Waspapi?*"

He smiles, but it is not one of the happy smiles.

"Oh, Blue Wing," he says. "I had a worry that this day might come. There is something I have not told you. Something that I thought you didn't need to know."

"What is it, Siringen?"

He comes up to me and puts his hands on my shoulders. This gives me worry.

He is putting the words in order inside his head. Then he begins.

"Blue Wing. The thing I have never said to you – because I thought it was best you didn't know... The thing I never said, is that I *was* nearby on the morning Jeremiah and Zephyr died. I was outside that bay just one or two hours before it happened."

"Did you see it happen? Is that what you haven't told me?"

"No. I had moved away by then. I only knew of their deaths when I came back to the shore."

"Then what is it you are trying to say?"

He pauses. "Let me finish."

His hands tighten around my shoulders.

"What I am saying is this… When I was calling sharks that morning, one of them that came to me was Xok. He had never come to me before. Never. Now everyone is fearful of Xok – you are right, he had killed people before your parents. So I widened the rope on the *kasaman* and used the bait fish to lure him in. I thought that if I could kill him myself, the village would be pleased and everyone would be happy."

"*Waspapi*…"

"Please, Blue Wing. Let me finish my tale. Xok went into the *kasaman* and I tightened the rope. He struggled hard and fought against it. I have never seen a shark fight so hard in my life. The sea was white with his struggle. But he never went to sleep. All the *taim* the *kasaman* was around him, he fought. Never giving up.

"So, I paddled over to him, my spear ready to take his life. I stood up in the canoe, trying not to fall out because the waves he was making were too quick and tough. I stood up and held the spear above him…

"But I could not do it."

I cannot say anything.

"You see, Blue Wing. He had never come to me before.

174

I have been out on these seas for many, many year, and I have seen many rogue sharks. And none of them have ever come to my calling. That was when I knew that Xok was *not* a rogue shark. That he is a shark like plenty of others. Only, he is hurt. Damaged by the people who fear him."

There is no sound in my ears except the sound of the waves on the beach.

"After a *taim*, he broke the *kasaman* in two and swam away. Out into the ocean."

"You let him go," I whisper.

"What?"

"I said, you let him go."

Inside, my heart has an anger like no other anger before.

Siringen looks like a frightened old man. But that doesn't stop the anger.

"You let Xok go. And then he swam into the shore and killed my mama and my papa!"

"Yes," he says. "I did. I let him go."

I look around, not knowing what to say. "You are responsible for their deaths! It is *your* fault almost as much as it is Xok's."

"It is *tru*."

I bite my lip hard and it starts bleeding. I can feel the blood running down my chin.

"Anyway, you didn't tell me this before because you felt *guilty*. Not because you thought I shouldn't know! You felt guilty that you were responsible for their deaths, so you kept it all hidden away, like a coward."

He stands still and says no words.

The anger inside me has turned into energy and I find myself walking around Siringen, not going anywhere.

"In fact," I say loudly, "that is why you invited me into your home. Not because you felt sorry that I had no family to live with, but because you felt guilty about taking them away from me. That's right, isn't it?!"

"*That*," Siringen says quietly, "is not *tru*."

"Don't keep lying to me, *waspapi*!" I change my words. "Don't lie to me, *Siringen*. You are full to the very top of your head with guilt about my parents. And all you are doing is making it easier for you to sleep in the nights on your sago mat. That is why I am in your home, and there is no other reason! So do not lie."

The blood is now flowing around inside my ears as well as down my chin, and even though Siringen says things to me, I cannot hear them. My eyes are wet too, so I turn away from him and run through the edge of the village, across the track, past the papaya grove and up into the mountain.

Through the forests I climb, over the rocks and under

the bushes – not caring if they scratch my arms and legs – until I come out on the very top, at the place where the sea and the sky are the same thing.

I stand there alone, on the top of the world, everything else below me. And I cry. I cry for my mama and I cry for my papa.

And I cry for the lie that is my life with Siringen.

WANPELA TEN WAN

The trees above are like pandanus umbrellas and the waterfall that pours into the lagoon sprays cold water all over us as we dive and swim and play.

Suddenly Maple's head comes out of the water beside me.

"He's probably as embarrassed as he is guilty, don't you think?" She has been thinking it over. "I mean, if he's the great shark caller of the village, surely he would know which sharks he should kill, right? There'd be some that you would just have to kill to protect the population, yes? Part of the job. And he made a bad call."

I do not take all of this in. She speaks too quick sometimes.

"Do you think anybody else in the village knows that he let Xok go free?" she asks. "Do you think he has told the chief of the village?"

I almost laugh at this, my mind remembering how Siringen and the Bigman are like always-battling cassowaries, pecking at each other.

"No. I do not think he has. I think he had buried it down inside him until it is as hidden as the heart of the mountain."

We swim over to the pebbles on the side of the lagoon, where Maple pulls a towel out of her rucksack and starts drying her body.

"Have you made it up with him yet?"

I shake my head and water flicks off my hair.

"I have not said words to him since, and he has not said words to me. He is trying to not see me too. Today he has gone to the village beyond the shoreline to see an old friend. Siringen never does those things."

"Probably thinks you need time to take it all in. Thinks you need some space."

"I will never take it all in, and there will never be enough space to make this *orait.*"

Maple wipes her face and looks at me. "I know how you feel. I don't think I'll ever get used to my mom not being around."

We get dressed into our clothes and begin the long walk back to the village.

"You thought very quick with your father yesterday," I say, climbing down over a *bikpela* hill of earth. "I don't think I could think so quick."

After Mr Hamelin had asked me to go home, Maple told him that she had lost her charm bracelet and that she was looking for it because it meant so *tru* much to her. With her hand under Mr Hamelin's bed, she let the bracelet slip off. Then, a few minutes later, she pretended to find it.

"It was all I could think of. I was going to blame it on Trinket, but that didn't seem fair somehow."

"But you still do not know what is in your father's chest," I say. "You are still no further along that road than you ever were."

"No, I'm not. And it's so frustrating. I feel like Dad's locked *me* inside that box and I can't get out." She looks at me with eyes that could knock over trees. "No matter what happens, Blue Wing, I'm going to find out what Dad's keeping hidden away from me. And I'm going to find out why we're here and why he wants me to take pictures of the sea – even if I have to trick it out of him."

"Good," I say. "That is *tru* good. You need to know. And I will help you."

"The thing is," says Maple, her eye catching some light as we start to come into the edge of the village, "if Siringen is feeling guilty, perhaps now is a good time to ask him to teach you the secrets of shark calling."

"Ha! I do not think he is going to do that."

"Why not?"

"You do not know Siringen like I know Siringen. When he has decided on something, it is almost impossible to make his mind flip."

"He changed his mind about not telling you he could've killed Xok."

"That is different."

Maple shrugs.

"The thing I find difficult to understand," she says, "is that you've been out shark calling with him millions of times, yes?"

"Well, *millions* isn't right, but—"

"So you've seen him do it, like, millions of times."

"Well. As I said, *millions*—"

"So why don't you just copy him?"

"What?" I think that my face carries the look of a confused fruit bat. "*Copy* him?"

"Just go out onto the sea and do whatever he does. Shake the coconut thing and do some chanting. See what happens."

"But Siringen wouldn't allow it. It would go against everything he ever says."

"Yes, but Siringen hasn't been exactly straight with you these last two years, has he?"

"No, but…"

"So why not just try it? If it's a disaster, just pretend it never happened. Siringen doesn't even have to find out about it. I mean, how will you ever know if you can do it, if you've never even tried?"

I look at her. She is smiling and it is a *bikpela* smile. So *bikpela* that I find myself having to smile too.

"But I do not have the equipment. I do not have a canoe."

"Can't you 'borrow' Siringen's?" She says "borrow" in a strange way.

"It would not be right. Even if he has told me lies, I could not take his canoe."

She takes off her bug sunglasses. "O-kay." Her smile gets even more *bikpela*. "What about reclaiming what is rightfully yours instead? Taking things back. How does that sound?"

I do not know what she is saying.

Moses always has everything he wants. The Bigman always makes sure that his only son – the future Bigman of the village – has everything he needs to keep him as uncivil and as *bikpela*-headed as himself. Televisions and games machines and computers, and watches that tell you how far you have walked. American clothes. Italian shoes. English hats. All these things are nothing to Moses.

So I do not feel bad taking something from Moses. Especially as the thing I am taking was once mine. Is *still* mine, in Maple's mind.

"There it is," I whisper.

The canoe my papa made for me is lying on a small strip of beach near the Bigman's compound. It has not been pulled properly onto the sand away from the sea and the waves are splashing against the front of the outrigging. If the tide comes in much higher it will be swept away. It is almost as if the canoe that my papa made for me is a piece of litter that has been dropped onto the beach and left for the birds to deal with. That is *tru* much like the Bigman and his family. They feel as if they can do whatever they like here and nobody will tell them anything else. It is the way it has always been.

There is nobody around, so we leave our hiding place behind a tree and walk out onto the beach.

"Cool to have your own canoe that your dad has made," says Maple. "I wish *my* dad could make something like this."

"Come on. We need to move quick, before someone sees us."

We bend over and start pushing the boat the *liklik* distance into the water. Once it is in, I help Maple climb into the canoe and then jump in myself.

I take up the oar – finding a half empty bottle of Pepsi in the bottom of the boat – and start to paddle out onto the sea.

Once we are far enough away from the shore, we both start breathing again.

"You know where these shark roads are?" asks Maple.

"Of course."

"What are the shark roads actually? I still don't really understand what you mean by shark roads?"

"They are the places where the sharks swim. Sharks prefer some parts of the sea to the others. That is why they swim along them. Siringen calls them the shark roads."

We paddle further out to sea. There are some fishermen on the ocean, but they do not notice us.

"It is a shame we could not bring a *larung*," I say, throwing some of the wild garlic into the water. "I do not know if the calling will work without a *larung*. But I could not take Siringen's. That would also have been wrong."

"But the...the coconut rattle thing just makes it look

as if there are fish swimming around. That's what attracts the sharks, isn't it? The splashing."

"Yes. I think so."

"So we should be okay with these." She flaps the two *bikpela* palm branches that she found. "These bad boys'll get the sharks to come! Trust me."

I smile. "Bad boys?"

"Yep!" She laughs. "Bad boys!"

It is quiet on the sea as I put the paddle back into the bottom of the canoe. We are all alone.

"Is this the place?" Maple asks. "Are you going to try it here?"

I nod my head.

"This is good. This is a good part of the shark road."

"Okay." She lifts one of the palm branches up. "Shall I start splashing?"

"Yes. You splash on that side and I shall splash on this side."

We hit the water with the branches, slapping the surface and making it white. It is harder work than either of us has thought.

"This feels silly," says Maple. "And it's making my arms ache."

"Keep doing it," I say. "We have to keep doing it. Siringen can do it for a long *taim*."

"Shouldn't you be doing some chanting as well?"

Softly I start to say things that sound like the things Siringen says. When Siringen chants I know that he chants the names of all the shark callers before him – a long line of uncles who passed on the magic to their nephews. A long line going back *wan-handet, tu-handet, tri-handet* year ago. Siringen has told me stories about plenty of them, so I know how to say their names. But others I am guessing and making sounds that sound right, hoping that it works.

I look behind me and I can see Maple smiling again.

"What?" I ask.

"I dunno. You just sound so weird."

"Are you laughing at me?"

"Well…"

"Yes. You are laughing."

"Perhaps just a little."

I smile. There is something about Maple that makes me smile and laugh too.

"Are you going to help me do this or are you going to laugh all day?" I say, pretending to be serious. "If you are going to laugh, you can swim back to shore, please." I point. "Go on! Swim back to the Bigman's beach!"

Maple laughs. "Do you want me to keep slapping the water with this branch, captain?"

"Please."

"Even though my arms are about to drop off and float away like little logs?"

"*Orait,* maybe you'd better stop. I think the *larung* must be plenty more easy to shake."

"Phew!" She throws the branch out onto the ocean and we watch it gently float away from us. "I'm not sad to see *that* go. Do some more of your chanting, Blue Wing. See if that works."

"You just want to make yourself laugh."

"No, no. I promise I won't."

I look at her like I do not believe her.

"Honestly! I won't!"

I turn away from her, dropping my branch into the boat, and chant some more. More quiet this *taim.* Maple does not laugh, or if she does, she keeps it down within herself.

"Look! Over there."

I look to where Maple is pointing. Something is coming through the water towards us.

"You've done it, Blue Wing! You called the sharks!"

I make my eyes go small to see more clear.

"No," I say. "It is not sharks. They are dolphins."

"So what? You called the dolphins. That's pretty impressive."

"No, it is not." I shake my head and my inside feels disappointed. "Dolphins are not sharks. Dolphins are interested in everything. They will come to see you even if you are not hitting the water with a tree and trying to remember the names of your *waspapi*'s ancestors. Dolphins are friendly. Sharks are not."

She is not really listening to me. She is too busy watching the dolphins jumping out of the water as they swim towards us.

"Yeah, but…dolphins are pretty cute, don't you think?"

The dolphins get nearer and then one puts its head out of the water.

"Oh, look at it!" Maple's voice sounds more like a squeak than ever before. She reaches out and runs her hand along the top of its head. "Isn't it adorable?"

I shake my head again. "It is a dolphin. That is all you can say."

"Oh, don't be such a meanyguts, Blue Wing. Look at him. Her. Whatever. Isn't he – or she – the cutest thing you've ever seen?"

I sigh. "It is a dolphin. And it is a girl."

The dolphin makes a dolphin noise and then dives back under the water.

"See ya, sweetie!"

I smile and look back at her. "'Sweetie'?"

"Yep."

"You are saying strange words for strange things today," I say. "Soon you will be calling me a baby."

"No, Blue Wing." She winks at me. "Today I am calling you Mistress Meanyguts for not loving the dolphins as much as I do. So there!"

Nothing comes. We wait for long *taim* but nothing comes. My heart feels like it is going down under the water with every minute that slips past us.

"Shall we go back?" Maple says after a long, long silence.

I am not laughing now. It is too sad a moment for me. My shark calling has not worked.

"Yes. We should get the canoe back before Moses sees that it is gone."

I take up the paddle and turn the canoe back towards the shore.

"What's that?" Maple nods at something floating in the water.

"It is just the palm branch you threw in. Nothing else."

I steer the boat to avoid it when—

Schlumpf!

It disappears.

"Er...what just happened?" asks Maple.

I take the paddle out of the water and look around at the sea. Something does not feel right. The air is too still.

"Did the branch go under the water or something?"

"Sssh!" I hiss. "Don't move."

I don't move and I don't breathe. I just watch the water.

Then I see what it is.

"There!"

To one side of the boat, a dark shadow is moving under the blue-green sea. It is a shark. It is a *bikpela* shark. A *bikpela* shark with a palm branch between its teeth. A shark I recognize *tru* too well.

"Xok!"

Maple makes a strange noise in her throat.

My heart starts to drum.

This is it! This is the *taim* I have wanted for *tru* too long. Xok has come to me so that I can do to him what he did to my mama and my papa. He has come to me willingly, so that I can kill him.

There is no spear in the canoe, and I swear under my voice that there is no spear in the canoe.

So I reach down and pull my knife out of its ankle sheath.

This is the moment. I will dive into the water and wait for Xok to turn to attack me. But he will not know what is happening because I will twist out of the way – I have been practising this for many months – and I will stab out with my knife. If I can stick one of his eyes that would be good. If I can stick one of his eyes it means that I can keep to one side and get him without him seeing me. I can escape his attacks – not that his attacks will hurt me – and I will slash out with my knife until all the fight and light has died within him and he sinks to the bottom of the ocean.

I start to stand up.

"Blue Wing!" Maple screams and I remember she is here in the canoe with me. "What are you doing? Sit down!"

"I must kill him! I have to kill him! I have never had a chance like this before."

The shark curves around and passes the boat once again.

"No, don't! Please sit down. You're scaring me."

"But this is my *taim* to avenge Mama and Papa. Can't you see? This is the *taim* for me to make it right."

"But…but if something happens to you, I'll be left

on my own." She looks vast-eyed and frightened. "And I don't want to be left on my own. Not with that…thing… waiting to eat me. Please, Blue Wing! Please! Don't be foolish. Stay with me. I'm scared."

I feel the handle of the knife in my hand. I grip it hard and imagine the blade going through the shark's tough skin, clouds of blood filling the sea.

I want to kill Xok, with all the life in my heart. I want to take this creature and put its evil to sleep. I want to do that more than anything in the world.

"Please, Blue Wing." Maple's voice has gone small and sad. "Don't leave me alone."

I stop myself jumping into the water. I think for a moment too long.

The shark passes the canoe again.

Now is the taim to jump, Blue Wing, I say to myself. *Now is the taim to do this.*

"Please!"

My legs stop me.

Now! Do it now!

"Blue Wing!"

I stay still. My mind thinks too much. Too, too much. And then…

The shark twists its body around and swims away out to sea, bored with us.

"No!" I shout. "Come back! I haven't finished with you yet! Come back!"

As I watch Xok swim away I feel thinner, like there is less of me.

"Please!" I say. "Please, come back! Let me make this right. I need to make this right. For my mama and my papa, I need to make this right. Come back!"

I drop my knife into the bottom of the boat and I find that I am crying.

WANPELA TEN TU

The council is sat in a wide circle around the Bigman. The elders are all wearing their traditional costumes, which is what they always do when there is an important meeting. Even the Bigman has his battle paint on his face and the cassowary headdress that doesn't fit him *tru* on his head.

Above the meeting place, the sky is getting darker and the stars are about to come out. It is a cool evening with no clouds.

I watch from behind my tree as the Bigman picks up the *taur* shell and puts it to his lips. He blows hard and a loud noise bursts through the clearing, out towards the mountain in one direction and out towards the sea in the other. This is to show that the meeting has begun.

Siringen stands up from the rock on which he sits and

takes his place before the Bigman. Siringen looks small. And he looks old, like he might die soon. This makes me feel worse.

"Shark caller Siringen," begins the Bigman, not smiling. "I have called this meeting of the village council because of what has happened today." I am far away from the elders and it is difficult for me to hear. "Do you understand?"

"Yes."

"This village and its community work around basic principles that were laid down by our ancestors. We live peaceful, respectful lives that do not intrude on the lives of others.

"Earlier today, the girl who you have been given some responsibility for took something that did not belong to her. She stole a canoe that now belongs to my son, Moses. Is this *tru*? Do you agree with what I am saying?"

"Yes." Siringen is not saying much.

"The girl took it out onto the sea and then left it far from the place where it was kept. Is this *tru*?"

"It is what you have told me so, yes, I believe it is *tru*."

"Oh, it is *tru*," says the Bigman. "I know it is *tru*."

"Then why are you asking me?"

"What?"

"If you know it is *tru*, why are you asking me?"

The Bigman looks annoyed. "Silence!"

I can hear a few of the elders trying to bury their laughs and I find a smile upon my own face.

"This is not the place for your disrespect, shark caller Siringen. My son was *tru* upset to find that his canoe had been taken. *Tru* upset. He has great love for that canoe."

But he doesn't know how to use it, I think to myself. *It is just a toy to him. One toy out of many.*

"I am sorry if the girl's actions gave Moses a moment of pain," says Siringen. "But isn't it a vital lesson for him to learn? That, sometimes, the things we love are taken away from us unfairly."

"What sort of rubbish is this?" The Bigman's headdress looks like it might fall off again. "The girl took something that didn't belong to her. That is all we are discussing. The question is, should we let you continue with your responsibility to this village, or should we pass that responsibility to another?"

An aeroplane flies overhead. A *bikpela* jumbo jet from Australia or Japan. The noise covers the words being said in the circle. Heads are being nodded and heads are being shaken. Some of the others are saying things but I cannot hear them. I try to make my ears stretch to snatch at the words but it is *tru, tru* difficult and I shake my angry fist up at the plane. Finally, after what I think is a long *taim*, the plane has gone further on its journey and the noise is less.

"…Hamelin?" I hear the Bigman finishing off his words.

"I have taken him to many places where the coral grows," says Siringen. "But he is wanting to go further. Out into the sea where the coral does not grow. I do not know why he wishes to go out so far in the sea. It does not seem right to me."

In my head I think of the locked box that Maple wants to break open. I think of the photos that Mr Hamelin wanted us to take from the top of the mountain. I think of the man in the town with the envelope. And I think of how these vines must all tie themselves together, but I do not know how.

"That is not for you to question, shark caller," replies the Bigman to Siringen. "It is simply your duty to aid Professor Hamelin in his work. Do whatever he asks, without wondering why you are doing it."

The Bigman moves uncomfortably on his rock and makes a *huff* noise through his mouth.

"*Orait*. The council need to decide if you are to continue with your responsibilities, and continue to look after Mr Hamelin." He stands up. "Please, elders. Make your choice."

Some of the men of the council throw stones onto the ground in front of them. Some throw them quick.

Some throw them slow. Some of the men do not throw stones at all.

The Bigman walks around the clearing and counts the number of stones thrown. From my hiding place I can see that there are more stones on the ground than in elders' hands and I am pleased.

The Bigman sits back down on his rock and puts his headdress straight.

"*Orait*, shark caller Siringen. The council have decided that you should still take this responsibility. But it falls onto your shoulders if anything like this happens again. Do you understand? It will be *your* fault."

Siringen says nothing, but turns and walks away from the clearing and the men in their battle dress. As he passes my tree, he sees me and we walk back towards the village in silence.

Back in the hut, I hand him his pipe and his tobacco. He takes them and starts to stuff the pipe full.

"So," I say after a long *taim*. "You still have responsibility for Mr Hamelin."

"Yes," he says, lighting the pipe with a glowing stick taken from the dying fire. "I *still* do."

Then he winks one of his eyes and I know that he is not mad with me. I know that I am not in trouble. And that everything is *orait* between me and Siringen.

"You know," he starts, his eyes suddenly changing and looking sad, "I am sorry that I let Xok go on that morning. It is something I have lived with for a long *taim*. If I *had* killed him, then…you would be living…living with your parents right now. Not with me. Not with an old man who has plenty more days behind him than ahead."

"*Waspapi*." I kneel on the floor next to him. "It is not your fault. I know that I said it was, but it is not. I was angry, and when I am angry I say things that should not be said."

"Truthful things," Siringen says.

"No. Things said in anger are not truthful," I say. "They are just ideas that haven't found the right words yet, so trying to put them into words early is wrong. They are like clouds – changing shape and not what they would ever be over *taim*.

"Mama's death and Papa's death and…well, they are not your fault. I do not blame you. Please, do not carry this rock around with you any more. Please."

I reach over and hold his old hand.

In one of his eyes is a tear, so I look down to the floor because I know Siringen is a tough man who would not like me to see a tear in his eye.

"Thank you," he says, and he squeezes my hand back.

WANPELA TEN TRI

"Oh, Blue Wing!"

It is Maple's voice.

I wipe my eyes and look around the hut. Siringen has gone. Out on the sea as normal, I think.

"Oh, Bloooo Waaaaayng!"

Maple's voice is like a song going up and down. It is not serious. It is like it is a joke.

"Come in!" I shout.

The door opens as I stand up from my sago mat.

"You're up late today," she says, her face with a frown, like she has worry about me. "That's not like you."

I take my sleeping T-shirt off and pull on a day T-shirt. "No. I think I slept *tru* good last night." I push my hand through my hair to make it go flat. "I slept *tru* deep."

"Oh, good. Anyway..." She pulls something out of

her pocket and turns it around in the air in front of me. "Look what I found."

I step towards her to see what it is. "The key! You found the key."

"Yes, I did!" Maple smiles like she has won a swimming competition. "Turns out Dad keeps it hidden inside the old grandfather clock."

"Have you looked inside the box yet?" I ask.

"No. Thought that this time it would be best to wait until Dad really had gone off on his boat – he's just left. And I also thought you might like to see it with me. You ready?"

The *bikpela* clock that stands in the corner of the room is *knicking* and *knocking* much slower than ever before. I can see from the dials that the *taim* is not right. It is at least three hours slow.

"Dad keeps meaning to fix that," says Maple, picking Trinket up from a chair and putting him onto her shoulder like a pirate with a parrot. "It annoys him the way it keeps losing time."

"Siringen says that the air will make it go wrong. He says it is too hot and wet here for the clock."

"He's probably right."

Maple pushes the door to Mr Hamelin's bedroom. My parents' bedroom.

She goes to the chest and kneels in front of it, putting Trinket down on the floor. Then she takes out the key from her pocket.

"Should you really do this?" I say, my thoughts staying on the council meeting the night before. "Is it *right* to do this?"

"What do you mean?"

"Well…whatever is in that box, your papa has put there for a reason. And he has *locked* the box for a reason. It might not be because he does not want you to see whatever is in there. It might be because it is *mobeta for you* not to see what is in there. He might be protecting you."

Maple holds the key in her fingers. She is thinking this over.

Then she shakes her head.

"The best way to protect me is to let me see what is in the chest and then help me to deal with the consequences. That's the best way to show love, isn't it? Not to just hide things away from me so I don't even know they exist."

"But you might get into trouble doing this." I think about Siringen and how small and old he looked in the clearing last night.

"Well that's something I'm going to have to live with."

Maple puts the key into the lock on the box and then turns it.

It clicks.

She looks at me and I look at her.

"Are you sure?"

She nods and then pushes the top of the chest open.

Books. Papers. Maps. Photographs.

"What is all this stuff?" says Maple, pulling some of it out and putting it on the floor next to the *kapul*.

I am too interested to stay away from it, so I kneel down next to her.

I pick up some photographs with a rubber band around them. Pulling the rubber band off, I start to look through them.

The photographs are all old, black and white. They look like they might be from World War Two. Photographs of *bikpela* ships with planes on their backs. Plenty of those photographs – some with words scribbled onto them. *Shokaku. Zuikaku. Shoho. Taiyo.*

There are photographs of groups of men – not smiling – wearing leather flying caps and goggles on their heads. Japanese men. All of them staring at the camera like it is not a joke.

"These are war photographs," I say, before I put the

rubber band back around them and sit them on the floor.

Maple has opened up a map. It looks old too. It shows much land and much sea around the land. I recognize a part of the land as New Ireland.

"That is *this* island," I say, pointing to the map. "*That* is the sea."

"Then what are all these things?"

There are red crosses all over the map.

"I do not know."

"Neither do I. It's so random."

She folds the map up and puts it near Trinket.

"What's this?"

Maple pulls out some sheets of paper held together by a staple in the corner. She starts to read out the first page.

"*Report into the sinking of the Imperial Japanese Navy aircraft carrier Kumano Maru by His Majesty's Australian Ship Nizam in The Bismarck Sea, New Ireland – January twelfth, 1945.* Wow. This looks fascinating!"

"Does it?"

"No. I was being sarcastic. Even though it's about the sinking of a ship – and theoretically it should be interesting – it's probably just a mind-numbingly boring historical document. The sort of thing my dad loves."

"*Lukim!* There are others like that." I pull eight or

nine stapled documents out. "They are all about Japanese ships that have been sunk."

Maple ignores me and starts to lift some heavy-looking books from the bottom of the chest.

A History of the Japanese Navy 1917 – 1956
A6M: The Story of the Zero Fighter
Ancient Artefacts of Ancient Cultures
The Life and Times of Emperor Hirohito
The Lost Riches of the Japanese Empire
The Wartime Diaries of Prime Minister Hideki Tojo
Sunk! A History of Submerged Treasure
A Beginner's Guide to Deep-Sea Diving

I look at all the words on the fronts of all the books and my mind starts to put together a story.

"What is all this trash?" asks Maple. "Why's my dad trying to hide away all these stupid books? What's so important about them?"

I pick up one of the books – *The Lost Riches of the Japanese Empire* – then I pick up another – *Sunk! A History of Submerged Treasure*. I put them both down on *A Beginner's Guide to Deep Sea Diving*.

"I think," I say, "that your papa is trying to find treasure."

Maple laughs. "What? No. That's not right. He's not a pirate! He—"

"He has pretended to be looking for coral... He has lied to Siringen and everyone else in the village because he is trying to find treasure that has gone down to the bottom of the ocean in a ship. That is what he is doing. He is trying to make himself rich."

Maple laughs. "That's ridiculous. My dad—"

"Your papa has come here to try and make himself rich."

"Don't be so stupid, Blue Wing. My dad's not interested in finding treasure."

"Then why does he have all this," I point to all the paper on the floor, "information about Japanese ships and treasure?"

"He's just interested in history. That's all." She speaks like there is a seed of anger starting to grow in her voice. "Probably just wants to write an academic paper on it or something. Remember – or have you forgotten? – he's a historian after all."

I pick up the map with crosses on. "This map obviously shows where ships have sunk. He is looking for these ships. There must be treasure on one of them and he is trying to find it."

"You are talking trash! We came here to get away from

my mom's death. To start again. Not to get rich. I think all this heat must have finally got to you." Maple shakes her head, an unhappy smile across her mouth.

"Then why does he pretend to look for coral? And why does he not want Siringen to travel out with him any more? And why does he go into town and give men money for things in envelopes? And why does he not tell you all about it?" I find that my finger is pointing at Maple.

She laughs again. "He's an academic and he does things for reasons. Just because you've never been to school in your life doesn't mean everyone has to be as irrational and stupid as you."

"But you are the one being stupid. It is you who have wondered what it is you are doing here."

"No, *you're* the stupid one. You don't understand my dad at all. In fact, you don't understand *me* at all!"

I sigh. "No, I do not understand you. I do not understand anything about you. Yesterday, you got Siringen into trouble, yet today you act like it has been nothing. Zero."

Maple suddenly looks confused and she puts her hands up like they are trying to catch something invisible. "What are you—"

"You came here to this island and you put on a face like a boar trapped in a pen. You acted like you had been given the whole world and then had it taken from you.

And I did not like you. Then I get to understand you – by being interested – and I think you are sad because you have lost your mama. And I think that it is something we have the same. You lost your mama and I lost my mama and my papa."

I stand up, making maps and papers fall onto the floor.

"But yesterday, you told me to take the canoe that was once mine, and I said no."

"You didn't say no for long! You went along with it because you *wanted* to go along with it. It was all to do with you being a stupid shark caller! Nothing to do with me."

I do not listen to what she has just said. "I said no, but you said we should. And because of that, Siringen has got into trouble with the Bigman. But you do not care."

"I didn't even know he'd gotten into trouble. How am I meant to know if nobody tells me?"

"You should listen more and stop thinking about yourself so much. That is how."

"Does that even make sense?" The unhappy smile is back.

"And your papa pretends to be an expert on coral when really he is trying to find gold to take back to America with him so that he can build a *bikpela* house."

"Big! The word is big! Not *bikpela*!"

"So he can build a *bikpela* house!" I say *"bikpela" tru* loud to make her annoyed. "I thought that he was a good person. I thought he was someone who would understand the island and the village and the people who live here. I thought he would see the way it all works and respect that. But now I know differently.

"I see that – just like all the men from America and England who come here to kill and shoot animals – I see that he is just here to take something away from us. He uses us like a place to eat and sleep before digging a piece of the island's heart away and going back to his comfortable home over the sea. That is what *he* is like. And that is what *you* are like."

Maple gets up too, standing straight in front of me. She looks *longlong*. "Like I said, you don't know anything about my dad. I mean, how could you? You've spent your whole life on this island, too scared to go into the town because – woah! – there are too many people for you!

"Get on a plane, go around the world, see a few places. You never know, you might find somewhere you prefer. You might just come back home and think, *You know what? Perhaps this isn't automatically the most amazing place on the planet.* Anyway, who'd want to live in a place with a local killer shark?"

She starts me to think. "I could have killed Xok yesterday! If it was not for you being scared in the canoe, I could have killed him. I was ready to jump into the water and to put my knife into him. But I stopped because you did not want to be left alone, like you did not want to go further into the mine. The whole reason for me being here is to kill that shark, and yesterday you stopped me doing it. It was the one chance I have had, and you took it away from me. Because you were frightened."

"Hold on!" She stands with her hands on her hips and has a confused face again. "So if you'd managed to *kill* the shark – something you seem to criticize people from England and the States for doing – you would have been *delighted* that we'd stolen the canoe? Am I right? You wouldn't care about Siringen getting into trouble then, would you? You wouldn't care about that. You'd've been pleased that the shark was dead and nothing else would matter. Yes?"

I shake my head. "I do not know what you are saying."

"I'm saying that you're a hypocrite. That's what I'm saying. You say whatever suits you at a certain time and change the facts whenever you want to."

"I do not lie!" I shout. "It is your papa who lies. And I think you do too."

I turn and walk out of the bedroom, my heart like a thunderstorm.

I see all of Mr Hamelin's clocks in the room next door. I think they are all *knick*ing and *knock*ing. The hands are all turning.

Except for one.

I put my head to its chest and listen.

I think the grandfather clock's heart has stopped.

WANPELA TEN FOA

I do not speak to Maple Hamelin. And she does not speak to me. But even though we do not speak, my mind is fixed on her and her papa like a burr on a dog's back. The days move like a stream passing and we do not see each other for what – inside my heart – feels like a long *taim*.

So I am surprised when, one morning, I see her running across from the papaya grove, no sun hat on her head, no bug sunglasses.

"Blue Wing!" she shouts. "Blue Wing!"

I cover my eyes from the sun and squash my eyes to see her.

She has worry on her face.

She almost falls and I find myself starting to move towards her to make sure she is well. Even though I want to tell myself that I am angry with her and do not want to see her, I move towards her.

"Blue Wing!" She sees me and runs faster. "Come quickly!"

"What is it?"

She comes into the enclosure, her hands grabbing onto my arms. Her breath escapes her and it is a minute before she can speak.

"It's Chimera! I don't think...she's well."

"What is wrong with her?"

"I don't know. But I went to see her in her cave and I found her. Collapsed. She's breathing, but I don't know what to do. My dad's out on his stupid boat again and... and..."

"Okay." I try to think quick. "Okay...I will come with you and see."

I run out of the enclosure, Maple close behind me. We take the difficult – but more quick – way up the mountain, our feet slipping over the steep, dry earth.

We move fast and soon we are near Chimera's cave and I can see something lying on the ground just outside the entrance. I think it is some rags, but I realize that it is Chimera.

"Chimera!"

I get onto my knees and bend myself down to her face. "You are right. She is breathing still. But it is *tru* small." I put my hand on Chimera's head. "She feels like she is a fire."

"What are we going to do?" Maple asks, her whole face looking scared.

I look around. "Bring me the water. There! And bring me a cloth."

Maple carries over the water in a pot and takes a strip of rag from the clothesline.

I let the rag soak in the pot and then wipe it across Chimera's face.

"I will keep her cool."

"What will *I* do?"

I think again. "You will need to get Siringen. He will know what to do."

"Where is he?"

"He is out in the bay on his canoe. I do not think he has gone far out. You will need to fetch him. Swim out to him."

"But…but what about Xok?"

"Xok?" I feel my face turn into confusion.

"What if he is out there? In the sea? What if he comes for me?"

I shake my head. "Maple," I say. "You are a *tru* good swimmer. I need for you to swim out to Siringen and tell him to come here."

"But Xok?"

I feel my chest to be angered. "Xok will not be there! There are million and million of litre of water out in the ocean. He will not be there! Trust!"

I see she still has worry.

"Can't I just get another adult?"

"Please, Maple! Be brave! For Chimera."

She looks at Chimera and nods her head.

"Okay. I'll go and get him."

She turns and runs back down the mountain towards the sea.

"And hurry!" I call behind her. "I think you need to hurry."

"Blue Wing?"

Chimera opens her eyes a *liklik* bit. Her head is lying on my arm.

"Yes, Chimera?"

"Blue Wing? Is that you? What are you still doing here? You should be gone by now. Isn't it *taim* you were gone?"

"Ssh, Chimera. You are not well. You are sick. Siringen is coming to help."

"Siringen?" Her eyes get more vast. "Siringen is a good man."

"Yes, I know he is."

"He is a *tru* good man." She tries to smile.

"He will be here soon."

After some *taim*, I see something move at the edge of the clearing.

"Chimera!"

It is Siringen. He runs next to me and puts his hand against her head.

"She has a fever." He looks at me. "You did the right thing keeping her cool, Blue Wing. If she gets too hot, she could die." He takes the cloth from me, puts it in the bowl and holds it against her head. "We need to get her home. I can take *mobeta* care of her there."

Suddenly Siringen stands up, bends over and picks up Chimera, throwing her gently over his shoulder.

"It is *orait*, Chimera," he says to her. "I am taking you home with me. You need to rest well."

Chimera is small and like a piece of dust, and Siringen – who is strong – carries her like she is zero.

"Has she said anything?" he asks as we walk towards Maple, who looks wet. "Or has she stayed quiet?"

"She was talking to me, *waspapi*," I say.

"Good. That is a good sign. She has not gone too deep."

In the hut, Siringen puts Chimera softly down on my

sago mat. Then he finds an old cotton sheet and puts it around her body. Her eyes are shut.

"Blue Wing. Maple." He pours some of the fresh water he keeps in the *bikpela* pot by the door into a wooden bowl. "I need to find the best plants to make the best medicine. While I am away, you both need to keep her cool. And if she wakes again, try to put some water on her lips."

I look down at Chimera, her body not moving, and I start to realize just how much worry I have for her. She might have died up near her cave. And she might die still. Nothing is really as clear as the sky yet.

"Shouldn't we get her to a hospital?" Maple asks. "I could get my dad to drive us into the town and she could see a doctor there."

Siringen shakes his head. "No. Chimera is the daughter of the medicine man. If we took her to a hospital and she got well then she would feel like she had failed to her papa. I know her mind. She would feel like it would have been *mobeta* if she had died."

Siringen smiles at Maple.

"Do not worry, Maple. I am sure she will not die. I am an old man and I know plenty of the old ways. I will get the plants – they are around the mountain – and I will crush them and boil them, and Chimera will drink them.

Then she will get *mobeta*."

Siringen leaves and the room goes quiet. Maple sits on the floor next to me as I hold a cloth to Chimera's face.

"I hope she gets better," says Maple, moving closer to me. "I'd hate it if she died too."

So would I, I think inside myself. *So would I.*

"Why were you going to see her?" I say.

"I wanted to ask her about my mom. I wanted to see if she could try to speak to her."

I look at Maple and suddenly I remember all her sadness. And it makes me feel *nogut*. Guilty. For being so rude to her. For not trusting her.

"I know she said that she couldn't, but if anyone can, surely it's Chimera. I just wanted to make sure. Because if I could tell my mom that I love her...just one more time... Well, I know it sounds stupid but..."

"No. It does not sound stupid. It sounds right."

Maple stops talking and looks down at the floor.

"And I just...I just want to say sorry to her."

"Sorry?" I ask, my voice quiet. "What do *you* need to say sorry for?"

Maple doesn't say anything. She keeps her eyes on the floor.

"Maple?"

She wipes a tear from her eye.

"Well…I'm the reason why she died in hospital."

"I do not understand."

She looks back at me, and pain is painted all over her face.

"When she was really ill in hospital…when it was found that the doctors couldn't do anything to save her… when Dad sat me down and gave me the talk that Mom wasn't going to improve and that we had to be brave… around that time…she should have come home to die. She should have been in a place that she loved and surrounded by people who loved her back. But she didn't come home to die."

"No."

"She didn't come back home to die, because I didn't want her to."

I wipe the cloth across Chimera's head and say nothing.

"You see, by then, it was like she wasn't even my mom. Her eyes stayed shut all the time. She didn't speak. Didn't smile. Didn't move, even. She didn't know me. She was a stranger. And why would I want a stranger in my house? So I told my dad that I didn't want her home."

Chimera moves a *liklik*.

"Quickly, put some water on her lips," says Maple.

I move the rag to Chimera's lips and squeeze it. Some of the water goes onto her lips and down her cheek.

"By the time I'd realized she should be at home, it was too late. There was no point in moving her." Maple takes the rag from me and holds it back against Chimera's head. "So she died in her hospital bed."

I watch her. She seems soft and kind – softer and more kind than I could ever be. She strokes Chimera's hand with her fingers and puts fresh water onto Chimera's neck and chest. It is caring.

I try to think of something to say to her.

"I do not think you need to say sorry to your mama. I think she would understand. If she *tru* loved you, she would not care where she left her life. All that would matter would be the feelings in your heart."

"You're right. In my head I know all this," she says, "but somewhere, something inside me needs more convincing."

Chimera moves again. Her eyes stay shut but out of her lips come words that are mumbled. We put our heads near to her mouth and listen.

"The very young... The gifted... The guilty," she says.

Siringen returns more quick than I had thought. In his arms are sticks of twisted wood and balls of rolled up leaves.

He takes one of his pots, fills it with water, makes a fire outside and begins to cut up the leaves and sticks.

"She will be *orait* if she drinks this medicine," he says, dropping the herbs into the boiling pot. "In the old *taim*, everyone knew about medicines like this. All the children were taught how to make them. They are nothing difficult. They always work. But these days, the children go too quick to the town doctors and take their antibiotics and pills."

"How long will it take for her to get better?" Maple asks Siringen, as he stirs the pot.

"Days. Weeks. I do not know." He looks at me. "But perhaps, Blue Wing, it is right she stays here on your mat until she is well enough, yes?"

"Yes, *waspapi*," I answer. "Do not worry. I will sleep outside."

After two hour, the medicine is ready. Siringen takes a small cup, lets it get cool, then sits Chimera up and puts the medicine onto her lips.

Her eyes open. "Hello, Siringen," she says in a weak voice.

"Hello, Chimera," replies Siringen, with a *bikpela* smile on his mouth.

I look at Maple and I see that, like me, she is smiling too.

WANPELA TEN FAIV

I see that Mr Hamelin has got the *bikpela* grandfather clock *knicking* and *knocking* again. I point to it, but Maple shakes her head.

"No. It will only slow down and eventually stop again. Dad keeps resetting it every morning, but it doesn't seem to help."

"He has all his other clocks, so he will never lose the *taim*," I say. "Maple, why does your papa have so many clocks?"

"That's another thing he's become obsessed with since Mom died. He says he needs to know the time all the time, if you see what I mean. He's even got a watch that can tell you what the time is in any part of the world *while he's underwater*! Pointless! I've got this," she shakes the charm bracelet on her wrist, "and he's got some stupid thing that cost eight-hundred dollars. I know which one I prefer."

I open the door to her hut and step outside. The heat is strong and the light is *tru* bright. The sun is hitting the sea and making everything blind.

"Blue Wing," says Maple and I turn around to look at her. "All this 'treasure hunting' business. I know it isn't right. It's not why we're here. But I know for a fact that Dad intends to go into town tomorrow morning to 'speak to someone'." Maple makes shapes in the air with her fingers. "So I thought, perhaps, we could stow a ride with him and then tail him around."

"What?" I do not understand much of what she is saying.

"What I mean is, we could hide in the back of the truck – he's got a cover for it now – and then we could follow him. What do you think?"

"Good morning, Blue Wing!"

Mr Hamelin looks different to when I last saw him close. His face looks tired, his body looks thin and his hair is even longer and unwashed. The hair that sits on his chin looks more like a lawatbulut tree than a beard, and the ends of his fingers look dirty.

"Good morning, Mr Hamelin."

"How is Chimera? Recovering well, I trust?"

"Yes. Thank you. Siringen is taking good care of her. She is awake and eating soups and will be strong soon."

"Good. I think she gave Maple quite a shock."

"Yes, but I think she is over the shock now."

Mr Hamelin smiles at me like he is trying to see inside.

Suddenly, Maple comes out of the door and onto the beach. She does not look at her papa even though she speaks to him.

"Okay, Dad. See you later."

"What are you two doing today?"

Maple still doesn't look at him. "Thought we'd take a walk over to the local burial ground. Go take a look at some gravestones."

"Sounds depressing. Have fun."

We cross over the sand and up towards the road.

"Okay. I reckon we've got about twenty minutes before Dad gets to the truck. By which time we'll be well hidden under the tarpaulin on the back."

"I hope this is not going to get Siringen into more trouble," I say.

"No. Don't worry. No one's ever going to know about this except us."

It takes a few minutes to work out how to unhook the cover on the back of Mr Hamelin's truck. We look around to see that there is nobody watching us and then Maple climbs into the back, and then I climb into the back.

I find difficulty in putting the cover back from the inside of the truck. It is not easy. So Maple helps me put the corner of the rubber cover into its place and then we wait.

Mr Hamelin takes more than twenty minutes to come to the truck. And, lying down in the back of the truck, it gets *tru* hot.

Beep, beeeep!

Clunk.

The locks on the car are opened, so Maple and I stay quiet and don't move. The car rocks as Mr Hamelin gets into the driver's seat. It is dark and I cannot see Maple's face, but I think she is either smiling *bikpela* or covered in worry.

Then the engine starts.

"Here we go," whispers Maple.

"Yes," I reply. "You know, I feel *tru longlong*, hiding in the back of a truck. Do you?"

"Yep. True *longlong*. Very, very silly."

The car moves. Slowly. But then, it turns quick and I roll over onto Maple. Then it turns the other way quick and Maple rolls onto me.

It is difficult to stop laughing.

"Sssh," says Maple when she has swallowed the

laughter. "My dad'll hear us."

But he does not. Because he turns on the radio. And he puts the music loud. I cannot hear the words of the song, but I can hear the thumping of the drum.

The roads on the island are covered with deep holes. I have always known this. When I walk along the road, I can see them. I step into them. But this is the first *taim* I have ever really *felt* them. Each *taim* the truck goes over one of the holes, it bumps hard and makes my back hurt.

"Ow!" says Maple as we go over a *tru* rough part of the road. "This is uncomfortable. I'm going to be covered in bruises soon. I'll be in so much pain I won't be able to follow Dad around the town!"

The journey feels like it is going on for too long. I think that the town must have got up in the middle of the night and moved further away.

Suddenly the truck seems to slow.

And the road gets rougher.

We are bouncing in the back of the truck now. Rattling between the rubber cover and the floor of the van. If we both survive the journey, I will thank Moroa!

I begin to think. The road to the town is *mobeta* than this. The holes are filled in sometimes. It should be more smooth.

Then my mind realizes. Mr Hamelin has come off the *bikpela* road and is driving along a track!

I try to tell Maple, but the noise of the truck and of our heads bumping is too loud.

I begin to wonder where Mr Hamelin is *really* going. Why has he taken the car off the road and onto a path not made for wheels? Why has he lied about going into the town? What is he trying to see? *Who* is he trying to see? There are too many questions stuck on Mr Hamelin and it is impossible to pick any of them off.

But still Mr Hamelin keeps driving.

And then suddenly, like a surprise, the truck stops.

The engine is turned off.

The door opens and closes.

Mr Hamelin says something – we cannot hear him through the rubber.

Someone else says something.

Then the two voices get small like they are moving further away.

"Where are we?" asks Maple, keeping her words a whisper. "I don't think we're in the town. There would be more noise."

"I think we are in the hills," I say. "We went up and down plenty *taim*."

"Let's take a look."

We push the corner of the cover off and the elastic jumps open, showing bright light. I pull the rubber further back and put my head outside.

"Well?" Maple asks.

"We are in a clearing. In a forest. I can see a hut."

"That must be where my dad has gone. With the other guy."

I climb out of the truck. My legs and arms and head are all full of pain, and I have to move too slowly.

Maple climbs out too. She is the same slowness as I am.

"You know, we've also got to go *back home* in the truck. I don't think I'm going to have any bones left in me by the time we're in the village again."

I look around the clearing. It is bare apart from some pots, a rug and plenty sticks tied up with string. The door of the hut is whole open and I can hear voices coming from inside.

Maple and I walk as quiet as we can across the ground to a window. We bend down as low as beetles and try to listen to the words being said.

"The man you speak of has long passed?"

"Yes. Many years ago." Mr Hamelin's words.

"Then it may be difficult to reach him. Let me have the photograph."

There is no speaking for a few seconds.

"*Soldia?*" The *namba tu* voice again.

"Yes."

"The old war. There were many who passed in the old war. They are like a thunderstorm with their words. Loud. It is difficult to pick out an individual drop of rain from all that noise. But I will try."

Maple looks at me and makes a face that says, *I am confused*.

I shake my head. We do not know what it is that is going on.

The hut is quiet, and it is like the two men inside have become asleep.

Then there is a strange noise.

A humming noise.

"It's the other guy," Maple whispers.

"Mmmmmm…mmmmmmmm…hommmmmm…"

Maple almost laughs, and seeing Maple almost laugh makes me almost laugh too.

"The man you wish to speak with… He died suddenly. He was young but he died suddenly. It is like he didn't even notice he had died."

"Yes…yes…I understand. But where is he?" Mr Hamelin sounds like he does not have *taim* to waste.

I look around at the clearing again and it reminds me of Chimera.

"The man inside," I whisper to Maple. "He is a spiritual man. Like Chimera. He talks to the dead."

Maple still looks confused.

There are some more noises like the spiritual man is trying to pull the dead *soldia* out of the air.

"The man you seek is in the sea. Not too far away from here."

"Where? Tell me where."

There are no words.

"Please. I need to know."

A few seconds go past and then the spiritual man speaks again, in a *liklik* deeper voice.

"He says he knows what it is you seek. And he knows your reason for seeking it."

"Then he knows how desperate I am to find it. And he knows how finding it can make me complete again. Please. For the sake of me and my daughter, tell me where it is."

Maple looks at me. I make my shoulders go up and down. I do not know what any of these words mean.

"Before he became one with the sea, he saw a bay with a hill on each side. On top of one of the hills was a tree. The tree was bent like a man picking something up from the ground. If you find that bay…you will find him. And if you find him, you will find that which you ultimately seek."

There is silence again.

"Is there any more detail? Something more substantial? I need something more substantial."

"There is nothing more. He has faded into the noise of all the dead. Although…"

"What?"

"Before he left me…he did ask a question…"

"What question? What are you talking about?"

"He said, do you really *want* to find it? Do you really think that it would help?"

"Of course it would help. How could it not?"

I imagine the spiritual man shaking his head.

"I do not know what it is you seek, so I cannot answer that."

There is noise inside the hut like the men are getting up from the floor.

Maple hits me with her elbow and we begin to walk as silently as we can back to the truck.

Suddenly, I think it feels wrong to be listening in on people speaking to each other, and to pretend to people we are in different places, and to hide in the back of a truck without the person driving knowing we are there. It is not right. It is not what Siringen would do.

Maple opens the rubber cover and begins to climb in.

But I stop.

"Quickly, Blue Wing. Before they see you."

"No."

"What? What's wrong with you?" She hisses like a *snek*. "Get in!"

"No. I am not getting in."

"Don't be stupid! They'll be out any second."

"Maple," I say. "The *taim* is here to make your papa tell you *why* you are here."

"No! Get in!"

"Please, Maple. It feels *tru longlong* – very, very silly – to be talking to someone lying down in the back of a truck. Please. Get out."

"Blue Wing!"

"They are coming. I hear them."

Maple looks at me with *bikpela*, vast eyes.

"Now is the *taim*, Maple. Please. Trust."

Suddenly, my mind sparks back to the other day when I was standing in my old boat, my knife in my hand, ready to kill Xok.

Now is the taim. That was what I thought as the boat rocked on the sea. *Now is the taim.*

But it was not the *taim*, because the *taim* slipped away and I felt like the chance was gone.

I blink my eyes and I shake the bad memory out of my head as I see the two men step out of the hut into the clearing. Mr Hamelin nods to the spiritual man who, I see, has many beads around his neck and plenty rings on his fingers.

As Mr Hamelin turns, he sees me.

"Blue Wing?" He looks the same way confused as his daughter. "What are you doing here?"

"Are you *orait*, sir?" asks the spiritual man.

Mr Hamelin ignores him and starts walking towards me.

"What? Have you…followed…"

Suddenly the cover on the back of the truck jumps up in the air and Maple sits straight.

"What the…!" Mr Hamelin is surprised and almost falls over. "Maple? What are you doing?"

"That's the question Blue Wing and I have been asking ourselves for the last ten minutes. What are we doing here? What are we doing in the middle of nowhere, listening in on a conversation about dead people through a window? And, you know what? Neither of us seems to know the answers."

"Did you hide in the back of the truck? Is that what you did?" Mr Hamelin's face is dressed in confusion.

"Yes, Dad, we hid in the truck. But that's not the point. The point is we *had* to hide in the truck to try and find out what's going on."

"What do you mean 'what's going on'?"

Maple sighs. "*This*, Dad." She throws her arms around to show the clearing. "All *this*. All this secretive stuff that you're not telling me about. Why we're here. What it is you seem to be looking for. Why you're driving out into the countryside to talk to dead men. All of it."

Mr Hamelin looks like a child who has been caught stealing *saksak*.

"Hmm…"

"Because, if I'm being truthful, I'm finding it a bit of a strain not knowing." I look at Maple's face and I can see a tear on her cheek. "Whenever I try and get into the subject you just change it straight away. Whenever it seems like I'm going to ask you about being here, you make some excuse and go out on your stupid boat. As if things haven't been difficult enough with Mom dying, you're…making things…a hundred times worse by not… explaining. And I hate it, Dad. I really do."

More tears are coming out from her eyes, but I do not say anything. These words and tears are not for me. It is like I am not even there.

Mr Hamelin should be holding Maple. He should see the tears and move towards her and hold her until she stops crying. That is what he should do.

But he does not.

Instead he still stands where he is, his face still confused like he does not know what to say.

Maple wipes her eyes and says something *tru kwait*.

"I just want Mom back, Dad."

Mr Hamelin looks straight at her and speaks with a voice that sounds as flat as the sea on a still day. "I know. I know you do. So do I."

"I miss her so much."

"Me too. I'm sorry I'm not much of a replacement."

I look past the two of them and notice that the spiritual man has gone back inside his hut.

"Please, Dad," says Maple. "Tell me what's going on."

Mr Hamelin rocks from one foot to the other.

"Mr Hamelin," I say, stepping forwards. "Maple needs to know why she is here. She needs to know why *you* are here. And something I have come to know about Maple since we met first is that Maple is *tru* brave and *tru* strong and she will not stop until she finds out everything. So, it is probably best for you and for her if you tell the things she needs to know." I smile at Mr Hamelin and hope he does not feel I have said something too much.

Mr Hamelin tries smiling back.

"You see," Maple whispers, "Blue Wing thinks we are here to steal sunken treasure. So, please, Dad, stop carrying everything around on your own and making us think the worst. Tell us."

Mr Hamelin looks sad. "You wouldn't believe me if I told you. Either of you."

"Dad!"

"Okay." He nods. "Okay. I'm sorry, Maple. Blue Wing. You're right." He pulls his long, dirty hair back from his face. "You're right. You both deserve an explanation."

PAT NAMBA TRI

THE PLACE
WHERE THE SAND
MEETS THE SEA

WANPELA TEN SIKIS

The journey back to the village is much more comfortable than the journey away from the village. Maple and I sit on the leather seats in the back and look out of the windows. Nobody says anything and I think Mr Hamelin is trying to put his words in order in his mind before giving them out to Maple.

Back in the village, Mr Hamelin parks the truck on the stony ground next to Mr Boas's Mitsubishi. Getting out, I smile at Maple. She smiles back but it is not one of the happy smiles, I think.

We walk down to the bay, across the beach and into the hut. On a soft chair in the corner of the room, Trinket – the *kapul* – is lying sleeping.

"Sit down. Both of you."

I pull a chair from under the table and sit down. Maple

does the same. Mr Hamelin takes off his jacket with the pockets and no arms and goes into his bedroom. I can hear him unlocking the wooden box.

He comes back into the room carrying some of the things we have already seen. He sits down too.

"Okay. Now." I can see that he still does not know how to begin this speech. "Where do I start?"

"At the beginning?" asks Maple, trying hard to smile.

"It is a good place," I say, smiling too.

Mr Hamelin nods. "Okay then. Let's go right the way back to the *very* beginning. Before any of us were born."

He picks a photograph up and holds it in front of our faces.

"Maple. Do you know who these people are?"

It is one of the very old photographs in black and white. But it is not a photograph of soldiers. There is a Japanese man standing next to a Japanese woman. They are next to each other, but they do not hold hands or look at each other or even smile. The man wears a suit and the woman is wearing something pretty that looks soft and goes all the way to the floor. Her hair is held with pins and I cannot see her hands because they go into each other's sleeves.

Maple shakes her head.

"I've no idea. Should I know who they are?"

"The man's name is Akemi. The woman – his wife – her name was Kishi. Akemi and Kishi Mori."

"Wait." Maple sits up. "Mori? Like Mom's birth name?"

"Yes. They were Miko's grandparents. *Your* great-grandparents."

Maple takes the photograph from Mr Hamelin. "Cool." She turns the picture over. "*1937.*"

"Yes. It was their wedding day."

"They don't look like they're exactly delighted to be getting married."

I look at the photograph she is holding and see that she is right. They do not look happy. But I do not say anything. It feels wrong for me to say too much right now.

Mr Hamelin shrugs. "A different world. A different time. The whole world was on the brink of war."

He takes the photograph back from Maple.

"Two years after this photo was taken, your grandfather was born. Takeshi Mori. Their only child. And soon after that, Japan decided to enter the Second World War. December 7th 1941. The attack on Pearl Harbour.

"Akemi – your great-grandfather – joined the Imperial Japanese Navy as a Zero fighter pilot. Zero fighters, at that time, were the best fighter planes the Japanese owned. They were carried on aircraft carriers around the

Pacific and they would attack US and British naval bases.

"As it turned out, Akemi was a brilliant pilot and was awarded a number of medals for bravery. Official records show that, during his service, he managed to take out thirty-seven enemy aircraft."

"Is that good?" Maple asks. I can see from her eyes that, like me, she does not know where this story is taking us.

"Oh, yes. It's very good," Mr Hamelin answers her. "He would have been considered one of the Emperor's best. Trusted with missions of the highest importance."

"Is *he* the one you went to the witch guy to try and talk to?"

Mr Hamelin ignores Maple's question.

"By early 1945, though, the war wasn't going too well for Japan, and Emperor Hirohito started to believe that it would soon be over, and that Japan might actually be invaded.

"Now, Japan is an old civilization. It has a rich history of art and literature, and the Imperial Palace in Tokyo is filled with many items that are considered culturally important. You know, national treasures."

"Treasure?" I ask.

"Yes," says Mr Hamelin, and I look at Maple, who looks back at me, her eyes not saying anything. "Treasure.

"Anyway." He makes the story move on. "Emperor Hirohito began to worry that, in the event of an invasion, all the riches would be taken away from Japan. So he came up with a plan. A secret plan."

Mr Hamelin stands up and opens the refrigerator.

"Would you both like a drink? Coca-Cola?"

"Yes, please," I say. Maple nods.

He takes two glasses and fills them both to the top. Then he puts them on the table in front of us. Suddenly I think back to the *taim* when Mr Hamelin cooked for us all and gave me Coca-Cola. At that *taim* it was me and Siringen who were telling the stories. This *taim* it is Mr Hamelin.

"As I was saying, the Emperor came up with a way of hiding the most important stuff. Far away from Japan."

I take a drink from the glass and the bubbles go into my nose. "Where did he hide them?" I ask.

"On an island. A few hundred miles south of here. The Japanese navy found a small, insignificant lump of rock in the middle of the ocean, far from anywhere, with a system of long, winding caves deep in the mountains. They built a runway so that planes could land there, and the idea was to hide all the important artefacts away in the caves. Keep them safe."

I do not understand much of this. But I understand

enough. And I understand that as Mr Hamelin's story moves on, Maple's great-grandfather pilot and the treasures in the cave will both come closer until they are together. I can feel it.

"The treasures – as you call them," Mr Hamelin looks at me with questions in his eyes, "would be put on board Imperial Navy aircraft carriers where only a few select officers and pilots would know the exact details of the mission. Then, once the ships had sailed to within flying distance of the island, the items – the smaller ones, anyway – would be transferred to Zero fighters and flown in. That was the plan."

"Wouldn't it be better to protect *people* instead of a bunch of dumb paintings and statues?" Maple says, with her lips touching the glass. "Surely people are more important."

"You would think so. But it wasn't the case."

"Did the plan work?" I ask. "Did the Emperor hide the treasures inside the mountain?"

"Not really, no. You see, by the time they found the hiding place and got it ready, the US and Australia – the British too – were starting to claw back control of the whole south Pacific area. Any planes trying to transport these things were seriously at risk of being shot down.

"And that's what happened to Maple's great-grandfather.

"Being one of the Empire's best pilots, Akemi was entrusted with one of the Emperor's greatest personal possessions. Unfortunately, flying over *this* area," he points to the ceiling, "two US Grumman F6F Hellcats attacked him."

"Two what?" asks Maple, a second before I do.

"They were fighter jets. American ones." Mr Hamelin picks up his story again. "Your great-grandfather's plane was badly damaged and crashed into the ocean somewhere off New Ireland.

"We know this because another pilot dispatched on that day, Naoko Hayashi, filed a report. Afterwards, he wrote a letter to your great-grandmother, sending his condolences. In it he described her husband's last brave moments and gave a description of the item he was transporting."

He takes one of the pieces of paper in front of him and lifts it up so that we can see it. It is thin and looks dirty, but the writing is pretty.

"What was it he was carrying, Dad?" Maple's eyes are not looking at the Coca-Cola now. "It must have been something important."

Mr Hamelin looks sad. "Maple, when your mother was...when she was in hospital...I started to look through all her family things. I thought it would be nice for her to see things from her past. Things she would remember. I thought it might help her. That was when I found the letter.

"I took it to some colleagues in the Japanese faculty at the university and got it translated. And what it said made me think…"

"What does it say?" I ask. I want to know more.

"What was it in the plane, Dad? What is it you're trying to find?"

Mr Hamelin puts the letter on the table and shakes his head.

"This is the point at which you'll start to think your old pop has lost his mind, sweetheart."

"What do you mean?"

Mr Hamelin puts his hand through his hair, pulling it tight into the band at the back of his head.

"Your great-grandfather was transporting a scroll."

I think I must look confused, because Mr Hamelin starts to explain the word to me.

"A scroll. Before books were invented, people would write on individual pieces of papyrus – a kind of paper. In Japan, longer sheets of papyrus would be rolled around a small wooden stick. A scroll. That's what Akemi was taking to the island. A scroll from the eighth century."

"A book?" I say.

"Yes. Sort of a book," replies Mr Hamelin.

"What's so special about this scroll?" asks Maple.

"Is it worth plenty of money?" I ask, and I see Maple look at me with worry in her eyes.

"I daresay it's worth a fortune," says Mr Hamelin. "But that's not why I'm trying to find it. I really could not care less about the money it could bring."

Maple's eyes look like there is *liklik* less worry in them.

"So what does it say on this scroll, Dad? You're really dragging this out, you know?"

"Sorry. I'll get on with it. I've done a whole ton of research since I found that letter and I believe the scroll was written by an eighth-century Japanese philosopher called Kūkai."

"But what does it say?"

Mr Hamelin is quiet again and stares at the backs of his hands.

"Nobody really knows what it says exactly, since there is nobody alive who has ever seen it. It was only ever meant for the eyes of the Emperor, and Hirohito died many years ago. I don't think—"

Maple looks annoyed. "I don't care about the detail, Dad. Just tell me what it's all about."

Mr Hamelin looks up from his hands to his daughter. Then he looks at me.

"Time," he says. "It's all about time."

Nobody says anything for a minute. Maple turns to me and makes her shoulders go up and down like this information has not made her any wiser.

"Time?" she says to her papa. "What? Like clocks?"

"Not quite."

"Well, what then?"

Mr Hamelin sighs and makes his eyes go back to the backs of his hands.

"Many people believe that time is like a piece of string. It starts way off in the distance down *there*" – he points to the door – "and continues all the way past us, finishing way off in the distance over *there*." He points to the back window. "If it ever starts or finishes at all, that is. It is linear. It goes in a straight line. It carries on ticking away, never changing, never speeding up. Always the same."

I look up at the old grandfather clock and I see that it has stopped *knicking* and *knocking* again.

"That is the way that time has always been viewed. But what if it *could* be changed? What if it was possible to turn the piece of string back on itself so that it wasn't just straight any more? What if it was possible to twist knots into it and to tie it up into whatever shape you wanted?

"What if it was possible to *control* time?"

I take a sip of my Coca-Cola. I notice Maple doing the same.

"What if time was something we could take control over and use in whatever way we wanted? Govern time, instead of the other way around. For millions of years we've followed the straight path, but what if that could change?"

"You mean like time travel? Go into the future and stuff? Like in films?"

"Yeah. I suppose."

I see Maple thinking.

"But that's just stupid, Dad."

"Is it?"

She smiles. "Of course it is. You can't just jump around in time whenever you feel like it."

"Why not?"

"Because…because, you just can't. It's stupid. It doesn't make any sense. Anyway, if time travel is invented in the future, why aren't there people from the future coming back to *this* time and telling us it can be done? It's impossible, Dad. It's stupid."

My head turns back from one to the other as they talk. Like they are throwing a ball between themselves.

"Einstein proved that, actually, time changes relative to how fast you are travelling through space." Mr Hamelin's looks are pinned to his daughter.

"Eh?"

"So why not go a few steps further and be able to *alter* time?"

"Because it's stupid, Dad."

I listen to both of them and I suddenly feel like I should not be here.

"But if it was true? Just imagine it. If the scroll holds great secrets about how time can be altered...adjusted... I mean, wouldn't you like to see your mom again?"

They both stay quiet, so I drink the end of my Coke.

"Wouldn't it be incredible if we could just do... something...and be able to have Miko with us again? And...and, Blue Wing...wouldn't you like to have your parents back? Wouldn't that be something great?"

I say nothing, but I think. I think of a book – a scroll – that can change *taim*. A book that can make things which have already happened go backwards like a car. A book that can bring back people from the dead. I think of my mama and my papa and I think of holding their hands once again. I think of them standing next to me. I think of their laughter.

And then I think that it cannot be *tru*. I am *sure* it cannot be *tru*.

Can it?

In Mr Hamelin's eyes I see the look of a man who is

slipping down a tree. It is like he knows he is falling but his hands are trying to stop him from falling. Trying too hard and hurting himself. Pulling out his fingernails.

"When your mother was in hospital, Maple…I started my investigation into all this. I got so caught up in it that, to be honest, it began to take over. All I ever thought was that if I could find that scroll and see what it says…Miko would be okay. She would live. But she didn't. And in those last few weeks I felt like I had neglected her. So, ever since, I've been trying to make it up to her by trying to find the scroll. If I can do that…"

He doesn't finish off his words.

"But, Dad…" Maple sounds small. "It's stupid."

Mr Hamelin stands up, knocking his chair onto the floor behind him. I see Trinket jump up, scared, like something would like to eat him.

"It's something I've got to do, Maple. In my heart, I just know that it's something I've got to do." Mr Hamelin picks up the chair and pushes it under the table. "You understand, don't you?"

Maple looks at me, the worry back on her face.

"O-kay. So…do you know where the plane crashed? That man you were talking to this morning…did he help you?" She asks the questions like she doesn't truly feel them in her heart.

Mr Hamelin shakes his head. "I don't know. He gave me some vague directions. It'll probably come to nothing. I paid him a lot of kina, but he might just be a fraud. I've met a couple of those already."

I try to remember the words the spiritual man had used.

"A *bay with a hill on each side. On top of one of the hills is a tree. The tree is bent, like a man picking something up from the ground.*"

Mr Hamelin stares at me. "What?"

I stare back at him, my eyes holding on to his like hooks. Then I smile.

"That is what the spiritual man told you. The place where the plane is. The place where this book of the long now is. And I know *exactly* where that place is, Mr Hamelin."

WANPELA TEN SEVEN

As I get nearer and nearer to Siringen's hut, I think to myself that I should not tell him anything that Mr Hamelin has just said. Saying these things to Siringen would seem wrong. These words belong to Maple and her papa and even I have felt like I was a mosquito on the wall that should not have flown in. These are things no one else should know.

Like my thoughts about Xok. They are *my* thoughts and – maybe – I should keep them in my head and not show them to anybody else. Not Siringen. Not Chimera. Not Mr Hamelin. Not even Maple. After all, nobody else knows what it feels like to be me. Nobody knows the *tru* feelings in my head and in my heart. Nobody knows how much I *need* to kill Xok.

The afternoon is late and hot, and I see that Siringen

has put something to cook in the underground *mumu* oven. Smoke blows out from it, moving like a *snek* out of a charmer's basket. It smells nice.

Inside the hut, Chimera lies on the sago mat, wrapped in a sheet.

"How are you feeling, Chimera?" I ask her. "Have you had enough water to drink today? Would you like me to get you some?"

She opens one of her eyes and looks up at me.

"I have had plenty to drink, thank you, Blue Wing," she says. "More than plenty. Your *waspapi* has stood over me and watched me drink until I think there is no more water left and all the islands must have joined up together."

"Have you eaten?"

"Yes. Siringen has made sure of it. He is a good man, and between you all, you have saved my life."

I do not know what to say to this, so I do not say anything to it.

"Has he gone somewhere? He is not here?"

"Lungadak." Her eyes seem to say *Lungadak The Idiot*, so I smile.

"What is he doing there?"

"Lungadak ordered him to go. Probably wants to tell Siringen that he does not like me and that I need to be thrown out back to my cave to die."

"No. Do not worry, Chimera. I do not think Siringen would do a thing like that. Even if the Bigman told him to."

"No. I know. Like I said, he is a good man. But I do not want to bring trouble onto his head. Siringen still has to live in this village."

"I do not think the trouble will matter to Siringen. Not if you are still sick."

She smiles vast.

I do not want to stay in the hut with Chimera. I like Chimera, but I do not want her to keep saying how we have saved her life and how grateful she is. When she says these things, I find it difficult to know where to place my eyes.

So I walk through the village to the Bigman's house.

I pass many people in the village. Children. Adults. Old men and women. Everyone is busy doing something. The children play games with pieces of white wood that have been washed onto the shore by the ocean, or play on the waves with fat, black, inflatable tyres. The women stand like guards over the hot flames of supper. Men gut fish or clean their tools, ready for the next dawn. Old men scrape out their tobacco pipes. Old women string wet cloths over wires or strip sweet potatoes. They are all busy and nobody sees me.

Nobody sees me apart from Miss Betty's daughter, who sits playing with some *bikpela* stones in front of her hut. When I pass, her eyes go up to mine.

"Hello, *liklik* one," I say, stopping and crouching like a dog ready to chase a stick. "What is your name?"

The girl grins and shows me her *namba wan* and *namba tu* teeth in her mouth.

"Grace." She struggles saying it.

"Hello, Grace. My name is Blue Wing. How old are you?"

"Two." She holds one of the stones up for me. "Stone?"

"Thank you. You are *tru* kind." I take the stone and hold it up to the sky. I pretend to look hard at it. "It is a good stone, isn't it? I think inside there might be gold or diamonds. Do you agree?"

The girl puts another of the stones towards her mouth.

"Do not eat it. It is not a fruit," I say, but she still holds it next to her lips anyway. "These stones…they are *tru* old, did you know that? They were made in the sea, million and million of year ago. And they will still be here in one million year *taim*, when all this will be gone." I point around to the village. Outside my eye I can see Siringen coming down the steps into the Bigman's compound. "Did you know that?"

The girl looks at me with a frown on her head.

"Sad? You sad?" she says.

"What?"

"Sad."

"Blue Wing!" Behind me Siringen whispers. "What are you doing?" He looks around like he is hoping nobody has heard him.

"I am talking to the *liklik* girl. Her name is Grace."

"I know her name is Grace." Still he whispers and still he looks around. "But now is the *taim* to stop. Come on. Let's go."

I stand up and wave at Grace. "Goodbye, Grace. I shall see you again."

She watches Siringen and me go.

As we walk away from the compound, I can hear the Bigman's jukebox starting up behind us.

"What did the Bigman call you to his home for?" I ask Siringen. "Was it about Chimera?"

"Yes." Siringen nods.

"What did he say?"

"He says he wants her to go from the village. By tomorrow night."

"That is not fair. She is sick and she needs *taim* to get better. If she goes back to her cave now, she will die."

"Yes. I know all this already."

"Well?" I ask.

"Well, what?"

"What did you say?"

"I did not say anything. I just listened."

I stop walking. "You said nothing?"

"Yes."

"Zero?"

He frowns like he is getting annoyed with me. "Yes."

"Why?"

"Because, sometimes, Lungadak likes to listen to himself. I think it is the thing he most enjoys – even more than listening to his jukebox. There is nothing *mobeta* to him than hearing the noises that come out from his mouth. If you let him talk, he will enjoy it so much that he will forget what he says."

"So, you are not going to make Chimera leave the village?"

Siringen smiles. "No. I am not. I took *you* into my home and managed, so why shouldn't I take *her* in? Anyway…" He smiles even more *bikpela*. "I think I like to have her around."

"*Waspapi?*" I ask, as the light starts to die out over the sea.

Chimera is asleep inside the hut and we have finished eating the wild boar that Siringen had cooked in the *mumu*. Siringen takes a betel nut and puts it into his mouth.

"What is it, Blue Wing?"

"Can people change when someone dies? Someone they love?"

"What do you mean?"

"I think I mean...can their mind change so much that they become a different person?"

"What a strange question. Why are you asking this?"

I shake my head. "Oh, no reason. I was just thinking."

Siringen starts to chew on the betel nut. His eyes stare at the wide sky above as he tries to put his thoughts into order.

"I think..." he begins. "I think that people are what they are when they are born. I think there are things that can happen to us along the shark roads of life that might change us – but only a *liklik*. People are like rocks on the shore. The sea will slam into the rocks day after day after day. Hour after hour after hour. *Oltaim*. But the rocks still look like rocks, they do not become something else. There might be a few scars and parts of the rock might crumble like dust into the sea. But they are still almost the way they were when they were created by Moroa.

"The same is with people. There is nothing that can

happen on this world that will stop a person being who they are. We are all born a certain way, and we all die a certain way."

His eyes move away from me like he might have said too much.

Then he says some more.

"Grief is the thing that can make a person change most, I suppose. When…" He looks out over the sea that flickers and glows with the phosphorescence. "When my wife died, I was still only young. *She* was only young. Twenty-two year. She got sick one year after we got married. Then a few months afterwards, she died.

"For a long *taim* I was angry. People in the village would know to keep away from me. Not look at me. I spent long days out on the ocean, alone. The sharks were the only things to flatten my anger enough.

"Then, slowly – so *tru* slowly – I got *mobeta*. I did not have to do anything to make it happen. The anger just started to seep down into the ground until, at the end, it wasn't inside me any more.

"It had gone."

I say nothing. These are the *namba wan* words that Siringen has ever said to me about his wife. I do what Siringen does with the Bigman, but for different reasons – I just listen.

"It is said everywhere that *taim* makes the wounds heal. All over the world it is said. But it is *tru*. If you wait long enough, you will find that nothing is *nogut* enough to make *everything* change. People will always go back to being how they were when they were born. Like death, it is unavoidable."

I think about Mr Hamelin. A man who has studied history, which has inside its heart the need for truth. The need to have fact. If something cannot be proved into a fact, then history must throw it away like a banana skin.

But now Mr Hamelin is holding on to an idea that is empty of fact. A dream. A cloud. It is like he has changed how he thinks. And it is death that has made him do this.

"You know, Blue Wing," says Siringen, "your papa was one of the best fishermen I ever knew – and I am old! His hand was touched by Moroa the day his own papa took him out onto the sea for the *namba wan taim*. Never could he come to shore without fish from that day into the future. A skilful man, Jeremiah. And your mama… Zephyr… Such a kind woman. Clever and warm. A good mother to you."

His eyes are sad again.

"Blue Wing, I am sorry that they died. It was not their *taim*, I know. And I know you blame Xok more than you blame anyone or anything else. But, please, if you wait for *taim,* you will find that any blame will disappear, and you will not want to kill Xok."

"Yes, *waspapi,*" I say. But still I am not sure that I believe him.

WANPELA TEN ET

We start off early. Mr Hamelin insists that we begin the search as soon as the light is over the mountain. So I take myself up from the place where I now sleep, just outside the hut, wash myself off in the sea, pick some already hot mangosteen from Siringen's fruit basket and eat on the way to Mr Hamelin's boat.

Mr Hamelin is already awake and putting his equipment into the motorboat. On the steps of the hut I see Maple feeding bananas to Trinket. She looks tired, like she has not slept much last night.

"This is far too early!" she says, trying not to yawn. "I'm not sure I can handle spending an entire day out on a boat. I just want to roll back into my bed, pull the mosquito net over me and go back to sleep."

"You were thinking about everything too much last

night, were you not?" I ask.

She nods. "It's a lot to think about, don't you think?"

"Maybe."

Mr Hamelin comes next to us. "Okay. I've packed it all ready. We'd better go. Now you *definitely* know where this bay is, Blue Wing?"

"Yes, sir. I know where it is. It is not too far."

"Wonderful! You know, girls, I think today is going to be one of the luckiest days of our lives."

I try not to let it show on my face, but I feel that Mr Hamelin is not being completely *tru*, deep inside himself.

The boat moves more fast than an outrigger, but not as fast as any of us would like it to. Especially Mr Hamelin. He steers the engine and keeps telling it to speed up, like it might listen.

In the boat sits plenty of equipment. There is so much that it is difficult to move around. Gas bottles. Black boxes with computers inside that can find metal at the bottom of the ocean. Face masks. Flippers that go on the feet. Long electrical sticks that can tell you the thickness of steel. Plenty of equipment that Mr Hamelin thinks he might need to find the book of the long now.

Maple sits at the front with me and we laugh when the

boat bounces like a lazy sloth over the waves that come at us in long lines.

After more than an hour, I watch the land carefully as it goes up and then down.

And then I see it.

At the top of a hill next to a small bay, I see a *bikpela* tree that looks twisted over on itself. As the boat comes more into the bay, I can see that the tree *does* look like a man who has dropped something and is bending to pick it from the ground.

"There!" I point, and Mr Hamelin stops the engine.

"You sure?"

"Yes. I am sure. That is the tree."

Mr Hamelin and Maple shade their sunglasses and look.

"You're right. This *is* it. Well done, Blue Wing. Well done."

Mr Hamelin takes us both onto the beach and leaves us there with a large plastic box filled with lunch.

"I'll be a couple of hours," he says as he climbs back into the boat. "I'm just going to survey the whole bay – see what's out there. I'm hoping that Akemi's plane isn't too far out in the open water." He has an excitement in his voice. I have heard it before in my own papa's voice, whenever he came back to shore with a *tru* full net or found a good strip of wood with which to fix his boat. The thought makes me smile. "With a bit of luck," says Mr Hamelin, "it will be sitting in the shallows."

He takes the boat back out into the bay.

It is quiet on the beach – there is nobody else around – so Maple and I find some shade under a palm tree and watch as Mr Hamelin moves the boat slowly to the left and then slowly to the right.

All the *taim* he is doing this, we are talking.

"Do you think what your papa says is *tru*? Do you think there is a book under the sea that can tell us how to make *taim* change?"

"Of course there isn't." She says it like it is just a moth flying near her head.

"Then why are we here? Why are we sitting on this beach watching your papa look for something that does not exist?"

There is nothing said for a long *taim*. Then, she turns her big bug sunglasses towards me and says, "Because he believes in it. Because it is the only thing that gives him hope."

"But it is not hope if it does not exist. It is just…as *you* always say…stupid. If it is not there, he will not find it. And that will make him more angry. Yes?"

"And if it *is* there," Maple says, "then, whatever it is,

it's not going to be able to bring my mom back from the dead. That's impossible."

"Then why is he doing it?"

"Because he believes that he has nothing else. It has become his aim."

I think about Xok.

I think about killing him.

I think about how that will make me feel.

But, no, that is different.

Xok is not the book of the long now.

Xok is real.

Xok definitely exists.

"Shall we eat all the food and leave him hungry?" Maple says, opening the top of the large plastic box.

"Well, maybe we'd better—"

She stops me talking by talking on top of me.

"I don't see why we should waste all this food on someone who's going to spend all day ignoring us, staring down to the bottom of the sea. Do you?"

"Well—"

"Here. Have a cold chicken leg." She holds out a piece of chicken. "Don't worry. He's got loads of them."

I take it from her and bite into it. She has one and does the same.

"Juice?" She takes a bottle of bright orange from the

box and then two plastic cups. Holding the chicken between her teeth, she pours the juice into the cups and gives me one of them.

"Thank you."

"Cheers!" She taps her plastic cup against mine. "You know," says Maple, "if Dad *does* find a plane under the water…well…there's going to be a dead body inside it."

"The dead body of your great-grandpapa," I say with a mouth full of chicken meat.

"Do you think he's even thought about that? Do you think he's even aware that there will be a seventy-five-year-old skeleton sitting in the cockpit? He'll probably have to move it to get to the scroll. Can you imagine? Ugh! Gross."

"I thought you said you did not believe there is a book under the ocean."

"Of course there isn't. I'm just theorizing."

"If there *is* a body," I say, "then maybe your papa should not move it. It has stayed there for a long *taim*. That is its resting place. I do not think anyone should come along and disturb it. It would be wrong."

"But perhaps the body could be rescued and taken back to Japan to be buried properly. Wouldn't that be a good thing?"

I strip the last piece of chicken from the bone and

place it carefully back into the bottom of the box.

"I do not know. Your great-grandfather has been under the water for seventy year – that is more year than he was alive. Maybe he thinks the bottom of the ocean is more his home than Japan ever was."

"Weird."

"Like I say, I do not know. Different people all across the world and all across *taim* have had different ways of thinking about death. On this island, there are still many who believe that when someone dies, they become a new star in the night sky. Plenty of fishermen still think that the sharks are our dead ancestors. Maybe they are right, or maybe they are wrong."

"I was always told that when you die, you go to heaven," says Maple. "Wherever that is. When I was tiny, I always thought that heaven was just the other side of the moon – a great big place where everyone was happy and having parties all the time, only you just couldn't see them because the moon was in the way. And you had to be good when you were alive otherwise you wouldn't go to heaven, you would go to hell instead. I always imagined that hell was somewhere underground – just a few metres under the metro lines. Hell was dark and hot and you'd get bits of dirt stuck in your sandwiches."

"Do you believe in those places, now that you are older?"

Maple makes her shoulders go up and down. "Don't know. I like to think that there's a heaven. I don't like to think that there's a hell. Heaven seems like a fair place to go once you're dead. A cool place to spend the rest of time."

She puts her own chicken bone back into the box.

"If there *is* a heaven…I just know that's where Mom would be."

I smile at her. "Yes. I am sure."

Maple pulls a small tub from the box and peels the top off it.

"Sausage?"

Mr Hamelin seems to forget that there is food to be eaten and stays out on the water for most of the day. So, after we have eaten, Maple lies back on the sand, puts her hat over her face and falls asleep.

I watch her as she sleeps. She looks full of peace, like there is zero in her mind to give her worry – even though I know that, when she is awake, there is plenty in her mind to give her worry.

I turn from watching her and watch the sea instead.

Ever since I was born, I have been watching the sea. It has been in my sight all that *taim*. Everywhere I look, the sea has been in my eyes. The only way to not see the sea is to push my head into a pillow or to go deep into a cave. And, even when I have done these things, I can always *hear* the sea. And smell it. So I cannot completely escape it.

Not that I would want to escape the sea. It is everything to everyone around this island. It brings food and life and work and pleasure. And it is good to know that it will always be there. It will not disappear across a night, or die like a person would.

The sea will never leave.

Not like people.

I think of my papa in his canoe, and my mama watching him.

They have left.

They have left the island and the world for something *mobeta* and *bikpela* than I or Maple or Mr Hamelin or Siringen or even Chimera knows about. They have left for a place that none of us can ever describe because we have never seen it. We can make up stories or paint pictures to describe it, but we will never know if we are right. Not until the moment when we too will leave and wave goodbye to all the people and things that we know in this world.

My mama and my papa have left.

And it is all *my* fault.

I think backwards to the *taim* two year ago when I made the *nogut* choice not to go to school. It was a choice that I should not have made. Because of that choice, Mama and Papa are dead. And, yes, I realize that Xok was the one who killed them, and I realize that Siringen set Xok free, and I realize that they were sent to find me by the Bigman, but if I had not made the choice to miss school that day, they would still be fishing and washing and eating and singing songs now.

We all would.

So I know it is really all my fault.

Nobody else tells me this. Siringen has never said that I should take all the blame. It is just something I know inside my heart.

It was *I* who killed my parents.

"Nothing. I couldn't find anything."

Mr Hamelin looks like he has run all the way across from one side of the island to the other. The breeze and the salt out on the ocean have made his hair stiff and looking like it needs to be cleaned. And his eyes look empty and tired, like there is nothing behind them.

"Oh, well," says Maple. "Never mind."

"No! It is not *never mind*!" shouts her papa. "I am trying to find this thing and *nothing* I do seems to be working!" He throws his gas tank to the ground. It only just misses Maple.

"Careful, Dad!"

"I was right." He hasn't noticed that he was close to hitting his daughter. "That guy in the mountains was just another fake. Just trying to get money from another stupid tourist!"

His anger reminds me *tru* much of Maple's.

"I've spent all day out on the sea trying to locate this plane and there's nothing out there! Not a single sign of it. Not even a broken-up piece of the tail. I am sick of it!"

He throws his diving mask and nearly hits me.

"Dad! Be careful. You nearly hit Blue Wing."

"What?" He looks down at the ground. "Sorry."

"That is *orait*, Mr Hamelin, sir. It is not a problem. But you might want to sit here and eat something... We have kept you some food." I take a chicken leg from out of the box and hold it up to him. "I think your empty stomach has made you angry, so you need to stop."

He looks at me.

Then he sits on the sand between us and puts his head into his hands.

275

"I thought I was going to find it today," he says. "I told myself this morning that I was going to find it."

"There is always tomorrow," I say. "Just because you do not find it today does not mean you will not find it tomorrow." I think I am suddenly sounding like Siringen. Maybe his words are sinking into me.

"But...*this* bay. I thought it was going to be in *this* bay."

I look over at Maple, who does not seem to be looking at her papa. Instead she is watching the sea like I was watching the sea when she was asleep. I do not think she is even listening to him.

"Mr Hamelin," I say. "The spiritual man said that this bay was the final thing that Maple's great-grandfather saw before he died. But it does not mean that he hit the water here. From what direction was he flying?"

Mr Hamelin points to the sky. "He would have been heading south." He draws a line in the sky with his finger from right to left.

"Then he might have crashed in the next bay along. So, tomorrow morning, maybe you should check there. Yes?"

Mr Hamelin nods. "Yes. You're right, Blue Wing. That's probably what happened."

Suddenly he looks *mobeta*, like I have put hope back into him.

"Thank you, Blue Wing. That's exactly what we'll do."

He takes the chicken leg from me and bites into it.

WANPELA TEN NAIN

"I don't know why you are encouraging him," says Maple as we walk from her hut to mine. "Isn't it best that he finds out he's being completely stupid as soon as possible? Realizes just how ridiculous he's being and stops it all?"

"But you said it gives him hope."

"No, I said he *believes* it gives him hope. And then you said there was no point in giving him that hope. Why did you change your mind?"

I look at her as we pass the lawatbulut tree that I used to play on when I was *liklik*.

"I think hope is *tru* important. Even when something is not real, hope keeps people alive."

"You're talking about killing Xok, aren't you?" She sighs. "You're not really talking about Dad, at all. You know, I wish you'd give that stupid idea up. I wish Dad would give up trying to bring Mom back, and I wish you would stop banging on about killing Xok. You've gotta move on. Both of you."

"But you are the one going to visit Chimera to see if she can speak with your mama. So *you* need to move on too."

We do not talk for the rest of the journey.

Outside the hut I can see Chimera sitting on the ground next to Siringen. Chimera has her blanket wrapped across her shoulders and is watching Siringen split open a coconut with his bush knife. They see us coming.

"Would you like some coconut, Maple?" asks Siringen.

"Yes, please. Thank you, Siringen."

She takes the half shell of the coconut from him.

"Blue Wing?"

"No, thank you, *waspapi*."

Siringen gives the other half to Chimera, who takes it close to her body, then he finds some metal spoons from somewhere and gives one to each of them.

"You have come again to see if I can speak to your mama, haven't you, girl?" says Chimera, her voice more strong than the day before.

"Yes." Maple sits on the ground next to Chimera. "I don't know why." She looks up at me. "I thought that

I might try one last time. It would be nice to know that my mom is happy. Wherever she is."

"Well, it was lucky for me that you tried to see me three or four days ago. Otherwise I would be long passed now."

I start to sit next to Maple, but Siringen stands up and makes his face go into a shape to tell me not to sit down.

"Come help me clean the shark gods," he says, his eyes showing me that there is no choice.

I follow him around to the side of the hut where the stone gods lie.

"Why did you do that?" I ask.

Siringen waves his hand up and down to say that I should speak more quiet.

"Whatever Chimera has to say to Maple Hamelin is not for you. It is between them. Now," he picks up some dried white coral and pushes it into my hand, "start rubbing these sharks."

I bend over like the tree on the bay and brush the coral gently over the first stone shark. Secretly, out of my ears, I am trying to listen to what is being said.

"Blue Wing!" Siringen stares like he is angry – but I know he is not really. "Stop trying to hear, and clean the shark. Scrub it harder. If we still want sharks to come to this island, we need to make the gods happy."

"Yes, *waspapi*. You are a sport spoiler, *waspapi*!"

He grins and I see his red teeth.

"So, what did you do with Atlas Hamelin today? Did he take you to see the coral reefs?"

"No, Siringen. He did not. Mr Hamelin is a professor of history and he is investigating the Japanese boats and planes that sank and crashed here in World War Two." I think this is enough of the truth for Siringen to take in.

"Ah. That makes some sense. But why would he say that he was interested in the coral reefs? I do not understand."

"No. Neither do I, *waspapi*."

He believes this and doesn't ask anything more about Mr Hamelin.

I finish cleaning one of the shark gods and move on to another.

After a few minutes, Maple comes around the side of the hut to see us.

"Everything good?" I ask.

"Oh, yes." She smiles and I am pleased she is smiling. "Very good."

She turns to Siringen.

"Siringen," she says, "I have not yet apologized to you for taking the chief's son's canoe without asking. I know that you got into trouble for it, and that was never what

I intended to happen. It was stupid of me – the idea was mine and not Blue Wing's – and I wish I'd not made such a terrible judgement call. So I would really like to say sorry." She puts out her hand for Siringen to shake. "Sorry."

Siringen looks at it for a few seconds and then drops the coral in his hand and shakes it.

"Thank you, Maple Hamelin. I accept your apology. Apologizing is a *tru* strong thing to do."

I watch as their hands go up and down before releasing each other.

"You see, Siringen," Maple says, "the reason why we stole the boat is because Blue Wing so desperately wants to become a shark caller. Ever since I've known her, it's all she's really talked about."

Siringen puts a frown over his face and listens to her.

"Honestly, Siringen, you should hear how she goes on about it all the time."

I look at Maple. What *is* she doing?

"It's 'shark calling *this*' and 'shark calling *that*'. She is *sooo* desperate to become one that she just doesn't shut up."

"Oh, I know all about that," says Siringen. "For two year it is all I have heard from her. We have argued so *tru* much about it."

Maple nods. "So why not let her become one?"

"What?" Siringen looks like someone has just stood on one of his toes.

"Let her become a shark caller. After all, she has already learned such a lot from you. Why not just finish off the job and allow her to become a shark caller? She might stop ranting then."

I look at Maple and she smiles *bikpela* at me.

Siringen shakes his head. "No. She knows why she cannot become a *tru* shark caller. We have discussed it a million *taim* before."

"What? Because she's a girl? Because you think that she will only use her skills to hunt down Xok? I think you underestimate Blue Wing. I think she is tougher than any boy, and I also think she is clever and funny and strong and caring. She will not kill Xok. I just know it. Even though she says she will and that it is her reason for existing, I think that she would never be able to do it. I think that deep down inside her she is smart enough to know that killing Xok will not do her any good at all."

I listen to these words and they remind me of the ones I spoke to Mr Hamelin outside the spiritual man's home. I listen, but I am not sure I *wan-handet* per cent agree with them.

Siringen sighs. "Maple Hamelin. You do not know the ways of the island. For centuries now, shark calling has always been passed along the line of history from one shark caller to his nephew. This is the way and it should always be the way."

"Even though you have nobody to pass it on to?"

Siringen says nothing.

"Even though, after you, the shark calling of the village will die out? Is that the way it should be? Is that what your ancestors would want? Surely it is better to pass it on to *somebody* than nobody at all?"

Siringen still shakes his head. "It will die out anyway. There is *liklik* point in passing it on to Blue Wing—"

Maple interrupts him. "But at least you would have passed it on. You would have done your duty and left the knowledge with someone other than yourself. Is that not a good thing? To teach someone something. To give someone your knowledge. Especially somebody who actually *wants* to learn."

Siringen looks at Maple like he had not realized what a shark she had in her heart.

I do not say anything. I have talked over and over again to Siringen about this and, if I say anything now, I think it will only remind him of those discussions and he will just say no. So I stay quiet.

"Well…" It is like Siringen is thinking about it. That is more than he has ever done before.

Maple pushes on.

"What harm can it do? If Blue Wing isn't going to kill Xok, what's the worst that could happen? She fails? She succeeds? What?"

Siringen's eyebrows go up and down. It is as if he is agreeing with her.

Still Maple speaks. "I realize I don't know much about it, but I think she would make a really good shark caller. And I think you do too."

Suddenly, Chimera comes around the side of the hut, her sheet over her shoulders. She walks slowly.

"Go on, Siringen," she says. "It is *taim* you gave the girl her lesson. You have held out for so long. Maybe even your old heart needs to break a little sometimes."

Siringen shakes his head and laughs.

"Too many women," he says. "How can I win with too many women? Too much sense." He grins at me. "*Orait*, Blue Wing. I lose."

The afternoon is dying into the dimming light of dusk when Siringen and I paddle out onto the still waters. Maple and Chimera watch us from the shore as we make our way quietly to the nearest strip of shark road. There are no other boats around — all the fishermen have finished their catching for the day and are right now either cooking up their fish or selling them to other villagers.

"You know, when we took Moses's canoe the other day," I say, "well...we saw Xok. He came near the canoe."

"Yes. I know," says Siringen, switching the paddle from one side of the outrigger to the other.

This surprises me. "How did you know?"

"Sometimes, in your sleep, you talk *tru* loudly."

"Do I?"

"Mmm. I can hear you from outside the hut."

"That cannot be *tru*. Is it?"

"Yes. It is *tru*. Anyway...it is good that you saw Xok. He came. You saw him. He went away. You did not kill him."

"Only because Maple stopped me."

Siringen looks me straight in the eyes. "Did she? Or did you stop yourself?"

I do not answer.

It only takes a few minutes to get to the nearest shark road. When we arrive, Siringen takes the paddle and lays it in the bottom of the boat. Then he hands me the *larung* rattle.

"You know how to use this," he says. "Hold it just below the surface and shake it hard."

I put it into the water and start moving it. It is easier

to use than the branch of a tree. The water begins to froth and fizz, and I seem to get *tru* wet *tru* quick.

I do this for some seconds and then I stop.

"You know," says Siringen, taking the rattle from me. "It is strange that Maple Hamelin believes that passing my knowledge on to you will keep the *tambu* alive." He smiles gently at me.

"I know, *waspapi*. It is not her fault. She does not know what I *tru* am. She does not know that I do not belong here."

"No, I know that. Do you think she will ever know the truth?"

"Maybe." I sigh. "Maybe."

There is no breeze on the sea. Late in the afternoon the breeze blows itself until it is no more. And when the breeze is no more, the waves become almost nothing. Almost zero. So the only noises that can be heard come from the island. Excited children's voices. The birds of paradise strengthening their lungs. Tiny slices of music from radios (or jukeboxes). But you would be mistaken to think that most life is back on the island. It is not. Because beneath us, under the ocean, there is plenty more life than there is on the land. But you cannot see it because it is hidden. The water keeps the truth from view.

"Now," says Siringen, sitting himself straight on his seat.

"It is *taim* to call the spirits."

"This is the bit I can never remember," I say.

"You cannot remember, Blue Wing, because I have not taught you. Now listen *tru* carefully. You must say the names in the correct order, otherwise the spirits get angry and scare all the sharks away. Are you ready?"

"I have been ready a long *taim, waspapi*."

"Okay. Repeat after me..."

Then Siringen begins his chant. A long, long chant, listing the names of all the shark callers in his line, beginning with Pilai-one-tooth, through Bogin and Begondi, all the way to his own uncle Abel. He sings the names and I follow, keeping *tru* close behind.

He does it again, and again I follow, my voice a *liklik* more strong and confident this *taim*.

Then he sits back.

"Okay, Blue Wing." His arm points out over the sea. "Begin."

I chant loud and without breaking the flow. Over and over I call the names. Over and over, until I feel that my throat is about to burn and set fire. I do not stop because I want this to work so much. I think back to the *taim* I managed to force Maple out of the hut by singing the papaya song over and over again. At that *taim*, she was like a shark too.

I chant, my voice good and strong.

And then...

"Ssh," says Siringen. "Listen."

I hear nothing.

"What?"

Still Siringen shows me to listen.

Then I hear it.

Everything is so silent and still that I can hear the small splashing of the surface being broken. I look to see where it is coming from.

A shark.

A *bikpela* shark. Not the same sort of *bikpela* as Xok, but *bikpela* all the same.

It is a *she*. I know it is.

"Congratulations, Blue Wing," says Siringen. "Your first real shark. And a tiger shark too. *Tru* impressive."

I watch as she goes under the boat and comes out the other side.

"I do not want to catch her in the *kasaman*," I say. "I do not want to catch any shark in a *kasaman*. Sharks are too beautiful for that."

"Do not worry," replies Siringen. "I have not even put the *kasaman* in the canoe. The *taim* for the *kasaman* and the *taim* for killing sharks has gone. Never to come back."

"Good."

We watch the shark cutting through the clear water of early evening. Siringen throws some of the day-old bait fish into the sea for her and she rises to the surface and takes them, snapping them quick into her jaws.

She stays with us for a while, hoping for more bait fish, I think. Then, once she realizes there is no more, and that the *bikpela* shoal of fish the *larung* and the chanting promised her is not going to come, she swims away, back out into the open waters.

"*Taim* to go back home," says Siringen. "*Taim* to go back to the ones we love and the ones who love us back."

"Thank you, *waspapi*," I say. "Thank you."

Siringen smiles.

"You are welcome, *shark caller* Blue Wing."

"Maple."

I move alongside her as we walk along the path back to her hut. Across the ocean, the sun is disappearing below the edge of the sea. The light has fallen low and it is getting harder to see the smaller parts of things.

"Maple. When you were with Chimera, what did she say? Did she speak with your mama?"

Maple turns and looks at me.

"No. I asked her if she could try again. I told her I wanted to tell Mom that I loved her and I was sorry for being so stupid. I said I wanted Mom to forgive me."

"But?"

"But Chimera said she couldn't connect with her. Said again that Mom must be happy if she couldn't connect with her."

"Did she say anything else?"

"Yes."

She doesn't say anything else, so I keep asking.

"What did she say?"

Maple looks away from me. "She said that the living should put the living above the dead."

"What does that mean?"

"What it says, I suppose. She means I should put my dad above my mom. Worry about him more because he's still alive."

I nod. "*Tru*."

"And she said I shouldn't be looking for forgiveness from Mom – she would have forgiven me the moment she…died, apparently. I should be looking for forgiveness from myself."

"You should forgive yourself? How do you do that?"

"Not too sure."

She picks a leaf from out of her long, straight hair.

"Perhaps you need to do the same thing too," she says.

"Forgive myself?"

"Yeah."

I find myself swallowing. "I don't understand."

Maple turns her face close to mine, her eyes serious like there is no joke about to come from her lips.

"Of course you understand. Don't do that 'not understanding' trash with me. You understand perfectly well what I'm saying."

I keep quiet again.

"It's not your fault that your parents died," she says. "It's not your fault. It was just a load of things coming together at the same time. That's all. Okay, you skipped school, but you weren't to know Xok was going to be around that day. You weren't to know your chief was going to tell your parents that you hadn't gone to school. You weren't to know that Siringen let Xok escape. You weren't to know that your parents were going to come and get you. You weren't to know any of that."

It is like she has read my mind while sleeping on the beach today. It is like she knows me *tru* well. "But I started it all off," I say. "If I hadn't missed school, nothing else would have happened. So it is still my fault, no matter what you say."

Maple shakes her head, her eyes even more serious.

"No, that's not right. You skipped school because you didn't want to sit a math test.

"Well, perhaps you didn't want to sit the math test because you don't like math, and perhaps you don't like math because the teacher gave you a hard time about it one day. And perhaps that teacher gave you a hard time about it because they were in a really bad mood that day. And perhaps they were in a really bad mood because...I don't know...because their cat had gone missing that morning. And perhaps the cat had gone missing because it decided to chase a mouse. And perhaps..."

I smile.

"But do you see what I'm saying? You can trace everything back. Everything depends upon something else. Like Dad says, time is like a piece of string that goes all the way back in one direction and all the way forward in the other. You can't just cut it to fit your own view of things. You can't just take a section and say that's how it was. You have to think of how it all slots together."

I find my head is nodding.

"And what about you, Maple Hamelin? Can you use these smart words to bring forgiveness down on your own head?"

"I don't know. It's always easier to see how to fix

somebody else's problems. It's much harder to fix your own."

"Then perhaps *I* should try."

Maple grins vast. "Go on then, shark caller Blue Wing. Try."

I think as we walk. Then I speak.

"You loved your mama. Like I loved my mama and my papa. Your mama took you on trips to Paris and taught you how to read books. Her blood is in your blood. You were bound together like two trees joined by a vine. There was zero you would not do for her, and there was zero she would not do for you.

"The problem was that, when she got sick, you learned quick that there was zero you could *really* do. It was all going to happen and it did not matter what you thought or what you did. It was like a wall was built right in front of you that you could not climb over. And your mama would have felt it too. She would have known that you wanted to help her to get *mobeta*, but that you couldn't do anything.

"But when there is a wall that you cannot climb over – a *bikpela* wall, *fo-hundet* metres high – it is *longlong* to try and climb it. If it is a wall so *bikpela*, then at some point, you will definitely fall. So all you can do is learn to live this side of the wall. Do what you can to make this side of the wall as good and as wonderful as your mama would have wanted it to be."

I look at her. There are tears in her eyes.

"But I didn't want her to come home. At the last stage of her life, I let her down."

"No. You did not. Your mama was on the other side of the wall then. Even though the machines were still breathing for her. Her eyes were closed and she was gone. What you were doing was keeping your side of the wall as straight and as normal as you could. So that you could live. So that you and your papa could have a future."

More tears are pulling down Maple's cheeks, so I reach across and wipe them away.

"I miss her."

"I know. It is good that you miss her. That will mean you will never forget her."

Suddenly she rubs her hands over her eyes.

"Ah. That's better. Stupid tears." She is pretending to be the *bikpela* tough girl again. "Make your eyes all blurry and you can't see anything."

I laugh. "Nothing is your fault, Maple. Your mama died. It is not your fault."

"No. I know."

A few minutes later we pass the lawatbulut tree and come out, down onto the small bay where my mama and my papa brought me up from a baby. A light comes through the windows of the hut and I can see the shadow of Mr Hamelin inside.

"Blue Wing," Maple says as she kicks off her sandals and picks them up. "Must you kill Xok? I mean, I know he killed your parents but…well…look at the way you reacted when you found out I had Trinket. You like things to be free. And killing Xok isn't really setting him free, is it?"

I look at her but I do not reply.

"Killing Xok isn't going to make you feel any better."

I still say nothing.

"And anyway," she says, her eyes difficult to see in the dark, "if this scroll *really* exists…and if it can *really* turn back time…then you wouldn't have to kill Xok, would you? There would be no need."

I stop walking.

"But you do not believe that the scroll exists," I say. "You are always saying it is stupid."

She stops too. "Perhaps it is. And perhaps it isn't. My brain tells me it's all trash, but…"

"What?"

"I've been thinking. All I know is that if it *is* true then there is a chance I'll get Mom back and you'll get your parents back. But if it *isn't* true…well…once Dad's seen that it isn't true, then there's a chance I'll get *him* back. You see what I mean?"

I do see. I understand everything. I watch Mr Hamelin's shape move in the light of the window.

The living should put the living above the dead.

"Maybe tomorrow we should not just sit on the beach and watch your papa drive his boat up and down the bay while we eat all the food," I say. "Maybe tomorrow we should help him find the thing he is looking for."

Maple nods. "Yes," she says. "I think we should."

TUPELA TEN

The day is as hot as the day before. Every day it gets more hot and every day it feels as if the rainy season is not getting closer, but moving further and further away. It is as if it will never rain again. The land, the sea, the trees – even the people – would like to feel the rain now.

And the engine of the boat seems louder today than it has before. Maybe it is because none of us says anything as we bounce over the water. But the engine is loud and it makes my head buzz.

Everything seems *bikpela* today.

I sit at the front of the boat at the place where it becomes a point. Behind me, Maple holds on to the sides to stop herself from swaying. At the back, Mr Hamelin stares across the water, the hope in his eyes more strong than even their colour. Vast and wide, it is like they are trying to stretch themselves around the entire world.

No one says anything. All we do is think.

About the plane.

About the scroll.

(About Xok.)

Mr Hamelin takes the boat along the coast to the bay this side of the bending tree. The waves are gentle but still they knock the side of the boat, so Maple holds on tightly. Many seabirds fly above us, wondering what we are doing and where we are going. Their cries and screeches almost as loud as the *phut-phut-phut*ing of the engine.

Finally, we arrive at the bay. Mr Hamelin turns the key and the engine sighs itself into silence.

"Okay," he says, and it is the *namba wan* thing anyone has said since we left the village. "Okay."

"How are we going to do this, Dad?" asks Maple.

"Do you have maps of the sea?" I say.

"Well, kinda," he says. "Yesterday I just sailed up and down the bay, slowly working my way out to sea. I used this to help me keep track of my progress." He reaches into a large plastic box and pulls out a flat black computer. He flips the screen up and presses a button. It flashes itself alive. "I use GPS to track my path. That way I don't end up covering old ground just because the tide has carried me back to shore."

I do not understand much of what he has said, but I see a green line on the dark screen and I realize it is the outline of the land. A small red dot glows, and I realize that is the boat.

"Nice," I say and Mr Hamelin grins.

"Look. Maple. Blue Wing," he says. "Thank you for coming out here with me. Helping me like this. It means so much."

Maple smiles a smile that doesn't go all the way up her cheeks, and I nod to Mr Hamelin in a way that says, *It is orait*.

"Shall we start?" he asks.

I nod again.

After one hour has gone past, we have still found zero. Maple and I crouch over the sides of the boat, staring down deep into the clear waters. Sometimes we slip over the edges of the boat and swim underneath. We see nothing but, when we swim, we stop our necks and our backs from hurting from staring too much.

As *taim* goes past us and the sun moves itself over in the sky, Mr Hamelin's temper gets hotter than the day. Sometimes he swears and we pretend not to have heard him. Sometimes his hand swings out into the water and slaps the sea for not revealing its secret to him.

"Oh, this is hopeless," he says at one point, and it is a surprise to me when Maple answers his words.

"We've gotta keep going, Dad," she says. "We can't stop now. We've gotta keep going."

This makes Mr Hamelin sit up straighter on his seat and he turns the boat back to search another part of the bay.

It is the movement of the sea that I notice first.

The waves and swells sweep in towards the beach. They move like lines over the bay and up to the sand. That is what normally happens. On all the beaches I have known, that is what happens.

And it happens here, on this bay.

But not in one area.

In one area, the sea swirls around like it doesn't know what it should be doing. It twists and spins like a *liklik* hurricane, white froth spitting at its centre.

"What is that?" I say, pointing. "There is something there."

"Where?" Mr Hamelin answers like there is no breath in his body. "I can't see anything."

I show him.

He twists the handle on the engine and makes the boat move towards the swirl.

"I have seen things like this before," I tell them. "When there is something heavy under the water – dead ships, oil cans – the sea moves around it in a strange way. There is something there. Something *bikpela*."

Mr Hamelin's eyes are focused on the place where the water moves differently and I can hear him whispering, trying to make the boat move more fast.

As we get closer to the swirl, Maple and I look over. The water is as clear as the stars. The waves try to make it harder to see, but almost straight underneath the boat I can see the long wing of a plane.

"Is it…" Mr Hamelin asks without finishing his words.

Maple turns back to her papa and nods. "It's a plane, Dad."

"Ha!"

I look along the wing until I can see the body of the plane. It looks old and green, like the bottom of the ocean is trying to wrap itself around it, but it is definitely there.

It is strange to see an aeroplane beneath the ocean. I have seen boats and ships under the waters, but the plane looks strangest of all because it was never built to be anywhere near the sea. It was built to be in the sky. I see the fish swimming around it and I think they are like the birds that would fly past when it was...alive. I imagine that we are in a *tru* small plane, flying a *liklik* higher in the sky than this one below.

Mr Hamelin switches off the engine again and drops a heavy weight on the end of a rope into the sea. On the other end he fixes a bright red ball-shaped buoy that floats on top of the water. Then he ties the boat to it.

"I have to check," he says. "I have to make sure it is the right plane." He reaches over and pulls his gas tank towards him.

"How can we see that it is the right plane?" I ask.

"There's a serial number – in Japanese – on the rear fuselage. I have to go down and check it."

"I will go," I say, standing up and kicking off my sandals. "I will go down and see if it is Maple's great-grandfather's plane." I pull off my T-shirt and jump over the side of the boat into the water, my own heart excited. When my head comes back to the surface, I see Maple and her papa looking down at me.

"You need a mask?" asks Mr Hamelin.

"No. Thank you. I can dive without one."

"Of course," he replies, smiling. "I forgot. You can hold your breath for ever."

"Well, not for for ever," I say.

"The long now," says Maple.

"What?" Mr Hamelin looks confused.

"Don't worry, Dad."

Mr Hamelin does not worry. Instead he carries on talking.

"If you swim towards the back of the plane, you'll find the serial number. It looks a little like this." He puts his fingers into a pocket on the chest of his wetsuit and pulls out a small, plastic-covered piece of card. He gives it to me and I look at it. There is a box with four lines of Japanese writing on it. "If it looks *exactly* like this… it's the right plane," he says. "Check that the symbols are the same."

It is Maple who has worry on her face.

"It is okay, Maple. I will be safe," I say to her.

"That's not what I'm worried about," she answers and before I have *taim* to think about what she means, I turn and kick myself under the water.

I pull myself down to the plane, the *liklik* plastic strip in my hand. As I get nearer, I can see that the glass where the pilot would have sat has been broken and that part of the screen into the cockpit is hanging on by a tiny stick of metal, swaying in the movement of the water. On the seat there are no bones to be seen.

I swim around the side of the plane. Even though it is not that far under the surface, the bottom side of it is down where it is dark. Suddenly a barracuda swims out from the side of the plane, straight past me, out into the open water. I turn and watch it as it moves away, scared of this unwanted stranger.

I make my way along the body of the plane. At the back I can see some marks on the metal. I brush small barnacles out of the way and I realize that this is the serial number of the plane. I hold the plastic in front of me. It is dark, so I have to move my eyes close to it. There are no words on the card that I recognize, only Japanese symbols. The first looks like two crosses next to two vertical lines. I look at the plane.

Two crosses next to two vertical lines.

On the card, the next symbol looks like a face with a moustache pointing down.

On the plane, the same face with a pointing moustache.

I go through the next few symbols.

They are all the same.

I check the last few symbols.

They are all the same.

I am certain. This is Maple's great-grandfather's plane.

My heart bangs hard inside my chest and I push up and kick towards the surface.

When I come alongside the boat I hold my thumb up to Mr Hamelin.

"It is the right plane," I say.

I have never seen Mr Hamelin look more happy.

"Well?" asks Maple as I dry myself off alongside her.

"What?" I answer back.

"Well...inside...is there...a body?"

I laugh and shake my head. "The glass at the front of the plane is broken. I think when the pilot crashed into the sea, his body was thrown out."

"Oh, good. Well. Er. No. Not good, obviously. That wasn't nice. But..."

I smile at her trying to struggle, like an inchworm on a log.

"Oh, you know what I mean."

"Got your snorkel and mask, Maple?" Mr Hamelin asks, pulling his wetsuit tighter around himself.

"Why?"

"Well, I'm not going to be able to do all this on my own. I need you both to help me. You see, the box containing the scroll should be somewhere behind the pilot's seat. There wasn't a great deal of room in those Zero fighters so the only place they could store anything was behind the seat. If I can get into the cockpit and shift the seat forward – which probably isn't going to be easy, considering it's been corroded by saltwater for the last seventy-five years – I should be able to get the box out. But I'm going to need your help." He looks at me like I should be agreeing. "Hopefully the scroll has been wrapped well in waterproof cloths. That way it might still be in good condition."

Mr Hamelin is excited and his mouth is finding it difficult to hold back.

Maple turns from looking at the water to looking at me. Her eyes seem to ask, *Is this tru? Is this real?*

I do not know what to say to her or what face to make at her – I cannot believe any of this myself – so I look away, back to the flying machine below.

"Do you think that other people might have been here before?" I ask as I slip over the side of the motorboat and into the sea again. "What if other people have already been here and taken the book away? That might have happened."

I see Maple looking at me as she zips up her wetsuit. I tell from her eyes that she knows what I am saying. Maple does not *really* believe that there is anything here. Neither do I. But Mr Hamelin does not seem to think in this way. If he goes down to the plane and there is zero there, his heart will find it difficult to understand.

"That's right, Dad," says Maple, agreeing. "If it's been down there for over seventy years, it's likely that in that time someone would have found it. The scroll might not be there any more."

Mr Hamelin says nothing. He pulls one of the gas cylinders over his shoulders and puts the diving mask over his face.

"Dad?"

He still says nothing.

"Dad!"

It is like Mr Hamelin cannot hear his daughter. It is like he has suddenly become deaf.

"Hurry up and get ready, Maple." He steps off the boat into the water, splashing both me and Maple. When he comes back to the surface, he lifts the mask away from his face. "Blue Wing and I can't wait for you. We're going down."

He rolls in the water until the flippers on his feet are kicking the air, then he disappears beneath the waves.

Maple makes one of her faces.

"Do not have worry," I say to her. "Your papa's mind is nailed onto the scroll right now. He will not listen to *anyone*. All you can do is help him find the book. That is all you can do."

She nods and plays with her snorkel.

"Come on. Come in." I wave at her.

She slips the mask over her head, then puts the snorkel into her mouth. She looks *longlong*.

"Come in, Maple."

Maple climbs down over the side of the boat until she is next to me, floating in the water.

"And there's no dead body hanging out the side of the plane?"

"No," I laugh. "No dead body."

"Good."

I dive back under and Maple swims along the surface, looking down on everything.

Mr Hamelin has finished swimming around the sides of the plane with his torch. As I join him, I notice him looking up at Maple. He holds out his thumb like he is asking, *Is everything okay?* I nod and hold my thumb up too.

As Mr Hamelin breathes through his mouthpiece, large bubbles come out and shiver their way up to the freedom of the surface. I watch them as they fight between themselves to be the first to reach it.

Mr Hamelin points to the plane and I can see that he wants to inspect the cockpit. He kicks with his flippers and I kick with my bare feet and soon we are holding on to the bent frame that would go over the pilot's head. Much of the glass has broken and fallen off over the plenty years, but there are still some pieces that stick out, trying to catch my fingers like the teeth of an angry crocodile.

Mr Hamelin shines his torch into the cockpit. I can see that there are levers and dials and buttons and switches and straps, all of them covered in a slippery black moss. I reach inside and pull one of the straps – it must be the safety belt – and it breaks away in my hand. A small shoal of tiny silver fish that were hiding behind it race out past my face.

I hold out the broken belt to Mr Hamelin, who shakes his head, so I let it go and let it sink to the bottom of the ocean.

Mr Hamelin keeps pointing his torch inside. He is trying to shine light on the area behind the seat. He pushes with his flippers to change his position a *liklik* bit and twists his head to see.

Suddenly something touches me on the shoulder. I turn around quick to see what it is. I find my eyes staring straight into Maple's eyes. She has taken the mouthpiece out – it is hanging on to the side of her mask – and has dived down to see what we are doing. I smile as good as I can without losing any of my breath.

Mr Hamelin hasn't noticed Maple. He is too busy trying to look behind the pilot's seat with his torch. He pushes his hand in and makes the seat move a tiny bit. He tries again, but it does not move any more. He keeps looking in, pointing the torch as far in as he can.

Without giving us any warning, he turns and shows us he wants us to go back to the surface with him. Maple and I both nod and then we swim up to the light.

Holding on to the side of the boat, Mr Hamelin pulls his mask off enough so that we can hear him speak.

"There's a box down there. In the cockpit. I can see it. It's kinda wedged between the seat and the floor. If I can get the seat to move forward some more, I'll be able to reach in and get it."

"Is it the book?" I ask.

"Yes. I think it is, Blue Wing."

"But it might not be, Dad," says Maple. "It might just be a toolbox or a lunchbox or anything. It might not have anything to do with what you're looking for."

Mr Hamelin sighs. "Please, Maple. Let me try."

I see Maple biting her lip in the same way that I bite mine. "I just don't want you to be disappointed. That's all."

Mr Hamelin continues with his story. "The problem is I can't move the seat one-handed. I need to try and move it with both hands. So I'm gonna need one of you to hold the torch for me."

I am about to say that I will do it when Maple jumps her words in before me.

"Okay, Dad. I'll do it. I'll hold the torch for you."

Mr Hamelin reaches across and squeezes his daughter's shoulder.

"Thank you, sweetheart. That means more than anything to me. Here." He hands his daughter the torch. "Point it onto the seat and the area just behind it. Keep a little away from me in case something loose comes flying out of the cockpit. And if you need air, just tap me on the back and let me know and I'll wait until you've come back up to fill your lungs again. Or you can have some of this." He shakes the mouthpiece that goes all the way back to his air bottle. "Okay? Ready? Blue Wing, if you could keep an eye on Maple…I would be very grateful."

I nod.

"Okay. Let's try again then, shall we?"

He puts his mouthpiece back in and pushes himself under the water, his flippers making the top of the sea foam once again.

"*Orait?*" I ask Maple. "You are taking my advice? You are going to help him, even though you do not believe in it?"

"Of course I am," she says, changing the position of the large torch in her hand. "I trust you more than anyone, Blue Wing. The things you say...well...they might not always be perfect, but they are nearly always right."

I do not know what to say.

TUPELA TEN WAN

Every *taim* I see or look at Maple I realize that we are both almost the same. I swim. She swims. She is sad. I am sad. She is happy. I am happy. She wants to see her mama again. So do I. It is like, even though she was born a long, long way from here, we are sisters.

Sisters.

Twins who had never met until just a few weeks ago. I do not know if she feels the same way, but I like to think that she does.

Maple can also hold her breath *tru* long. Almost as long as I can hold *my* breath. As Mr Hamelin holds himself in position next to the seat, Maple points the beam into the cockpit. I am keeping myself floating next to her. I watch her carefully. If Mr Hamelin's eyes are on the box, then my eyes are on Maple.

There is *liklik* for me to have worry about, because Maple is strong and tough – even though it is not obvious when someone meets her for the *namba wan taim*. They might think that she was spoiled or delicate, someone used to getting everything she wants. But they would be wrong. She has had to be tough because of everything that has happened to her. If she was not tough before her mama died, she has definitely become tough since.

But still I keep my eyes on her. Because she is my sister and that is the sort of thing sisters do.

Mr Hamelin uses both his hands to try and push the plane seat forward and then back. The bubbles from his mask seem to become many. I do not think he is having much success. He reaches into the cockpit and tries to move a lever. His arm pulls quickly up and down.

Still nothing moves. He punches the side of the plane in anger. Maple watches him as he swims over the top of the cockpit to the other side. There, he tries the same things with different levers.

The first one does nothing.

The second one also does nothing.

But the third one snaps off in his hand.

He holds the lever in front of his face and it looks *tru* silly. I feel like I want to laugh, but I cannot because of the air in my mouth. Maple looks at me and I know that she feels exactly the same way. She wants to laugh too.

Sisters thinking the same things.

Mr Hamelin throws the broken lever over his shoulder and tries moving the seat again. From the other side of the plane, with the torchlight pointed towards him, I can see the need in his face. He *needs* to get to the box inside. He will do anything to get to it.

He bangs hard on the seat – more bubbles screaming out from his mouthpiece. He pushes hard. He twists it hard.

And then…

The seat jerks forward. Only a few centimetres. But enough to give Mr Hamelin hope.

He pushes in exactly the same direction. Not so hard this *taim*. It moves again. Much further. Far enough to get inside the cockpit.

Suddenly, Mr Hamelin goes darker and I realize that Maple and the torch are returning to the surface to get air. I kick my feet and follow her.

Out in the open air, I tread water alongside Maple. A few seconds later, Mr Hamelin's head comes out of the water. He pulls his mask off – his face covered with excitement.

"We're nearly there, sweetheart! Nearly got it. When

you're ready, bring the torch back down so I can see exactly what I'm doing and we'll bring this baby out into the real world once again. Ha!" He slips his mask back over his face and dives below.

"Ready?" I ask.

"Yeah," she replies. "Okay."

The current is not so strong at this *taim* of the year, so it is a simple thing to stay in the same position under the water. Still, it is *mobeta* to hold on to something if you can.

Maple holds on to the frame of the cockpit and I put my hand out to something cold and made of metal on the wing. After a minute or so, I look at it and I realize it is one of the plane's machine guns. I take my hand off and swim to the front, near the broken propeller.

Mr Hamelin's legs are sticking out of the cockpit, his flippers like the bottom of a frog's feet. Again I feel like I want to laugh, but Mr Hamelin's seriousness takes it away and I keep the air in my lungs.

Slowly, Mr Hamelin comes backwards, away from the cockpit. Maple shines the torch straight at his hands.

In them he holds a box.

It is only a small box, wooden and about the size of

something that holds cigars, but Mr Hamelin carries it like it is made of glass.

Some of the light from the torch shows his face. He looks like a child who has found the most precious and most beautiful rock in the entire ocean. No bubbles come from his mask. He is too amazed and is holding onto his breath. I watch him as he forgets to kick, his body slowly starting to sink down to the bottom of the sea. Suddenly, he remembers and kicks himself back up into position.

This is it. The thing he has been searching for. The reason for coming to the island. This blackened box that looks too small to carry anything important. This box that holds secrets to the way that *taim* works.

This box that holds the book of the long now.

For a few moments we are all still. Only the tiny organisms in the sea move around us, catching the light. We seem trapped in a moment, unable to carry on with our lives.

Could it be tru? I ask myself. *Could everything that Mr Hamelin said be tru? Is the book of the long now a real thing?*

And then...

Something terrible starts to happen.

One of the corners of the box snaps off in Mr Hamelin's

fingers. He stares at it the same way he stared at the lever in the plane that came off in his hand. Only, this *taim*, I do not feel like laughing.

And then...

The piece of box crumbles. It falls apart and turns to dust within his fingers. All that is left of the corner is a cloud in the sea that joins the tiny organisms in the sway of the tide and the light.

Mr Hamelin's face changes. His eyes become vast as he realizes he needs to save the rest of the box.

But he moves too quickly and he moves too hard and, as his hand comes to cover the open corner of the box, the whole thing disintegrates in front of him.

It has spent too many year rotting in the bottom of the ocean and cannot tolerate the sudden movement.

I notice something starting to fall from the disappearing box. It looks curled round and like paper, but as Mr Hamelin tries to catch it, it too begins to turn to dust. His fingers reach it and hold it for a second, but then it melts like chocolate in the sun and is gone for ever.

There is nothing left.

Where once, only a few minutes ago, there was something – something real that you could see and feel – there is now nothing.

Zero.

Even though this is a place of silence, I think I can hear Mr Hamelin screaming. He spits out his mouthpiece and snatches away in the sea at the clouds of disappearing dust. He looks like someone *longlong*, dropped into the water, who doesn't know how to swim.

My heart feels like it wants to burst for Mr Hamelin, but Maple and I watch it all and there is nothing we can do.

TUPELA TEN TU

I do not climb back into the motorboat. Instead I stay in the water and listen to the words spoken between Maple and her papa. I think it is best. They do not need me staring at them as they talk in the boat. I feel the need to stay invisible.

"It's all gone." It is Mr Hamelin speaking. "All I've tried to do for the last year. Everything's gone." His voice is *tru* sad.

"No, it hasn't, Dad." Maple is trying to put some happiness into her words. "It hasn't gone."

"Of course it has. All the research I did. Coming here. It's all been pointless. And now we'll never get to see your mom again." I think he is crying. "And all because I was stupid enough to rush the box out!"

"But the box had been under the water for so long,

it was bound to just fall apart. There was nothing you could do to save it." Maple's voice is soft, like she is trying her best to make her papa feel better. "Saltwater and time had already done their damage. There was never going to be anything you could do. It was ruined before you even got there."

"I'm sure there could have been a way of bringing it up without damaging it. Robots or something like that. But I was too damned keen to read what the scroll said. Stupid. So damned stupid of me. And now I'll never see Miko again."

"Dad!" She sounds less soft and more angry now. "Please stop going on about not seeing Mom again. It's creeping me out."

"But I won't see her. *We* won't see her."

"That was the case the moment Mom passed away. You can't just wave a magic wand or chant a few magic words and – abracadabra – there she is again. She's gone, Dad." Her voice is weak like she is starting to cry also. "Gone for ever. Perhaps when we die we'll see her again, but…until then…she's not coming back."

"The scroll…"

"Please, Dad. The scroll was *never* going to bring Mom back to life. You know that. I think that deep down inside, you knew that all along. It was just some sort of weird hope that made you believe the scroll was real."

"It *was* real."

"Okay, perhaps it was a real thing…but it wasn't going to be what you wanted it to be. It wasn't going to be some incredible cure for death. A few words from an ancient Japanese philosopher or something, but not the secret to life and death. That doesn't make sense."

Mr Hamelin mumbles like he hasn't heard what Maple has just said. "It *was* a real thing."

"DAD!!!"

I almost jump out of the water.

"Dad! When are you going to learn?" Maple's crying has now become louder and more obvious. "When are you going to understand that the key to getting over Mom's death is *not* to bring her back? When are you going to realize that everything you need to recover is right in front of you…has been right in front of you from the day Mom died?"

"What are you talking about?"

"Me, Dad!" There is a sound like Maple is hitting her chest. "I'm talking about me! All this time I've been here, needing you to help me – wanting to help you – and all this time you've been miles away inside your head and inside your weird dream, not even noticing I am here." I hear her wiping the tears away from her nose.

"Mom's gone. She's dead. She's in heaven or wherever. And I'm okay with that. I just want my dad back."

"Oh, Maple!"

I stretch my head out of the water and I can see that Mr Hamelin has set his arms around his daughter. They hug for a long *taim*, rocking left and right in the boat, making small waves splash against the smile that is growing across my face.

"I'm sorry. I'm so, so sorry. All I ever wanted was the best for us both."

"I know, Dad. I realize that. But you've been going about it the wrong way."

"Have I?"

"Yes. You have. You know you have."

They keep holding on to each other, making the boat rock.

Maple speaks again. "The living should put the living above the dead. That's what Chimera says. And she's right. The dead are gone. We should respect them, we should remember them, but we shouldn't chase them. If we chase them, then everyone else in our lives starts to disappear. It is almost like they are dead too."

Her words make me think of my own mama and papa. Gone for ever now. Never to be brought back by a magic book. And I think of Siringen. Good, kind Siringen who has helped me and guided me over the last two years. Maybe I should have put him above my dead parents. Maybe I should have put him over my thoughts of revenge.

Maybe.

I keep myself floating and let Maple and her papa talk.

"My wonderful, wise girl," says Mr Hamelin, kissing Maple's head. "How did you get to be so wise?"

"I've had to grow up. I've had to *learn* to be wise."

"You've had to learn too young. You shouldn't be so young and not have a mother to love you and take care of you."

"No, I don't have a mother…but I *do* have a father. And he can do pretty much the same things. If he puts his mind to it."

"Oh, sweetheart. I've been so stupid. I've not helped you much through all this, have I?"

"No, Dad. But you can start now."

Mr Hamelin holds Maple by the shoulders and looks into her eyes. Then he sighs. "Today's the first day of the rest of your life. That's what they say, don't they? Well from now on I'm putting you first. I should have done it right from the start, I realize, but if I start now… It's not too late, is it, Maple?" He sounds sad. "Tell me it's not too late for me to begin. To be a better father."

"Don't worry." I can hear the smile in her voice. "I'm not suddenly expecting you to become Superdad, Dad. I know we're still gonna have difficult days. But if we can help each other...well, that would be good."

"I love you, Maple Hamelin."

"Hey, I love you too, Atlas Hamelin!"

They hold each other for a long *taim*.

"We're gonna be good, yes?" says Mr Hamelin.

"We're gonna be the best," replies his daughter.

I dive under the boat. Deep down into the sea. I am still smiling as I pass over the tail of the plane and along its wings, over the smashed glass of the cockpit, over the nose and the broken propeller, between two large barnacled rocks to the place where Akemi's bones lie on the ocean floor, as alive with the life of the sea as any strip of coral.

TUPELA TEN TRI

Back in the boat, Mr Hamelin looks like somebody else. His face is less tired and he smiles like he has a reason to smile. It is as if all the sadness and all the pain inside his heart has been pulled out and thrown into the sea.

And Maple looks like a girl who does not know what anger is. She stares at her papa like he has suddenly returned home from fighting in a battle.

"Blue Wing," says Mr Hamelin, turning to me. "I think I need to apologize to you. I have been very… distracted recently. And you have been a much better friend to Maple than I have been a father. Thank you."

"Please, Mr Hamelin," I say. "Do not apologize. Maple has been a good friend to me too. It makes me happy to see her happy. If you can keep making her happy, I will not accept an apology."

Mr Hamelin pats me on the shoulder and turns away, his eyes on all the equipment lying in the boat.

I move closer to Maple.

"This is *mobeta*," I whisper. "You and your papa. It is *tru* good."

Maple nods like her neck is rubber. "Yes. At last it all feels..." She thinks for a word. "I dunno... Right, I suppose. Everything is as it should be. I mean, I know Mom should be here but...hey...I've got my dad. And that's pretty good."

"I am pleased. It feels like it has taken a *tru* long *taim*." My hand reaches out and holds one of hers. "I know that it really isn't a long *taim* but...well...it *feels* like a long *taim*."

Her hand squeezes mine. "I know what you mean."

"Okay, girls. I think we should call this a day. Let's go home." Mr Hamelin begins lining up the gas bottles on the boat.

Maple starts to take off her wetsuit.

"Oh!" she says. "Oh no!"

"What is it?" I ask.

She holds up her wrist. "My charm bracelet. It's gone."

"Is it in the boat?" Mr Hamelin stops what he is doing and turns around. "Perhaps it's just fallen off in the boat."

We move things in the boat to see if it has slipped behind something.

But, no. It is not there.

"Did you leave it in your hut?" I ask.

"No. I definitely had it when we got on the boat. I remember it on my wrist when I changed into my wetsuit. And I'm sure I had it when we found the plane. At least, I think I did."

"Well, if it's not on the boat, it must have come off when you were in the water," says Mr Hamelin. "If that's the case, it could be anywhere down there."

Maple looks sick. "But I need it. It was from Mom."

Mr Hamelin looks serious. "Perhaps you don't need it."

"What?"

"Well… It's like the scroll. You don't need it to remember Mom. Everything you need to remember her by is in there." He taps the side of her head with his finger. "The charm bracelet…it's just a *thing*, after all."

"Yeah, but it's a *thing* that she gave to me. It's more than just a way of remembering her. It's something she actually wanted me to have."

They say nothing for a few seconds.

"I will look for it," I say, and before anyone can say anything else, I jump over the side of the boat into the water. "I will return it to you, Maple. I promise."

I take a last deep breath and I pull myself down to the bottom of the ocean where it is *tru* dark. The fish that like to sit in the darkness all swim quickly away from me as I move my fingers through the sand and stones and plants that cover the seabed. I feel more than I can see, but I feel nothing that could be a charm bracelet.

Light flickers above me and I turn to look up. Maple has dived into the sea, holding the torch. I watch as she swims down towards the plane, the beam from the torch moving left and right.

I drag myself along the bottom of the sea, my fingers sifting the floor. If the bracelet had fallen off Maple's wrist while she was near the surface, it could have been carried far by the sway of the tide. It is *tru* what Mr Hamelin has said about it being anywhere.

But I must find it. However long it will take. I have promised my sister, so I am determined inside my heart.

Maple is looking around the underside of the plane and I am moving further away. Small creatures I do not know the names of run away from my hands and I work myself further out to sea.

Suddenly I hear something. It is *tru* muffled here at the seabed but I try to listen.

"Mwwaah-bwah! Bwaah Wahh!"

I cannot make out the noises, but I think they might be coming from Mr Hamelin.

I look up and before I can see the bottom of the boat, I see something far off in the distance. Something coming closer. Something *bikpela*.

A dolphin?

No. It is not a dolphin.

It is a shark.

Not just a shark.

It is Xok!

I watch his movement. He has noticed the light from Maple's torch and is heading straight for it.

Maple!

I push myself away from the seabed, up towards the surface. If I can get myself between Xok and Maple... maybe...

I reach down to the knife on my leg and I pull it from its sheath.

I swim hard.

"*Mwaah-bwahl! Blah Wahng!*" Mr Hamelin is screaming from the motorboat.

Xok is coming in quick, but I am more quick. I come up to his level and I face him head on. I look back over my shoulder and I see Maple, still swimming next to the plane with the torch. She has not seen Xok swimming towards us.

Suddenly there is a splash and I see Mr Hamelin in the water without his mask and air tank. He shouts towards me, making bubbles come from his mouth and then turns to swim down to his daughter. He is frightened, I can tell.

The shark is cutting through the water. I think of Xok ahead of me and Maple and her papa behind me and I realize I have been in this position before.

The last *taim*, I was caught between Xok and my parents. The last *taim*, I stayed quiet and still. The last *taim*, Xok passed me and killed my mama and my papa.

Not this *taim*.

I shake my arms and my legs wildly in the water. I thrash hard. It is like I am my very own *larung* coconut rattle, attracting the shark. I cannot shout any noise, but it does not stop me from trying.

Because I want Xok to come to me. I want him to forget all about the girl with the torch and the man trying to pull her back up towards the boat. I want him to come to me instead.

I grip my knife tight in my fingers and kick to keep myself where I am.

I need Xok to come to me so that I can kill him.

You will not hurt my friend! I shout in my mind. *You will not go anywhere near her. Attack me instead. I will show you how death feels.*

I think my movement is working. He slows down and swims towards me, not understanding what I am.

And that is when I see his eyes.

For the *namba wan taim*, I see his eyes.

There is something about them.

I think they are not the eyes of a monster.

They are wide and shiny and bright.

And scared.

Xok is scared! I think. *He attacks. He kills. Because he is scared.*

And then, other words go through my mind.

Siringen's voice. *Xok is not a rogue shark. He is damaged.*

Maple's voice. *Blue Wing. Promise me you won't kill Xok.*

For a second, I do not know what to do. All these last two years I have held on to the idea that I need to kill Xok. To take revenge. To stop him. It has been my reason for being here.

Or so I had thought.

Blue Wing. Promise me you won't kill Xok.

But, no. I *need* to kill him. Would Maple have said that if she knew that Xok would kill her if I didn't kill him?

If it is a choice between protecting my friend and letting a scared animal live, I will choose Maple every *taim*.

Maple.

My sister.

Who I have learned to love.

I make the muscles in my arm go tense. I feel the bumps and grooves on the wooden handle of my knife. I hold my breath even tighter.

But the voice keeps coming back.

Promise me you won't kill Xok.

Promise me…

Promise me…

I see his scared eyes getting nearer.

Promise me…

Over my shoulder I can see Mr Hamelin and Maple, half the way back to the boat. If I can keep Xok on me for a *liklik* longer, they will be safe.

Promise me…

Promise me…

And then the voice changes.

You won't kill Xok.

"Mama?" I say, even though I am below the water. "Mama? Is that you?"

Xok comes nearer.

"Mama?"

He is close to me now. Straight in front of me.

The moment has come to decide. Kill Xok or let him live.

Kill Xok.

Or let him live.

It is like a burning in my head.

I struggle.

"Oh, Mama."

I let the knife slip from my hand.

Xok's nose is right in front of me. He looks like he does not understand what it is I am. I reach up and put my hands on the sides of his head.

We float in the water.

Still.

Together.

Like we are one creature.

Then I speak. And even though this is a place of silence – and has always been a place of silence – I can hear all of the words I say.

I know you are scared, I say. *All your life you have been scared. Nogut men hurt you, made you angry and scared. Treated you badly. But the nogut men are gone now. They are far, far away. They cannot hurt you any more.*

So you need to stop trying to hurt them back.

Leave them behind.

You see, you and I, we are the same. I was hurt and I thought that the only way I could get mobeta was to kill the thing that hurt me. Destroy it. If it was dead, then I would be free.

But it is not tru.

It is not my reason for being here. I see it now. It has taken me a long taim and it is only now in this second that it has made itself as clear as the stars.

My reason for being here is to accept what has happened. And to forgive you.

He stays completely still, but I know he understands what I am saying.

And your reason for being here, on this Earth, is not to kill. I know it feels like you should kill, but you should not, and you know that already.

Your reason is to realize that there is a life mobeta than this one you are living. Away from the shore. Far out to sea, where the water gets tru deep and the people are few. There you might be happy. There you might become loved. You might have a family. You might be accepted. In that place, you will start to forget all the nogut things that have happened to you and begin to see that not everything has to be bad. I know it. I know that if you go to that place, you will never want to come back here, where people fear you. You will find your peace.

Let me take you.

I stroke my hand across the top of Xok's head. I feel the ridges and cuts and scars of his long, tough, cruel life.

I will lead you there. I know you trust me.

The people call you Xok, but I know that you do not know this name. You don't know any name. Besides, at the end of taim, no name matters. Not even the names of kings and queens and chiefs. Names can be forgotten. Names are unimportant. All that matters – all that stays behind – is what we did while we were still here. The good that we did. The others we helped.

So, come with me. Let me take you out to sea, to the place where I know you will find your peace. Come.

I am not scared.

I feel lighter than I have ever been.

Everything is good.

I let go of the shark's head and swim above him. I twist and hold on to his fin. He lets me. It is like he knows me. He does not fight or struggle. He understands.

We both understand.

Okay, I say. *Let us go.*

The shark flicks his tail and turns in the water. I can see that Mr Hamelin and Maple are no longer in the sea and I am pleased.

Maple, my sister, is safe.

Let me take you home, I say as he swims away from the plane, pulling us out together into the deeper water. *Let me show you where you belong.*

TUPELA TEN FOA

I have become the sea. I have become the air. I have become the light that fills all the spaces between all the things. I am the softest leaf that falls and I am the heaviest rock that refuses to move. I am the rain and I am the sun and I am the snow.

All these things – and plenty more – I have become.

After I leave the shark, I take to the breeze. I race the wind back to the island, over the ocean and all the life within it. Over the fishermen reeling in their nets. Over the birds that dive and steal the shiny silver fish from the sea.

Over Maple, who does not understand.

When I arrive at the village, I sweep onto the land. Outside Siringen's hut I see my *waspapi*, Chimera and the Bigman in an angry talk.

Nobody sees me now.

So I listen in.

"I told you, she should be gone!" The Bigman is the angriest of all. "Two days, I said. Two days I gave you to get her back up to her cave. She should not be here."

"Lungadak," says Chimera. "It would be nice if you would not talk like I am not here. I am alive and I am here, you know?"

The Bigman looks at her with a snarl over his face.

"That is the problem. You are *here*. When you should be back up...*there*." He points to the mountain. "*That* is your home. You need to go back."

Siringen does not smile at all. He stares at the Bigman like he is interested in watching his anger. Then he talks slowly and quietly.

"Lungadak. Son of Meuri. You have come from a long line of great village chiefs stretching back into the far-gone days. This honour I am sure you will pass down to Moses, so that the rule of the village will stretch off into the far *future* days."

The Bigman straightens up and looks as important as he can.

"There have been many great leaders in your family, Lungadak. Many men who have ruled with fairness and kindness and honesty. Your father, Meuri, for example, was a good man who helped make the village strong by putting in place rules that should never be broken. Am I right?"

The Bigman looks suspiciously at Siringen. "Yes. He... was a good leader."

"He also opened up the village to the outside world, fearing that isolation from the rest of life would be *nogut* for us. Yes?"

"Yes. I suppose he did."

"He was a man *tru* much ahead of his *taim*," says Siringen seriously.

"That is *tru*. He was."

"Like the *taim* thirty year ago when he set the rule that the people of the village could marry people from outside of the village. You remember that one?"

"Er..."

"Because it would mean a whole new future for the village. Fresh blood. Fresh hands. Fresh eyes."

Chimera looks almost as suspicious as the Bigman.

"What are you saying, shark caller?" The Bigman frowns.

"What I am saying is that your father – Chief Meuri – gave the ruling that if a man from the village married a woman from *outside* the village, then both were allowed to live their lives *in* the village."

The Bigman smiles. "Are you saying you are going to marry the witch?"

Siringen turns to face Chimera, then talks straight to her. "Chimera. I do not really know what romance is... All I really know is the sea and the ways of the shark. But I would *tru* like it if you would come and live with me, here. I think you would be happier down from the mountain, and I would be happier with you to lighten up my hut."

Siringen looks like he has said something rude.

"Ha!" The Bigman laughs. "You have finally gone *longlong*, Siringen!"

Chimera moves closer to Siringen and then...

...she takes his hand in hers.

"Yes, Siringen. I would be *tru* happy to marry you. And do not worry about the romantic ways...I do not understand them fully myself." She leans close to him and kisses him on the cheek.

Siringen smiles for the *namba wan taim*.

I do not know if I can smile or laugh or punch the air, but I believe that I do all three.

Beyond the hut, I can see Mr Hamelin's boat struggling towards the shore.

"Ah, but you have forgotten something, shark caller," says the Bigman. "You need the permission of the village chief to be married. And I refuse to give it."

"No." My *waspapi* shakes his head. "We only need your permission if we wish to be married *here*. If we marry outside of the village…well…you have to accept us."

The Bigman looks as if his head is finding it difficult to put all the information together.

Chimera nods. "It is *tru*, Lungadak. That is what your papa wrote."

The Bigman looks even angrier. "But you will not find anyone outside of the village to marry you. I am certain of it."

"I have already spoken to someone I know in the village over the hill," says Siringen. "We will be married there."

"You are doing this to attack me! That is why you are doing this. You are pretending to marry this…this witch… just because you want to make me mad."

"No, Lungadak," says Siringen. "I wish to marry Chimera because I have found that to have her around makes me happy. Since she has been here in my hut, I have had a greater purpose." Siringen looks at Chimera. "You see, taking care of her has made me feel like I am not just waiting to die. It has made me feel like I have plenty more years ahead of me."

"You have many more years, Siringen," says Chimera. "And we shall spend them here, together."

The Bigman looks horrified. "Ach! It makes me feel sick." He tries to find more words to say, but cannot.

"You cannot change the law of your father, Lungadak," says Siringen. "And I do not think you would really want to."

Mr Hamelin's boat gets nearer.

"Okay, okay. It is *tru*. There is nothing I can do to change that. But..." The Bigman looks at Chimera. "Please. One thing I ask. No medicine. No waving feathers about and chanting and making healing smoke from tree bark. Let the people go to the doctors in the town."

Chimera nods. "Yes, Lungadak. I will give you this."

The Bigman nods back at her. "Good."

"And I will take the tourists out to see the sharks," says Siringen. "Not to kill. Just to see. To watch. For accepting us, Lungadak, I will do this happily."

The Bigman nods again. "Okay, shark caller. That is good."

Suddenly there are shouts from the sea. The three of them turn.

"That is Professor Hamelin and his daughter," says the Bigman. "What do you think is wrong?"

I can see Mr Hamelin and Maple jump from the boat

beforc it has even got close enough to shore. They do not wait to pull the boat in – they leave it to float as they run through the water towards Siringen.

"Siringen!" shouts Mr Hamelin. "Chief Lungadak! We need a search party! We need to get help!"

I can see that Maple is crying. I want to reach out and brush her cheek with my hand and to tell her that everything is fine and is as it should be. But I cannot.

"Oh, Chimera!" she cries and runs to the old woman, who wraps her arms around her.

"My dear! What is it? What is wrong?"

"Professor Hamelin? Is everything *orait*?" asks the Bigman.

Mr Hamelin stands before them and tries to catch up with his breath. "We need to notify the coastguard. As soon as possible. Get the helicopters out. See if they can find her."

"Who?" The Bigman looks confused.

"Blue Wing," cries Maple into Chimera's dress. "Blue Wing. She's gone."

"Blue Wing?" The Bigman shakes his head.

"It was the big shark," Mr Hamelin explains. "The shark you call Xok."

"We were diving. Trying to find my bracelet. When he came. I think she tried to put herself between us and Xok. I think she was going to kill him. We got to the boat and…"

Siringen crouches before Maple. "*Did* she kill him?"

"What?"

"Did she kill Xok?"

Maple shakes her head. "No. She didn't. She didn't kill him."

"Ha!" Siringen jumps up and claps his hands. "She did it! She stopped herself from killing him!" He is smiling vast, and the thought that I have made him do so makes me smile vast too, and I feel pride rushing down into me like a waterfall.

Mr Hamelin, Maple and the Bigman watch Siringen jumping around, with their mouths open wide.

"But she's out there somewhere!" Mr Hamelin points to the sea. "The shark went away and Blue Wing didn't come back to the surface. All I can…imagine…is…"

Chimera smiles too.

"Do not worry, Mr Hamelin."

The Bigman makes himself look important again. "What is all this rubbish?" he asks. "Is this some sort of joke of yours, Siringen? Another way to make me mad?"

"What are you saying?" says Mr Hamelin. "A young girl has just been—"

"Blue Wing?" says the Bigman. "Blue Wing? That is

a name I have not heard in a long *taim*. Two or three year, I should think."

"I don't understand what you are saying." Mr Hamelin looks like he feels he is wasting valuable *taim*. He keeps looking back at the ocean as if he needs to be out searching it.

"Blue Wing. Poor girl. Missed school one day. Her parents went looking for her. Zephyr and Jeremiah. Good villagers from good families. They found Blue Wing swimming in the sea. But there was a shark. Xok. They ran in to try and save their daughter. I know all this because I saw it all from the hill. I watched it all happen."

"Please," says Mr Hamelin, "we are wasting time. We know the story of Blue Wing's parents. How they ran into the sea to save her but the shark swam past Blue Wing and killed them both."

"Yes. It was a terrible thing," says the Bigman. "Terrible. I saw it all. I will never forget it. The way the shark came into the shore and...well...took the papa and then the mama. And then, after the sea had become red, the way the shark turned and attacked the daughter."

"What?"

"Yes. There was nothing I could do. I was too far away to help. Not that I know anything about controlling sharks – that is your area of expertness, Siringen. But that poor girl. Would have been quick, I suppose. That is a small mercy. She would have been killed like *that*!"

He snaps his fingers.

"We managed to find some of them later – parts of their bodies, I mean. So we buried them together in the graveyard on the other side of the village."

The Bigman shakes his head.

"No, it was a terrible thing. An entire family destroyed like that. All three of them at once. That was a *nogut* day for the village."

Maple stares at the Bigman.

"Blue Wing…is dead?" she asks.

"Oh, yes," says the Bigman, like he is saying nothing more than the hour on the clock. "Two or three year ago – I cannot remember exactly. I would have to consult my journal."

Nobody says anything for a while.

At last, the Bigman coughs. "Well, it is *tru* good to see you and your daughter again, Professor Hamelin, and I hope Siringen has been taking care of you. If there is anything else you need, I am sure the shark caller and his bride-to-be will be willing to help."

He turns and glares at Siringen and Chimera, before walking back along the beach towards his compound.

I see that there are more tears on Maple's cheeks.

"I don't understand," she says, looking from Siringen to Chimera. "Blue Wing is dead? She…she wasn't really here?"

Mr Hamelin's mouth is open. His eyes look confused.

Chimera brushes her fingers through Maple's hair. "Do you remember all the things I told you about ghosts?" she asks. "Do you remember how I said that ghosts are the dead who have something they still need to do to feel worthy of their death?"

"Yes."

"Well, that was Blue Wing. When she died, she could not accept it. She had stopped herself from going over to whatever is the next world because she could not accept her own death. She felt that she needed to *kill* Xok to make her death worthy. But she was wrong. What she needed to do was *forgive* Xok.

"And that is what she has done today."

Suddenly, Maple pushes away from Chimera and races past Siringen's hut.

"Maple!" calls Mr Hamelin, but she does not stop. She runs hard and furious past the back of the trade store, between the papaya grove and the tool sheds.

I fly alongside her and see the tears falling like water down pandanus leaves.

Maple pushes her feet deep into the earth, across the

field resting from sweet potatoes, across the place where the old farming equipment is left to rot in the sun, along the pebble pathway into the wide, stone-covered burial ground.

There she crouches and wipes the dust and dirt and grass away from some of the small stones. She tries one. Then she tries another. I am alongside her, watching. Behind us, Mr Hamelin, Siringen and Chimera are walking their way up to this place.

I would show her where the stone she is looking for is, but I can't, so I let her take her *taim*.

Eventually, she finds it. In the far corner, where it has sat for the last two years.

She moves some of the dust out of the words scratched into it.

Jeremiah Tangaro

Zephyr Tangaro

Then she pulls a lump of grass up and wipes the earth out of the last line on the stone.

Blue Wing Tangaro

She kneels in front of the stone and lets her fingers trace the letters of my name.

Behind her, Chimera, Siringen and Mr Hamelin stand silent.

"But...she couldn't have been a ghost," says Maple.

"I held her hand, she wiped tears from my face." Maple's hands touch her wet cheeks. "I spoke to her, I watched her eat. She couldn't have been a ghost."

Siringen nods. "She was."

"Not everybody could see her," says Chimera. "Remember – *the young, the gifted, the guilty*. I could see her because it is in my blood to see. Siringen...well, Siringen could have killed Xok before it killed her and her family. He carried heavy guilt with him for that. Some young ones in the village would have seen her also, I am certain."

"So it was a surprise when she found out that you – Maple and Atlas Hamelin – could see her too." Siringen smiles. "It was a surprise to all of us."

"Guilt," says Maple. "We both felt guilty because of Mom. That's why we could see her."

Mr Hamelin kneels alongside his daughter and puts his arm around her. Then he kisses her on her head. "It's okay, sweetheart."

Maple smiles at her papa.

"She was never really here, Dad."

"I know, Maple. But *I'm* here. I'm *really* here. And I'm not going anywhere."

They hug.

I am the breeze that bends the grass and lifts the dust

and carries the birds. I fly high to the sky and low across the ground.

I watch as Chimera and my *waspapi* hold each other's hands, their faces happy with their own joy and the joy of my release.

Thank you, waspapi, I whisper. Thank you for watching over me – it is tru, you are a good man. Now it is taim for you to watch over someone else.

I come down, alongside Maple and her papa.

Thank you, Maple, I say. You made me see the world from a different position. You gave me friendship and happiness and strength, when I needed these things most. For these things I will always love you.

I wish that I could reach across and touch her wet face or her hand or her hair. But I will never be able to do that again.

Do not cry, I say. Do not cry, my greatest, beautiful, clever, loving friend. All is good. All is as it should be. I am going where I need to go.

Maple looks up, like she might have heard my words, but then she looks back down at the stone with my name on.

"I love you, Blue Wing," she says through tears. "You were my best friend." Mr Hamelin pulls her tight. "No. You weren't my best friend. You were my...sister."

If I could cry, I would.

Goodbye, sister, I say.

"Goodbye."

"Blue Wing!"

It is a voice. Calling me. The voice of a woman I have known since the day of my birth.

"Blue Wing!" she calls again.

"Hey, Bluey!"

A *namba tu* voice joins her, making me want to smile. The voice of a man I have known *tru* well all my life.

The voices are coming from the beach outside my old hut.

I look at the faces of Chimera, Siringen, Maple and Mr Hamelin. They have not heard the voices. Only I can hear them.

"Blue Wing!"

"Hey! Bluey!"

The *taim* has come.

I must go now.

I look into the eyes of Maple and whisper one last thing. *I will make sure I say hello to your mama for you, and I will tell her how brave and how beautiful you have been. I will tell her to be tru proud of you. Maple, my sister. Keep being brave.*

I leave them all.

I fly across the land to the place where I grew up.

The place where I was born.

And there I see them.

Walking out of the sea towards me, their faces bright with the sun and their smiles.

"There she is," says the man.

"Blue Wing!" The woman waves to me.

I rush across the sand to them. They stand with their arms stretched out to me.

"Mama!" I cry as I put my arms around her waist and feel her warm hands pull me close. "Mama!"

"Oh, Blue Wing. I have *tru* missed you," she says, her breath hot on my head. "We have so, so missed you."

"My *liklik* Blue Wing," says Papa. "What took you so long?"

"Papa!" I put one of my arms around him too and hold on to them both like I might fall off the world if I should let them go.

"We have waited a long *taim* for you," says Papa.

"Yes," says Mama. "It has felt like the long now."

"I know, Mama," I reply, my face close to her chest. "It took me *taim* to know the truth. That is all."

"Never mind," says Papa. "You are here now. With us."

"Where you belong."

"Mama. Papa," I say quietly. "I am sorry I went

swimming on that day. I am sorry I missed school and that—"

Mama takes her arms from around me and puts her finger to her lips. "Ssh, Blue Wing." She smiles. "What do any of these things matter? We are all together again."

"Come, *liklik* one." Papa puts out his hand for me to hold. "We should go."

Mama stands the other side of me and takes my other hand. "Yes. The *taim* has come for you to meet everybody else."

Slowly we turn together, the end of the afternoon sun hanging over the water, and we walk into the sea.

EPILOGUE

THE LONG NOW

From here, I can see everything.

It is like sitting on the top of the mountain and being able to see all the way around the world in every direction. North. South. East. West. And all the directions in between.

There is no distance I cannot see. No place I cannot reach.

And there is no *taim*.

I can see everything that there has ever been, and I can see everything that will ever be. Mr Hamelin's piece of string is *tru*, *tru* long, but my eyes and my reach are even longer.

From here, I see the village.

I see the changes that will happen.

I see the Bigman pass his cassowary headdress on to Moses, who follows his papa's lead by making the village as modern as possible. I see him sell the stretch of beach on which my hut sits to a *bikpela* American hotel company. I see the trucks and cranes and diggers tearing up the trees and the rocks and the sand and putting cold metal rods and girders in their place. I see the bricks and glass and pipes and wires. I see the new hotel. I see the guests.

But before all this – before I see the hotel – I see plenty other things.

After I am gone, Maple and Mr Hamelin stay long enough to be the guests at Siringen and Chimera's wedding. I see Maple throwing rice and giving Chimera a small bunch of fresh frangipanis, and I see the pig that is roasted in their honour.

I see the years that Siringen and Chimera have together. Happy years. Good years. Long and loving years. Until, in the end, one passes, quickly followed by the other.

I can see across all the rivers and all the oceans and all the countries to America. I see Mr Hamelin taking up his position as a professor of history again. I see Maple enrolled in a good school, surrounding herself with good friends.

I see her smiling.

As years pass, I see Maple standing dressed in a cap and gown. I see her working *tru* hard in her city. I see her swimming hard. I see the man she marries. I see her children.

And I see that she never forgets.

When she is older, and her children are close to the ages we were when *taim* brought us together, she stays in the hotel that has been built on our beach.

I watch as the eldest girl plays in the small waves, feeling them brushing over her toes.

So I dive. Down deep to the *tru* bottom of the ocean. And I look for something.

Near the wreckage of the plane, I find it.

I let the sea take me into the shore and, as I get near, I let the thing be carried by the waves.

Maple's daughter kicks water up into the air, making rainbows. Then she stops and looks down at her feet. She bends over and picks the thing up. It shines brightly in the light of the new day.

"Mom," she says, holding it up to the sun to study. "Mom. Look what I've found."

Maple stops collecting shells in a bucket with her other daughter and comes alongside.

"What is it, Cerulean?"

The daughter gives Maple the chain.

"Oh!" Maple's eyes go vast as she turns it over in her hand. "Oh my."

The charm bracelet has not changed, even though it has spent over twenty years below the waves. Each of the charms is still there. The Eiffel Tower. The book. The clock. The diving woman. The bicycle. The star. Each of them with a meaning between Maple and her mama.

I watch Maple's face fill with tears.

"Oh, Blue Wing," she cries.

"What's a blue wing?" asks her daughter.

Maple does not answer straight away. She lets the tears roll down her face, onto the sand as she slips the charm bracelet back over her wrist.

"Blue Wing!"

"What have you got there, Mom?" The youngest daughter brings her bucket full of shells to the always changing place where the sand meets the sea.

Maple takes a breath and smiles. "Celeste. Cerulean. Shall we go inside? There's a story I think I need to tell you."

They walk towards the hotel as I turn back to the *bikpela* blue.

Beyond the moonlit borders, beyond the leaping place, beyond the shark roads, Xok is waiting. He is young now. He has no scars. And sometimes, on days like this – when the sun is a rude and uncivil person – we swim the forever sea together.

AUTHOR'S NOTE:
GROWING UP IN PAPUA NEW GUINEA

Dear Reader,

I was born and raised for most of my childhood in Papua New Guinea. When people hear this, they often ask lots of questions like: did you get malaria? Did you meet crocodiles and sharks on a regular basis? Did you have your own canoe? Yes and yes and a canoe called *Bird of Paradise*! I thought maybe it would be easier to write a book about my memories of growing up there, and this was my inspiration behind writing *The Shark Caller*.

When I first came to the UK, I wore three jumpers during the summer, and met an English grandmother who made chocolate puddings and talked about snow and primroses – extraordinary behaviour! Here are a few more memories of my everyday life in Papua New Guinea – and I'd love to hear how they are different or similar to what you do.

- For breakfast I ate mango, paw-paw, sago pudding, sweet potato patties or flummy dummies (fish in batter). There was no chocolate and we drank a lot of fresh coconut water.

- There was no formal schooling in the village where I was born. Children played and helped grown-ups with daily chores such as collecting wood for cooking fires, catching fish or trading feathers and shells with

ACKNOWLEDGEMENTS

Eternal thanks to the PHENOMENALLY talented Becky Walker – my BEST EVER editor and an absolutely super nice person.

The legendary Peter Usborne for "badly wanting" to publish this book.

Everyone at Usborne who has contributed to the birth of *The Shark Caller* including Nicola Usborne, Rebecca Hill, Jenny Tyler, Christian Herisson, Arfana Islam, Anna Howorth, Lauren Robertson, Katarina Jovanovic, Sarah Cronin, Anne Finnis, Sarah Connell, Jacob Dow, Will Steele, Stephanie King, Jacqui Clark; and Stevie Hopwood gets a special mention for her amazing Quality Street origami skills!

Saara Katariina Söderlund for the stunning cover illustration and Katharine Millichope for the superb design.

Matilda Johnson and Sarah Stewart for sensitive and insightful proofreading.

My brilliant early readers – Sophie Anderson, Michelle Harrison, A.M. Howell, Sarah Lean, Jenny Pearson, Nicola Penfold, Holly Webb and Eloise Williams. Thank you for taking time out of your own busy writing lives to pen a note about *The Shark Caller*.

The altogether magnificent Family Bookworms for simply existing because by simply existing you make my world a shiny, happy place.

Alison at Books for Topics for being a lighthouse in the sometimes rocky world of publishing. Kevin Cobane for all your enthusiasm and your grin-worthy great gifs! Scott Evans for being the omnipresent and omnipotent Mr E Primary! Sarah Forestwood – geographically distant but close to my heart. My motley mix of fantastic early reviewers – Kate Heap, Erin Lyn Hamilton, Ashley Booth, Penny Thomas, Hannah Fazakerley, Stephalittlebutalot.

Julia Churchill for all her magical ways and for popping the MS through the letterbox on Saffron Hill.

Mark, Benji and Loveday for always being amazing in their own right and helping me to attempt amazingness. Also for being long-suffering sounding boards!

And finally to YOU, the reader, who it's really all for. Keep reading, keep smiling, keep following your dreams...

between their own, different languages. Pidgin languages are rarely written down, and often change as they are spoken and used.

How did you find the reading experience of the book with some words in Papuan Pidgin English? Try saying them out loud to see how they sound when spoken!

4) Zillah has described grief being like "a shark", "a very dangerous animal that must be handled with awe and respect". Think about a time when you have felt sad; do you think this description matches how you felt? What other descriptions or comparisons do you think might also convey this feeling?

5) Did the ending of the novel surprise you? Look back over the text, and see if you can spot any clues that Zillah included which suggest something might be different about Blue Wing, and discuss how you think the author handled Blue Wing's character.

BOOK CLUB QUESTIONS

1) The friendship between Blue Wing and Maple is a central theme of the book, but it starts with them both fiercely angry and suspicious of the other. At what point do you think their relationship changed and why?

2) Time is an important theme in the book, and Blue Wing uses the Papuan term "the long now" to describe "for ever". The author, Zillah, wrote the story in the present tense to heighten this sense of "the long now"; that "for ever" is made up of every second, every minute as it passes. Talk about what you think "the long now" means to you, and how this phrase might make you look at the idea of "for ever" differently.

3) Both Blue Wing and Siringen use a form of Papuan Pidgin English. Pidgin English is the name given to a variety of languages that have evolved from English and other local languages, with many different forms across many countries. Pidgin languages evolve between different groups of people who are looking to find or develop a common tongue

USBORNE QUICKLINKS

For links to websites where you can find out more about shark callers and sharks, the threats facing sharks today, and Papua New Guinea and its beautiful landscapes, go to usborne.com/Quicklinks and type in the title of this book.

At Usborne Quicklinks you can:

• See photos of shark callers in their outrigger canoes

• Take a video tour of Papua New Guinea

• Find out about sharks today and how you can help them

• Test your knowledge of sharks with a quiz

• Listen to words and phrases in Papuan Pidgin English

Please follow the internet safety guidelines at Usborne Quicklinks. Children should be supervised online.

The websites recommended at Usborne Quicklinks are regularly reviewed but Usborne Publishing is not responsible and does not accept liability for the availability or content of any website other than its own, or for any exposure to harmful, offensive or inaccurate material which may appear on the Web. Usborne Publishing will have no liability for any damage or loss caused by viruses that may be downloaded as a result of browsing the sites it recommends.

HOW MUCH DO YOU KNOW ABOUT SHARKS?

Sharks play a huge part in keeping our oceans healthy, however a recent estimate suggested that at least 100 million sharks are killed by humans every year. This can be for their fins – which are considered a delicacy by some, for their skins, or for sport. Sharks are often seen as a threat to humans, and they can be very dangerous, but in fact, we pose a much greater threat to them than they do to us.

Did you know:

- The biggest shark is the Whale Shark. It can grow up to 17 metres long! The smallest shark is the Dwarf Lantern Shark, which can be as small as a human hand.
- Sharks do not have any bones. Instead, their skeletons are made out of a type of cartilaginous tissue, which helps them float.
- Sharks can go into trances – as Xok does. This is called tonic immobility.
- You can find sharks in oceans across the world, from the Pacific Ocean (near Papua New Guinea) to the Arctic Ocean!

occasional tourists in exchange for fish hooks, razor blades, peanuts and raisins.

- We washed every day in the sea or freshwater creeks. The toilet was the long drop – a small hut at the end of a fallen tree hanging over the sea.

- I was never worried about sharks (they are quite shy creatures) but I was worried about freshwater crocodiles. They frequently snatched the last person crossing the river. Nobody ever wanted to be the last person!

- There were snakes, beautiful beetles, butterflies as big as your hand and colourful parakeets. Oh, and mosquitoes. Lots and lots of mosquitoes! Interestingly, there were no horses.

- My house was a wooden hut on stilts. This was to protect from snakes wriggling up under the floorboards.

- There were no books. Occasionally one might come with the trade ship. When I came to the UK I was very behind in Maths. On the plus side, I could beat all the boys at arm wrestling!

- We rose at sunrise and went to bed at sunset because of mosquitoes. We told the time from the position of the sun. There were no clocks or watches. We ate when we were hungry not because it was dinnertime. We ate when we had caught or collected something. There were no shops.

To find out more about Zillah, you can find her on Twitter at @ZillahBethell and tell her your own stories too!